Hula maidens, tiki bars and murder.

Just another day in paradise...

Em Johnson, manager of Kauai's popular Tiki Goddess Bar, is once again up to her coconuts in trouble. This time, hunky detective Roland Sharpe, who moonlights as a fire dancer, asks Em to take her fearless, sleuth-happy Hula Maidens undercover at the Kukui Nut Festival's hula competition. Can Em and the Maidens discover who's knocking off the dancers in a rival troop?

Em studied Jackie Loo Tong and wondered if he'd go as far as murder to win a hula competition. She glanced at her watch. Kiki would gossip forever if they didn't get moving.

"It's nice to meet you Jackie," Em interrupted, "but I'd better get back to work. Kiki?"

Kiki bid Jackie Loo Tong aloha with another big hug and a kiss, and then she and Em climbed into the car.

Kiki turned the key in the ignition. "He seemed pretty excited to hear the Maidens are competing again. Maybe this *is* a good idea."

Em was staring out of the passenger window thinking. When she got back to Haena she would call Roland first thing.

"People take these competitions pretty seriously, don't they?" she asked.

"Of course," Kiki said. "Hula is life."

Em thought about Jackie Loo Tong bragging about his own *halau* and his certainty of winning now that Mitchell was gone.

Hula might be life, but could it be the death of someone?

Two to Mango

Book 2: The Tiki Goddess Series

by

Jill Marie Landis

Bell Bridge Books

This is a work of fiction. Names, characters, places and incidents are either the products of the author's imagination or are used fictitiously. Any resemblance to actual persons (living or dead), events or locations is entirely coincidental.

Bell Bridge Books
PO BOX 300921
Memphis, TN 38130
Print ISBN: 978-1-61194-131-9

Bell Bridge Books is an Imprint of BelleBooks, Inc.

We at BelleBooks enjoy hearing from readers.
Visit our websites – www.BelleBooks.com and www.BellBridgeBooks.com.

10 9 8 7 6 5 4 3 2 1

Cover design: DonT.
Interior design: Hank Smith
Photo credits:
Fronds (manipulated) © Alhovik | Dreamstime.com
Glass © Otnaydur | Dreamstime.com
Flower © Fixer00 | Dreamstime.com
Mango © Almoond | Dreamstime.com
Tiki © Annsunnyday | Dreamstime.com

:Lmtt:01:

Dedication

To Kristin, Susan Elizabeth, Jayne, Stella and the "Other Jill,"
Goddesses all and Godmothers to this series.
You wouldn't let me give up or give in.

To Stella, who read the final draft for typos in record time.
(That's what you get for trying to hide out in paradise!)

To Kehaulani and the Hui Hula Sisterhood
Dance on!

Dear Readers,

Aloha from the land of palm trees, gentle breezes, rainbows, sunshine, Mai Tais, murder, mayhem and the Hula Maidens.

The Hawaiian words used here and in the other *Tiki Goddess Mysteries* should be self-explanatory. Since there are only twelve letters in the Hawaiian alphabet, words often look alike but have many different meanings. Hawaiian words are not pluralized, so where I have written *leis, muumuus*, and have added an "s" for clarity, *kala mai*, pardon.

Slang phrases such as: *for reals, oh shoots, lots of stuffs*, and *choke* (meaning crowded . . . "It's choke in the ballroom.") might be mistaken for typos, but they aren't. "Lucky you live Kauai!" is also a local saying.

Though the Hula Maidens and the rest of the cast of characters, including David Letterman—the taste-testing parrot—spend lots of time with cocktails in hand, this is a work of fiction. Please drink responsibly and always, always have a designated driver, a taxi waiting, or have someone phone a friend for you when you have no business behind the wheel.

For more recipes, tips on island style living, tiki lore, and updates about what adventures await the Hula Maidens, please stop by and visit www.thetikigoddess.com

Until next time, Tiki On!

—*Jill Marie Landis*

"There's naught, no doubt, so much the spirit calms as rum
and true religion.
—*Lord Byron*

1

Wardrobe Malfunction

"Thanks to you and your nipple, Lillian, we'll never dance in this town again."

Mournful silence filled the Tiki Goddess Bar on the North Shore of Kauai as Kiki Godwin pinned Lillian Smith with a cold, hard stare.

As the self-appointed leader of the aging troop of dancers known as the Hula Maidens, Kiki had gathered the women for an emergency meeting after their recent disastrous appearance at the Happy Days Long Term Care Center.

A recent transplant from Iowa, rhythmically challenged Lillian squirmed on the sticky seat of the red vinyl banquette. She had the sense not to argue, but when a telltale tear slipped from behind her black rimmed, rhinestone encrusted glasses Kiki went in for the kill.

"I'm afraid you have single handedly ruined us, Lillian." Kiki shook her head and let go a long suffering sigh. "There's nothing else I can say."

Lil let out a wail and leapt to her feet. Her hot pink rubber flip flops slapped an even tattoo against the floor as she ran out of the bar and onto the front lanai. Unfortunately, her sobs were still audible.

Kiki kept the troupe of not-so-talented over-the-hill dancers on a tight rein. They danced for free, but it was still hard for them to get gigs. Audiences expected lovely young Polynesian dancers, not a bunch of wrinkled old *haoles* with underarm bat wings.

If Lillian's shocking wardrobe malfunction truly had ruined their already questionable reputation, they would no doubt be confined to dancing solely at the Tiki Goddess Bar. No more appearances at pancake breakfasts, shave ice wagon blessings or the Annual Hanalei Valley Slug Festival. No more invitations to dance at the occasional private party.

The four other Maidens attending the emergency meeting watched Lillian's hasty departure in subdued silence. The bar didn't officially open until eleven, so no one outside the group of dancers was there to witness Lillian's shame except Sophie Chin, the twenty-two-year-old bartender.

In the mid-morning light, the place looked as tired as an old drunk after a night of heavy binging. The painted plywood floor was scuffed down to bare wood. Foam padding oozed from the stained upholstered seats of chairs that once graced a nearby hotel banquet room. Small round cocktail tables were unevenly spaced along a narrow vinyl banquette beneath the open windows.

Before the lunch crowd rolled in, Sophie filled the ice bin beneath the bar and then stocked fruit juices for the tropical concoctions the place was famous for. The minute Lillian started bawling Sophie dried her hands and tossed down the dish towel.

"A little harsh, don'tcha think, Kiki?" She called across the bar.

Kiki considered Sophie for a moment. Younger by forty years, the girl still had enough gumption to stand up to her. The kid was nice enough, but she had no class. Her jet black hair was short, spiked, and sported neon green tips, but she changed the color on a whim. A row of silver rings pierced her right brow, and if that wasn't bad enough, a fairly new and colorful tattoo of an Asian mermaid was entwined around Sophie's left wrist and forearm.

Not to her taste, but Kiki still couldn't help but be a little jealous. Sophie was everything Kiki wasn't anymore: young, healthy, and one heck of a hula dancer. Born and raised on Oahu, Sophie could claim a stew pot of mixed heritage. She was what the natives called "local." All Kiki could claim was that she was a *haole,* but her heart was Hawaiian.

"You think that was harsh?" Kiki tried to subdue the girl with a look. It didn't work.

"The poor woman is in tears," Sophie pointed out.

"That poor woman is always in tears. I *told* Lillian how to tie her *pareau* so that it wouldn't slip off. Halfway through our tribute to Elvis medley at the old folks' home, I looked over, and there she was with her right nipple sticking out. The left was close to peeping out too. If I hadn't danced over and blocked her from view she wouldn't have noticed until her *pareau* had rolled down to her ankles."

"Kiki? Oh, Kiki?" Suzi Matamoto, short, Japanese American and an aggressive realtor, waved her hand.

Kiki took her time, slowly cocked her left brow and tried to stare Suzi down.

"What *now?*"

Suzi cleared her throat. "I've always thought we're kind of old to be wearing sarongs anyway."

Kiki took a deep breath and tried to calm herself. She started to count to ten but only made it to five.

"Actually, Suzi, I've always thought *you* were a little old to wear your hair down past your hips. *I'm* the costume designer," she reminded them all.

2

"If I say *pareau* then that's what we wear. If I say paper bags, we wear paper bags. Got it? And stop using the word sarong. It's *pah-ray-oo*."

By now they should have it in their hard little heads; she was in charge of costuming. Kiki stared down each of the women gathered around the rickety cocktail tables and caught the dangerous glimmer of insurrection in their eyes.

"That may be." More headstrong than the others, Suzi went on undeterred. "Lillian doesn't have anything to hold her *par-eh-ooo* up with."

"No *chi chis*." Flora Carillo shook her head and sighed. The hefty Hawaiian who owned the local trinket shop in the Hanalei Village was seated at the far end of the banquette. "She get nut'ting up top."

Another pitiful wail floated in from the lanai.

"Next time I'm in town I'll buy her some double sided tape out of the treasury," Kiki said.

Before the agenda got away from her, Kiki turned to Little Estelle Huntington. The ninety-two-year-old was perched on her electric Gad-About scooter gumming the celery stick garnish from her cocktail. Though she didn't dance anymore, Little Estelle never missed a chance to accompany her daughter, Big Estelle, to all Hula Maiden meetings and performances.

"Little Estelle, go out and tell Lillian to cut the waterworks get back in here," Kiki said. "The sound of sniveling floating on the trade winds is driving me crazy."

Little Estelle polished off the dregs of a Shark's Tooth Frenzy, the closest thing to a Bloody Mary on the four page Goddess drink menu, then revved the battery powered engine and did a one-eighty on the scooter. She used the empty tables as a slalom course, weaving her way out to the lanai.

Kiki noticed Sophie was no longer lining up hurricane glasses but headed around the open end of the bar. Kiki liked Sophie as well as she liked anyone and was usually careful not to piss her off—especially since Sophie had voluntarily coached the Maidens through a particularly complicated new hula for the Annual Hanalei Slug Festival.

Truth be told, they could use Sophie as a full time choreographer, but they were all too stubborn and outspoken. They never had any luck keeping hula teachers longer than a month. Kiki knew it was best to stay on Sophie's good side and ask for help only when it was vital.

Legend had it Sophie had once danced at the Merrie Monarch Festival, the Olympics of hula held on the Big Island of Hawaii every spring. Even so, Kiki didn't appreciate the young woman running interference for the other Maidens. She'd hate for there to be rebellion in the ranks, but she doubted the others could get it together enough for them to put Sophie in charge.

As if anyone else would ever even attempt to corral such a mixed bag of nuts.

Sophie handed Suzi a Goddess coaster for her mimosa then picked up Flora's empty rocks glass. Kiki was almost convinced the kid was going to stay out of it until Sophie paused, fingered the front of her neon spiked hair and planted a hand on her hip.

"Kiki, I don't think you need to worry about Lil's accidental striptease at Happy Days. The doctors and nurses are used to exposed body parts. Besides, it's not as if the patients are going to remember anyway."

Suzi looked up from texting long enough to clarify. "They call them guests, not patients."

"Guests?" Big Estelle looked at Suzi. "Why? Because they at their last big luau?"

"Lined up for that all-expense paid vacation to heaven," Flora added.

"*Guests*," Suzi said, "as in hotel guests. Or residents."

"Hotel? You can check in, but you can't check out," Kiki mumbled.

"Unless you're my mother," Big Estelle sighed. Little Estelle had managed to escape the California retirement home her son left her in, charged a ticket to Kauai and moved in with her seventy-two-year-old daughter. Big Estelle's handicap modified van was scooter accessible. She wasn't allowed to drive off without her mother and the Gad-About locked and loaded.

Sophie might be right, but Kiki still wasn't convinced they wouldn't all be ostracized for indecent exposure. Showing some *chi chis* in public was one thing, but not when the *chi chis* in question were over sixty years old.

"We can't afford any more gossip," she said.

"Too late for that," Suzi mumbled.

Just then, Trish Oakely came strolling in with her camera slung over one shoulder and a backpack full of photography equipment dangling off the other. As the official photographer for the Tiki Goddess luau and catered events, Trish was an unofficial Maiden. Work demanded she miss too many practices for Kiki to allow her name on the active roster anymore.

Kiki greeted Trish with the price of being tardy—a cool nod. The others greeted her with alohas and exchanged air kisses and hugs all down the line. Big Estelle slid over to make room for Trish on the banquette.

"You'll never guess what I just heard." Trish slipped her camera strap over her head and carefully set the Nikon on the seat beside her. "Mitchell Chambers died last night."

Kiki had opened her mouth to take up where she left off before Trish's big news broadcast. When the announcement registered, Kiki snapped her mouth shut and choked down a sob that bubbled up from deep inside. The wave of emotion surprised her as much as Trish's shocking news.

Hula was the only thing that ever moved Kiki to tears. Hula was life. She wasn't afraid to die, but the thought of never dancing hula again was the most terrifying thing she could imagine. Pulling herself together, Kiki grabbed her clip board and pen.

"When's the funeral?"

"I'm not sure. Mitchell just died last night. They found him dead in the taro patch behind that new Thai restaurant in Hanalei."

"Yeah, I hear the food's terrible." Flora was digging around in a huge *lauhala* straw bag. She pulled out a Gatorade bottle and took a swig and then drew out a ball of yarn. She was constantly knitting toilet paper covers to sell at island craft fairs, or "crap fairs" as far as Kiki was concerned.

Flora was also famous for refilling her plastic Gatorade bottles with emergency alcohol so she didn't have to pay for extra drinks at the bar.

"What happened?" Kiki asked.

"You know his heart was really bad. Mitchell wasn't ever in the greatest shape. Probably a heart attack." Trish shook her head.

"That's an understatement," Suzi said. "Probably a heart explosion. He must've weighed four hundred pounds."

Flora's knitting needles stilled. "Mitchell was my cousin's sister's uncle's nephew."

"Great!" Kiki shot a fist into the air and then scribbled a note on her clipboard. "Call and tell them we'll be more than happy to dance at the funeral."

Lillian was trying to sidle back into her place without attracting attention. As Little Estelle rolled in from the lanai, her scooter careened off of one of the carved tiki barstools.

Little Estelle squinted at the carved face on the stool.

"Excuse me, buddy," she said before she parked next to her daughter's table. She signaled Sophie to bring her another Shark's Tooth Frenzy.

"You really should slow down, Mother," Big Estelle warned.

"I was only in first gear."

Big Estelle sighed.

Lillian was delightfully cowed, but her eyes were red and puffy. She wore a perplexed look behind her bejeweled glasses as she patted her cotton candy hairdo into place and then raised her hand.

"What Lillian?" Kiki figured it was best to let her have her say so that they could move on. "What's the matter now?"

Lillian whispered, "I was just wondering . . . do people actually dance hula at funerals?"

Kiki could almost forgive her. The woman still had Iowa corn silk between her teeth, which also accounted for the pink tint of her hair.

"Yes, *Lillian*. People *dance* at *funerals*. Do you think I would have *volunteered* us if it wasn't *done?*"

"Oh. Sorry."

"Right. *Sorry.* Now Flora, will you please call the family and tell them we'll be there?"

"Mitchell was a *kumu.* He had his own *halau* . . ."

"I know he had his own hula students. I also realize he wasn't just any *kumu,* he was renowned. One of the best teachers in Hawaii. But that doesn't mean we can't dance at the memorial as a sign of respect. Time is of the essence, though. I want us on that program before it fills up. Plenty of *hula halau* will come from all over the islands and probably even the mainland to pay tribute."

"Do you really think they'll want us?" Suzi asked.

Kiki thought about it for a moment.

"Flora, tell them Kimo will donate three trays of his famous miso *mahi mahi* for the memorial luau." Kiki wasn't above bribes. Her husband Kimo wasn't only head chef of the Tiki Goddess, but half Hawaiian, or *hapa haole,* depending on who you were talking to. He was as well known for his spectacular pupu platters, entrees, and island style cuisine as Louie Marshall, owner of the Tiki Goddess, was for his legendary cocktails.

"Why *wouldn't* they want you all to dance?" Little Estelle piped up from the Gad-About. "Once word gets out that Lillian was flashing her boobs at the Happy Days Care Center, they'll all be lining up for the show."

2

Call to Action

Em Johnson emerged from the crystal clear water off Haena and paused to take in the deep blue sky and sun-kissed morning and thought, *lucky I live on Kauai.*

She wrapped her long blond hair around her hand, twisted the water out, and, as the surf lapped around her calves, she looked for her beach towel. She'd left it on the sand somewhere.

Movement drew her eye to the curved trunk of a coconut palm a few feet from the waterline where Detective Roland Sharpe was holding her aqua striped towel. Tall dark and handsome, he looked like a page out of one of the Studly Hawaiian Men calendars that tourists bought by the dozens.

Roland was a man of few words who rarely smiled, but Em figured that might be out of self-defense since one glimpse at his rare smile could be devastating. It didn't help that he moonlighted as a fire knife dancer, tossing flaming knives to the sensual beat of native drums at parties and luaus. The sight of him all oiled up was enough to tempt her into forgetting the vow she made when her divorce was final; she was through with men.

Roland's gaze skimmed her bikini. Dripping wet and self-conscious, Em picked her way around the worn coral and rocks lining the beach in front of her Uncle Louie Marshall's cottage on the beach. It was just a coconut's throw from the Tiki Goddess Bar. He had owned the local gathering place and watering hole since the '70s.

When she reached the tree, Em held out her hand, and Roland handed her the towel. She whipped it around her body and tucked in the ends.

"Taking the morning off?" He crossed his arms across a bright aloha shirt. She tried not to stare at his biceps beneath the hems of his short sleeves.

"Sophie came in early to set up. I'm hoping to get some office work done; pay some vendors and take care of catering bookings."

Leisure mornings were few and far between since she'd taken over the management of her uncle's bar. She had no intention of staying on Kauai when she first arrived, but the island had slowly worked its magic on her. The lush green mountains with their silver ribbons of waterfalls, the sound of the surf lulling her to sleep at night, the crystal clear ocean and laid back lifestyle of perpetual summer were all too much to resist.

She'd met Roland a few months ago when their next door neighbor's body had been dumped in the luau pit behind the bar. He'd been assigned the case. Not only had she met Roland, but another perk of having a dead body turn up on the premises was that business had doubled overnight. Thanks to all the media coverage, the Tiki Goddess was *the* happening place to be, not just on the North Shore but on all of Kauai.

"Looks like Kiki's got her gang assembled," Roland said. "I saw all the cars in the lot when I came in."

"Honing your detective skills?" Em headed across the sand toward the screened-in lanai that fronted the house. Roland followed along, the thick rubber soles of his utilitarian black shoes sinking in the soft sand. She knew he'd rather be barefoot.

"Are they practicing?" He sounded hopeful. Everyone on the island knew the Maidens were hula challenged.

"Kiki called an emergency meeting." Em hadn't paid much attention when Kiki told her why. "Something about a wardrobe malfunction. Lillian's *pareau* slipped and exposed her . . ."

"Stop." His hand shot up to cut her off. "I don't need to imagine any of those women naked in my head."

"Don't worry. I don't know all the details, but it's probably not that bad. With that bunch there's always an emergency."

Following island custom, Roland slipped off his shoes when he reached the bottom step. Em brushed the sand off her feet before she opened the wood framed door to the screened in lanai. He followed her inside.

"I heard they're dancing here every night now," he said.

"Thank heavens they don't all show up. Get too many of them on the stage and it turns into a wrestling match. There's not enough room for all of them in the front row."

Roland was careful not to let the screen door bang.

Uncle Louie's parrot, David Letterman, was in a wrought iron cage in the living room just off the lanai. The red macaw started pacing back and forth on his perch. Bobbing his head, he shrilled out a garbled, "Where's the jigger? You wanna another jigger full, Dave?"

Dave taste tested all of Louie's tropical concoctions.

"That would drive me nuts," Roland winced. "Does that thing ever shut up?"

"Only when he's passed out or watching TV."

"Awk! Awk! This one's a keeper, Dave!"

"Why is he talking to himself?" Roland glanced over his shoulder. The huge cage took up one corner of the spacious living room beside a bamboo tiki bar on wheels.

"He repeats whatever my uncle says to him."

Roland looked around the interior room. "I didn't see Louie's truck in the lot. Is he gone?"

"I'm pretty sure he's at a sleepover at Marilyn Lockhart's."

She tried not to worry whenever her Uncle Louie stayed out all night without calling. A seventy-two-year-old shouldn't have to check in, but since their neighbor's murder, even though the killer was behind bars, Em liked to know when her uncle was going to pull an all-nighter with his significant other.

"That explains the frown." He pressed his forefinger against the crease between her brows. "I knew Kiki had a beef with her, but I didn't think you did."

"Kiki doesn't like her because Marilyn left the Maidens for another hula group. They call her the Defector. I personally don't have a problem with Marilyn as long as she doesn't hurt Louie."

"What makes you think she would?"

"I heard she's a serial bride. We've lost count of how many husbands she's had." Em frowned and pressed her finger against the frown lines between her eyes. "According to Kiki, until Marilyn came along, Louie hadn't dated a woman seriously since Auntie Irene died."

The former Irene Kakaulanipuakaulani Hickam, Louie's Hawaiian wife, had been instrumental in helping Louie establish the Tiki Goddess. And though he was often broke, Louie kept the place limping along as a tribute to her memory. A life-sized portrait of Irene still graced the wall behind the stage, and every night at the end of the hula show, Louie led the crowd in a song he'd written to his late wife.

He hadn't changed a thing in the bar in the eleven years since Irene had been gone—which accounted for the dilapidated condition of the place. His habit of lending money to people who rarely paid him back curtailed any improvement projects. But his generosity was something Em was trying to curtail. Admittedly, without much success.

Em added, "Kiki is more worried about the bar than Louie. She's afraid Marilyn will get her hands on the place and turn it into an upscale restaurant. If she ever did, there goes the Maidens' main venue for performing."

"Kiki's always worried," Roland noted.

"So what's up?" She didn't mind him showing up unannounced.

Roland smiled. "Maybe I came by just to see you."

"Maybe not. You're on the clock. I saw the KPD issue cruiser in the driveway."

It would be great if he *had* come by just to see her, but he never stopped by on the county's dime.

They'd had an encounter on the beach one night shortly after she and the Maidens had helped solve the murder/kidnapping case. Not an encounter, actually. It was only a few long, hot kisses and some pretty determined groping on a moonlit beach and was as far as they'd gotten before she put the brakes on and told him it was too soon after her divorce for her to get involved.

At first she thought maybe she could, but she couldn't. And she hadn't.

"It's not official business," he insisted.

She cinched up her towel and tried to concentrate on what he just said instead of the way his gaze kept slipping down to her towel.

"Oh, really?"

"I need your help."

She tried not to sound disappointed. "You need some catering done?"

He could have called for that. Stuck out on the far reaches of the North Shore, the Goddess wasn't exactly centrally located.

"I never in a million years thought I'd be saying this after what happened the last time you all got involved, but I need help with a case."

"With a case?"

"Case of rum!" David Letterman shrieked. "Unload another case of rum!"

Em fantasized riding alongside Roland in his unmarked squad car, pulling drivers over for seat belt infractions and expired car registrations. That was as close as she wanted to get to crime solving after what happened before.

"I need you and, unfortunately, Kiki's bunch of coconuts."

"The *Hula Maidens*? You have to be kidding."

"Mostly you. But I could use them as a diversion."

She started to laugh, but he was wearing his stoic detective face.

"You're not kidding, are you?"

"Nope," he said.

"You made me promise to drop the Nancy Drew act, remember? Besides, last time the Maidens tried to help you solve a murder, I ended up kidnapped. If it hadn't been for Kiki and the girls I'd have been shark bait." She'd never forget the way the women had come to her rescue in the nick of time.

"I had all it figured out. I was on the way," he reminded her.

"They got there first, remember? I'm not a cat. I only have one life."

"Hear me out, okay?"

"Do you want some coffee?"

"No, thanks."

Saltwater was pooling on the *lauhala* mat at her feet. "Well, I need some. And I need to change. Have you got five minutes?"

He glanced at his watch. "Sure."

"Have a seat. I'll take a quick shower and get dressed. I'll think better after a mug of coffee."

"Don't get dressed on my account."

"Ha ha."

She was back in eight minutes, showered, changed and towel drying her hair with one hand, a mug of coffee in the other. She took a sip of the dark *Molokai* brew.

"Sure you don't want some?" she asked.

"No, thanks."

"Okay, so go ahead. What's up?"

"Last night a guy named Mitchell Chambers died in the taro patch behind Fit to Be Thai-ed."

"I heard the food is awful."

He shrugged. "I doubt it was the food that killed him."

"I've never heard of him. Did he live around here?"

Roland shook his head no. "He was thirty-five, a well-known *kumu hula* who lived on the West Side. According to his friends, he was feeling really down after a visit to his doctor. He had congenital heart failure, and his prognosis wasn't good. They took him out to eat in Hanalei. In the middle of the meal he started sweating profusely and was nauseous and said he wasn't feeling well and stepped outside for some air. When he didn't return, they went to get him and found him dead."

"Dead in the taro patch."

He nodded. "He'd been under a doctor's care and died within twenty-four hours of an exam at the clinic. He was morbidly obese and on various heart medications. The coroner declared it a coronary, and there will be no autopsy. The family is dead set against it since the coroner deemed it unnecessary."

"You don't sound sure about it."

"I can't shake the feeling there was some kind of foul play involved."

"You think he was murdered? Why?"

"Six weeks ago one of his female dancers, Shari Kaui, died. She was barely thirty. Same *halau*. What are the odds two of them would drop dead so close together?"

"She just dropped dead?" Em snapped her fingers.

"She suffered from an autoimmune disorder, and her symptoms were pretty severe."

"But you think she may have been murdered?"

While Em waited for an answer, Roland turned to face the porch screen. Em followed his gaze. They watched the ocean roll slowly over coral worn into flat slabs in companionable silence.

"There was no sign of foul play. Her symptoms were normal for someone with hemolytic anemia that had worsened: fatigue, dizziness, shortness of breath and eventually, heart failure. The toxicology report didn't show anything suspicious but then again, you have to know what to test for if you're looking something out of the ordinary in her system. I've got nothing but a hunch to go on," he admitted. "But it won't go away. It all seems too coincidental to me."

"That's all you have? A hunch?"

"My grandmother was what you'd call psychic." His expression dared her to laugh.

"You think you're psychic too?" She couldn't believe it. He was the most no-nonsense guy she'd ever met.

"Let's just say I've learned not to ignore a hunch."

"We don't need any more murders up here." Em ran her fingers through her damp hair. She sat down on the rattan sofa and curled one leg under her, drank more coffee.

"After that last fiasco, are you sure you want the Hula Maidens involved?"

He had to be totally desperate to even think about it.

"I need someone who can get close to Mitchell's students. I don't want the Maidens to know you're snooping around, though. It would be great if they signed up for the hula competition that Mitchell's *halau* is sponsoring so I have someone on the inside."

"Won't they cancel the competition now that he's gone?" Em could only hope. The Maidens were only loveable to those who knew them well. Most of them were as contrary as old nanny goats, not to mention too rhythmically challenged to carry off a competition hula.

"I heard some of his dancers talking outside the morgue last night. They were all full of the-show-must-go-on and he'd-want-it-that-way kind of talk. Will you talk Kiki into it?"

"You want me to have Kiki enter the Maidens in a hula competition and then slink around looking for a killer? They're going to wonder what I'm doing there."

"They can't know what's up. I'd like you to blend in, work behind the scenes, just see what you can pick up."

"But I can't hula."

"I'm willing to bet you could dance as well as they do after an hour lesson. But don't worry, all you have to do is hang around. Help with costumes or something and keep your eyes and ears open."

"Be part of their entourage?"

"Exactly. The Maidens will make a perfect diversion without trying."

"What about Sophie? She's younger, tougher, and she can hula."

"I don't want her in on this."

"Because she was your number one suspect last time?"

"You believed that right up until the end, too. The less we broadcast it, the better. You know there's no such thing as a secret on this island." He got up and walked to the sofa, totally focused on her. He was the first and only man she'd been attracted to since she'd dumped her husband in a messy divorce in Orange County, California.

She was getting warmer and not from the coffee. Em smiled up at him.

"I'd rather work with just you," he said.

"Really?" He was six-two, and Em had to tip her head back to meet his serious dark eyes.

"Really." He was staring intently now. "But you can let Sophie in on it if you absolutely have to."

Slowly, he reached toward her. Em held her breath.

Roland slipped his hand beneath her coffee cup, tipped it upright and stepped back again. "You were about to spill that on your lap."

"Thanks." She cleared her throat, stared down into the coffee mug to hide her embarrassment. "So what do I do?"

"First you have to convince Kiki to enter the women in the *kupuna* division of the Kukui Nut Festival Competition."

"*Kupuna?*"

"Senior division. She'll probably jump at the chance."

"And then?"

"Get them signed up, and we'll go from there."

"I'm on a need to know basis, is that it?" She wished he'd move back. She was starting to sweat, and it wasn't from the humidity.

"All you need to know right now is that you're about to spill that coffee again."

3

Convincing Kiki

Em walked Roland out to his car and then cut across the parking lot to the Goddess. Kiki and the Maidens' cars were still there. Sophie looked up when Em walked into the bar from the back office.

"How's it going?" Em glanced over at the Maidens.

Kiki was talking. No one was listening. Flora was crocheting, Suzi was texting, Big Estelle was glaring at her mother, who was draining a Shark's Tooth Frenzy, and Lillian was blowing her nose. Even Trish was there, but the photographer was fiddling with a long telephoto lens.

"High drama as usual. You want anything? Orange juice?" Sophie asked.

"No thanks, I'm fine." Em headed over to the table where Kiki was frantically making notes on a clipboard. Kiki paused the minute she saw Em. Her cheeks were flushed—from either too much bronzer or too many drinks—Em couldn't tell.

"Have you heard?" Kiki glanced out the window alerted by the crunch of Roland's car tires on the gravel drive as he left.

Em nodded. "You mean about the dead *kumu*? Roland just told me. Sounds like a great loss to the hula community."

"It's terrible." Kiki glanced down at her clipboard. "We're planning to dance at the funeral."

"Wow. You were invited already?" Em knew the coconut wireless worked fast, but this was warp speed. She also knew the Maidens hadn't made many friends when they'd showed up uninvited to dance at opening day of the Annual Goat Hunting Tournament.

"Not yet, but we will be. Prior planning prevents poor performance."

"If only that were true in our case," Big Estelle mumbled.

Kiki shot her a dark glance.

"Are you entering Mitchell's competition?" Em hoped she sounded casual.

At the far end of the row of tables, Flora immediately dropped her knitting and took a swig out of her Gatorade bottle. Big Estelle gasped.

Trish winced and shook her head at Em with a don't-go-there look on her face. Suzi stopped texting. Little Estelle let out a bark of laughter and frantically began to toot the Gad-About horn.

"Enter the competition?" Kiki set down the clipboard. "Absolutely not."

"Why not?" Em glanced at the faces gathered around the cocktail tables. Only Lillian seemed to be as in the dark as she was. "You all love to dance."

"We entered that Kukui Nut Festival competition two years ago and got the worst scores ever given," Trish confessed.

"*You* danced too?" Em tried to imagine. Trish usually never appeared anywhere with them except at the Goddess.

"Those scores weren't *my* fault." The photographer shrugged.

"Nobody's fault really," Suzi said softly.

"We are not ever competing again and that's that." Kiki drained her wine glass and held it in the direction of the bar. Sophie came to collect it for a refill.

"We *were* pretty lousy dancers back then," Big Estelle volunteered.

"As opposed to *now*? None of you has a clue what you're doing." Little Estelle never let them forget she'd danced as a Rockette. She was a trooper. A *real* professional.

"But now we have our Sophie," Lillian chirped.

Sophie handed Kiki another Chablis then held up her hand.

"Hold it right there. I only volunteered to teach you a new dance for the Slug Festival. That's it. What you need is a real *kumu* hula."

Flora burped and shook her head. "Tried already. Nobody wants us."

"Well, you need someone strong enough to keep you all from wasting time arguing over minutia."

"We are *not* entering the competition," Kiki reminded them. "Let's get back to the funeral plans."

"You couldn't have been that bad." Em had seen them when they were "on" and were halfway decent. Those times were few and far between.

"Oh, yeah. We were bad." Flora nodded so hard her jowls bounced.

"Why not enter this year and redeem yourselves?" Em suggested.

"It wasn't just the dancing," Suzi sighed. "They hated our costumes. We wore strapless *holoku.*" At Em's puzzled expression she added, "Long muumuus, like ball gowns with six foot ruffled trains. We draped the trains over our wrists but everyone kept tripping. Flora got tangled up like a mummy and fell over."

"Broke our number one rule," Big Estelle said. "Never fall down."

"At least my top stayed up," Flora noted. A pitiful little moan escaped Lillian.

"I think the judges objected to the fruit baskets on our heads more than the gowns," Trish added.

"Fruit baskets?" Em tried to picture it.

"Real fruit. A pineapple, some bananas, lychee." Little Estelle chuckled. "And mangos."

"Killer mangos," Trish mumbled.

"All glue gunned to a rattan paper plate holder and tied to our heads with long strands of raffia." Suzi sighed. "Chiquita Banana style."

Flora picked up her knitting needle. "Took hours to make 'em," she grumbled. "We barely started dancing when a mango fell off Trish's head and hit the Defector smack on the toe. She limped off stage in the middle of the dance."

"So much for the show must go on." Little Estelle snorted. "I once had to dance with a broken toe. Had to cut my shoe open to get the thing on my swollen foot, but did I let that stop me?"

"You're kidding," Em said.

"No, I'm not kidding. Why would I?" Little Estelle's face fell into a frown.

"I meant the part about Marilyn. I can't imagine her with a fruit basket tied to her head or hobbling off stage after a mango maiming."

"It was one of the reasons she quit." Suzi tucked her iPhone into her purse and stood up. "I've got to show a property. Are we about finished, Kiki?"

"I'll email you the funeral details soon as I get them. Flora, don't forget to call and get us on that program."

The Maidens got to their feet and started digging in their purses for money for their drinks. Em noticed Lillian's eyes were swollen and her makeup smudged but knew it best not to ask why.

One by one the women paid for their drinks and edged out from behind the tables, gathered up their oversized purses and tote bags with their hula notebooks and left the bar. Little Estelle, trailing along behind on her electric scooter expressed her impatience by revving the motor and honking the horn.

Once the room was quiet, Em tried encouraging Kiki again.

"What if I help?" She volunteered. "Would you enter?"

"You can't hula." As if she smelled a rat, Kiki watched her with a critical eye. "Why is this so important to you?"

Em shrugged. She was convinced she'd have to tell Roland Kiki had outright refused to enter the gals in the competition.

"You're all so much better now. Wouldn't it be great to vindicate yourselves? Besides, I'm sure you can find someone to coach you." She glanced at Sophie who mouthed *no way*. "It's a shame not to try again," Em added.

"We'd only have three weeks to prepare." Kiki had a far off look in her eye.

Em took the expression as a good sign.

"We don't do well under pressure." Kiki seemed to be talking to herself more than Em. "Competition brings out the worst in us. We don't play nice with each other as it is."

"Maybe if you learned a very simple dance, executed it perfectly, and didn't overdo the costumes?" Em suggested.

"You think?"

"Better than giving up all together."

Kiki's shoulders slumped. She let go a long suffering sigh. "I guess we couldn't do any worse than last time."

"Or you could do so much better."

Em watched Kiki gather her purse and notes and slip her purse straps over her shoulder. As usual she was decked out in aloha wear, a floral print tank top and matching wide legged capris. Fuchsia was her signature color of the month, and she'd pinned an artificial spray of fuchsia flowers along her left temple. Though she was on the far side of her mid-sixties, she wore her long salt and pepper hair to her waist.

Kiki picked up her glass and downed the remaining half of the wine. "You might be right," she nodded. "Maybe we *should* enter. In Mitchell's memory."

Worried she would get the Maidens in over their heads, Em didn't feel as relieved as she would have liked. Roland was going to owe her big time for this. She felt even worse when Kiki paused on her way out.

"Did I ever tell you how glad I am that you answered our distress call and moved to Kauai, Em?"

"Not officially, but I know." Em did know how thankful the Maidens were, especially Kiki. They'd sent Em a one way ticket to Kauai at one of the lowest points in her life because they needed her help. The idea that the Maidens would lose their beloved Tiki Goddess because of Uncle Louie's poor management had inspired them to track down his only living relative.

"Well, officially, thank you. Now I've got to run. I'm sure there's a deadline for contest registration, so I'll get right home and check online. What with Mitchell unexpectedly ending up dead, they might extend it."

Kiki hurried out, and Sophie started collecting empty glasses and wiping condensation off the tables. A rental car full of tourists pulled into the parking lot, a sign that the lunch crowd was rolling in.

"So what's up with that?" Sophie wanted to know.

"What do you mean?"

Sophie clicked a stud pierced through her tongue against her front teeth and held up her finger. "Okay, let's see. First your no-nonsense detective shows up."

"He's not *my* detective."

"Whatever." She held up a second finger. "Then you casually stroll in and start pushing Kiki to enter a competition that's being held by the same *halau* whose *kumu* just so happened to fall over and go *maki.* You were shoving so hard Kiki's actually considering it. Something is definitely not right here, and it has something to do with Roland Sharpe."

"I know there's still some animosity between you and Roland but . . ."

"Some? Being arrested on murder and kidnapping charges will put girl off for a while."

"But you were vindicated," Em reminded her.

"Thanks to the Hula Maidens."

Sophie still hadn't budged and was waiting for an explanation.

"Let's just say we may be in for a bumpy ride." Em fell silent and indicated the front door with a nod.

A family of tourists piled out of a minivan and two sedans and began to file in. Lobster red, still in swimsuits, tank tops, and flip flops, they left a trail of sand behind them as they walked in and looked around the empty bar with trepidation.

One of the mothers was dragging a five-year-old along through the door by his wrist while he screamed through a snorkel, his tears trapped behind his swim mask. If not for his mom's iron grip on his wrist and a hearty yank he would have tripped over his flopping fins and landed on his mask.

"Brentwood, I don't care if you scream until you're blue in the face. Everyone is starving, and we are *through* snorkeling for the day."

His swim fins slapped the floor as he snuffled along behind her. The group of fifteen claimed chairs as Em welcomed them with an aloha and went to collect menus from the bar.

A second later, one of the older boys lost a coin toss and had to take snorkel-boy to the bathroom, while Brentwood's harried mother collapsed into a chair. One of the men, apparently the leader of the pack, walked up to Em. His gaze flicked over the liquor bottles lined up behind the bar.

"Do you serve kids in here?"

"Of course, but not alcohol." Em smiled and handed him a stack of menus. "We're a bar and a restaurant. Kids can only be inside until nine p.m. when Chef Kimo stops cooking."

After that the lights went down, the music got louder, the crowd got younger and the place morphed into a full-fledged bar complete with an occasional brawls and bottle throwing—but only on the worst of nights.

"Why do I get the feeling I should be worried about this hula competition thing?" Sophie was behind the bar looking for a pen. She had her order pad in hand.

"I'll tell you later when things slow down," Em promised.

Before Sophie walked away the older boy ran back in from the restroom.

"Mom! Brentwood's snorkeling!" He hollered.

"What?" His mother jumped up, frantic. "How did he get out? He's not supposed to be in the water by himself."

The teenager yelled back. "He's not. He's in the bathroom with his head in the toilet bowl!"

4

The Defector Begs

"Big crowd tonight." Kiki's husband, Kimo Godwin glanced out of the door between the bar and the kitchen. The hefty *hapa*-Hawaiian wandered back to the stove and drizzled *shoyu* over a huge wok full of fried rice.

"Your Saturday shrimp and rice special always brings them in, honey." The fact that the Goddess was *choke* with patrons delighted Kiki. "I'm so excited to make my big announcement tonight."

Kimo paused, wooden rice paddle in the air. His usually smiling brown face was marred by a worried frown.

"You sure this is a good idea, Keek?"

Kiki took Kimo's place in the open doorway, surveyed the crowd again. Then she took a deep breath and nodded. "I do. We're ready. The girls will never be more ready than this." She paused and then gasped. "Oh, no."

"Oh no, what?" Kimo left the stove to look over her shoulder.

"The Defector just walked in. Why does she always have to ruin everything?"

"Ruin how?"

"Look at Louie. He starts grinning like an idiot whenever that woman is around."

"You keep saying he's losing it. Maybe that accounts for the grin."

"We only told Em that to get her to move over here and help him out." They'd taken a chance sending Em a one-way ticket and a plea for her to take over for her "senile" uncle—who wasn't senile at all—not officially anyway. No more than the rest of them anyway.

But falling for a gold digger like Marilyn Lockhart certainly qualified him.

"I've got my own pupu platter full of worries tonight," Kiki mumbled. "No need to add *her* to it." The Maidens had made such a poor showing at the Kukui Nut Competition before that Kiki had no reason to think they'd do any better this time. Not unless she could get Sophie or someone else to coach them.

"Looks like Danny's ready to get things started," Kimo nodded toward the stage where Danny Cook, the guitarist, and his sidekicks were tuning up.

"I'll go give the girls the high sign."

She was headed toward the ladies' room that the Maidens commandeered as their dressing room when her nemesis, Marilyn Lockhart, slipped away from Louie's side and came prancing over.

In her silk Mandarin cut gown, gold designer sandals and armload of heirloom bangle bracelets, Marilyn was as out of place in the Goddess as a vegetarian at a pig hunt.

"Kiki, you're looking lovely tonight."

When Marilyn fairly cooed, Kiki knew the Defector was up to something. It was hard to tell by the woman's expression how sincere she really was because she'd had so many Botox injections that only her lips moved. Her smile never reached her eyes.

"Excuse me, but I've got to get the dancers . . ." Kiki tried to walk past but Marilyn took a step to effectively block the way.

"I've never seen anyone combine that shade of neon green with purple and orange before," she told Kiki. "Who knew it would actually work with your complexion?"

"Thanks." Kiki tried a head fake but couldn't get around her. "I think."

Marilyn reached up and straightened the huge spray of artificial flowers artfully attached to the right side of Kiki's head.

"Your flowers were slipping."

"The Maidens are waiting for their cue." Kiki looked everywhere but at the Defector. When the woman failed to move, Kiki finally met her gaze and was shocked.

Marilyn's eyes were glistening with unshed tears.

As Kiki stared in awe, Marilyn slowly wiped a tear from the corner of her eye with a perfect crimson acrylic nail.

"I've been thinking about dancing again." Marilyn spoke so softly Kiki had to strain to hear her in the crowded barroom.

"I thought you *were* dancing . . ." Then Kiki suddenly remembered. "Oh! You were in Mitchell's *halau* last, weren't you?"

Marilyn's face took on a sorrowful expression, at least Kiki thought she was trying to. It was hard to tell.

"Oh, I quit that *halau* a while ago," Marilyn admitted.

"Oh really? I never heard." Kiki realized her jaw was hanging open and snapped it shut. In a town without secrets the news had the effect of a nuclear bomb. Something wasn't quite right. Kiki knew Marilyn never started a conversation unless she wanted something. The woman wanted something now, and she wanted it bad.

"Why did you quit?" Kiki asked.

"I didn't get along with Mitchell's *alaka'i*. Shari Kaui was a headstrong little bitch."

"Marilyn, I'm shocked to hear you say that." Actually Kiki wasn't shocked at all. Marilyn couldn't get along with anyone in power, and the *alaka'i* was a *kumu's* second in command.

"It was an honor for you, virtually a beginner, not to mention a *haoli*, to have been in Mitchell's *halau*," Kiki reminded her. "You shouldn't speak ill of the dead, you know. It must be awful for them, losing Shari and then Mitchell so close together."

"I'm sure. I've been hoping that you and the others might allow me to rejoin the Maidens again. I still have most of my costumes . . ."

Kiki had no idea what else Marilyn said after that. The woman's lips were flapping, but Kiki's head was spinning. When she finally recovered her wits, she yelled across the room to Sophie.

"I'll take a wine." Then she had a change of heart. "No! Make that a double vodka martini with two olives." Suddenly she remembered they were about to go on. "You want to *rejoin?*"

"Yes." Marilyn smiled as far as she could stretch her frozen lips.

"You want back in the *Hula Maidens?*"

Marilyn nodded and even showed her teeth. Sensing an emergency, Sophie hurried over and put a martini glass in Kiki's hand. Kiki drained it and stared at Marilyn.

The nerve of the woman. She'd put the Maidens down time and again by telling anyone who would listen that the women couldn't dance their way out of a wet paper bag. It was a cardinal Maiden rule not to bad mouth your hula sisters outside the group. They might be lacking in talent, but one thing they had by the truck full was loyalty to each other. When one of them was in need, they all showed up.

Kiki tugged down the hem of her sarong and hiked up the top, set the martini glass on the bar and shook her head.

"Marilyn, I don't think . . ."

"Before you decide, will you *please* just ask the others?" Marilyn glanced toward the ladies' room.

"You have got to be kidding me, Marilyn. You really do." Kiki turned and walked away without looking back.

5

The Big Announcement

Thirty minutes later Em was circulating the tables greeting tourists and locals with the same warm welcome. Time and again returning visitors wanted to share stories about meeting Uncle Louie's wife Irene, the consummate hostess. The lovely Polynesian's reputation for warmth and generosity had made the Goddess the tourists' "home away from home" that it still was today. Once you walked through the door, whether you were a *malihini* or a *kama'aina*, a newcomer or an old timer, you were part of the family. Em worked as hard as Louie to make everyone feel the aloha.

Outfitted in his long white linen pants, vintage Aloha shirt, black *kukui* nut necklace and white Panama hat, Louie looked every bit the island planter and colorful host. But he *was* absentminded, and tonight he was more distracted than usual.

He'd seated Marilyn Lockhart alone at a reserved table near the stage and had barely left her. Em's anxiety amped up as Louie walked up to the table with a bottle of champagne and two glasses. He rarely drank anything that didn't involve a whole lot of rum, fruit juice and a paper umbrella.

Marilyn gave Louie a tremulous smile, and they toasted each other, ignoring the dancers on stage, which was just as well. Most of the Maidens were trying to circle to the right when Lillian suddenly went left and wound up face to face with Kiki.

Lil stopped in her tracks which caused Suzi Matamoto to careen into her, and a train wreck ensued. Suzi stomped her foot and marched off the stage.

It was so crowded in the bar that Little Estelle had been forced to leave her Gad-About in the van, so Big Estelle had left her at a table right in front of the stage. Little Estelle started banging her aluminum walker up and down, trying to get the girls back on beat. The attempt was lost on the Maidens. No one could recover the tempo. Disaster loomed as they flailed around.

Thankfully Danny Cook, leader of the three piece Tiki Tones band noticed. He suddenly cut the song short, which only made matters worse.

The five women left on stage executed five different endings from a deep bow and curtsy to Flora's flinging both arms overhead in a desperate move that started a series of off-the-Richter-scale underarm quakes.

Twitters of laughter rippled around the bar as the Maidens filed off stage as fast as they could. All but Kiki, who was furious, headed directly to the ladies' room. She hovered in the short hallway between the bar and the restroom, collecting herself.

Em quickly made her another martini.

It was time for Louie to take the stage in his nightly tribute to Irene, the woman he referred to as his one true love, his Tiki Goddess. Everyone in the room waited expectantly. But tonight as he took the mic, Louie didn't face the life-sized portrait of Irene that hung behind the stage. He barely glanced at the image of his late wife. He was smiling down at Marilyn instead.

Em watched the Defector raise her champagne flute and silently toast Louie.

Em's gaze shot to Kiki, who hadn't missed the exchange either. Kiki's eyes slowly narrowed, her mouth hardened. The rest of the Maidens had collected themselves and filed back in. Suzi and Big Estelle joined Louie on stage. The others were forced to remain on the floor and join hands with the public. Soon tourists and patrons stood and linked hands, forming a huge circle around the room.

"And now," Louie said, "for all you *kama'aina* and *malihini* alike, it's time for our traditional finale. The Hula Maidens are going to sing along with me as they dance to the Tiki Goddess Song. This is a number I wrote back in 1973. It's dedicated to my late wife, my very own hula gal, Irene Kau'alanikaulana Hickam Marshall."

As Louie began the Tiki Goddess Song, Kiki glowered at Marilyn.

> "Brown-skinned girl of my dreams
> Standing there by the shore
> Dancing 'neath the moon beams
> I'll never love anyone more."

When Louie began the chorus, everyone sang at the tops of their lungs.

> "My Goddess. My Tiki Goddess.
> I'll never love anyone more.
> My Goddess. My Tiki Goooddess.
> I'll never never, never, never, never
> Love anyone moooooore."

Everyone sang with the off-key enthusiasm inspired by too many tropical drinks which dissolved inhibitions. No sooner had the last strains of the tune died away than Louie smiled at everyone gathered around the room. He was lifting the mic to his lips again when Kiki elbowed her way through the crowd.

"Louie! Oh, Looouie!" She called out in a sing-song stage voice and waved frantically, cooing as she tried to capture Louie's attention.

"I have a big announcement to make!" Kiki climbed up on stage and tried to reach for the mic, but Louie held on tight.

"I'd like to make an announcement first," he said.

Kiki shook her head, forgetting the mic was on. "I don't know how you found out, but you're *not* stealing my thunder."

Her words echoed around the bar. Most of the tourists were still on their feet. The locals sat down and were back to eating and drinking with one eye on the stage.

Kiki grabbed the mic and tugged. Em got ready to referee, but ever a gentleman, Louie finally shrugged, smiled, and handed over the microphone.

It was an unwritten rule that fist fights over the mic were reserved for Karaoke night.

Kiki tapped the top of the mic and then blew on it to make sure it was still on.

"I'm sure you are all dying to know what the Hula Maidens have been up to." She'd honed her stage voice to the carefree chirp of a coy schoolgirl.

Chairs scraped across the floor as the tourists took their seats. Locals who knew Kiki knew her announcements tended to go on forever. The old boys' club, regulars straddling tiki barstools with their backs to the stage, were studiously contemplating the labels on their beer bottles. Only the newcomers, the *malihini*, and the Maidens were actually listening with rapt attention.

"Well, you all know how much my girls love to dance and how we've danced at so many recent events: The Slug Festival, the shave ice truck opening, Flipper Thompson's baby's one year luau, not to mention our up and coming appearance at Mitchell's funeral."

She paused and scanned the crowd, then nodded. "Yes, it's true. We've been invited to dance at the funeral." She clapped her hand and started a short burst of applause. "Not only that, but in a few weeks the Hula Maidens are going to compete in the Kupuna division at the Kukui Nut Festival Competition!"

The room was full of noise, the clink and clank of flatware against thick ceramic china and the constant whir of dual blenders. Kiki kept smiling, waiting for a response that hadn't happened.

"Whoo hoo! Yes!" Kiki shouted into the mic so loud that an ear splitting whine shrilled with such a high pitch it rattled Em's fillings. "We're competing again, and we'll need all of your support. Next week we'll be selling pork *lau lau* out on the highway to help with our expenses, and I'm expecting *all* of you to buy at least four orders. *And* tickets for the competition will be available from all of our dancers very, very soon."

"The more excitement we generate in the audience, the better our chances to get high scores, so we're counting on *all* of you to be there. The event will be held at the hotel that used to be the Hilton, before it was a Hyatt. That was before it was a Marriott. Anyway, I think it's called Island Holidays Hotel this week, but whatever it's called, you know the place, near Wailua golf course and the prison. We'll have maps and brochures so you won't miss it. *And* all of you tourists who will still be here in three weeks, well, you've *never* seen anything like this competition. It's *real* hula. The *real* deal. So be there or be talked about."

Kiki took a deep breath. "As some of you know, most of us started dancing over nineteen years ago . . ."

Afraid Kiki would rattle on until she emptied the place, Em started forward, intending to somehow cut her off, but Louie was already there. A brief tug-o-war ensued before the mic popped loose, and Louie caught it.

"*Mahalo*, Kiki, for that exciting news," he said.

She glared back, but he ignored her. When he raised his champagne glass, Em could swear her uncle's eyes were glistening. She held her breath, aware of what was coming but not wanting to hear it.

"As you all know," he began, "my lovely Irene passed on over a decade ago. She'll always be the love of my life, but recently another woman has entered my world, a beautiful lady inside and out who makes me smile and puts a real spring in my . . ." He wiggled his brows and laughed. "A spring in my *step!*" he finished.

"We know what's really been springin' up lately," Little Estelle yelled from behind her walker. "But please! Spare us!"

The crowd howled. Louie waited for them to calm down before he went on. Em found herself staring at Marilyn thinking, *Oh Louie, what have you done?*

All the color had drained from Kiki's face leaving two huge blotches of adobe bronzer on her cheeks.

"I'm pleased to announce that I've asked Marilyn Lockhart to be my wife, and she's graciously accepted." Louie took a bow as cheers went up around the room. The tourists were thrilled to be included. The old boys at the bar groaned and ordered another round. The Maidens stood in stunned silence, staring in horror. Louie might as well have announced he had ten minutes to live.

When he saw Marilyn on her feet, raising her own champagne flute in his direction, he offered his hand, and she gracefully stepped onto the stage. She could barely smile but there was no hiding her triumph. She stood there next to Louie reminding Em of a recent photo she'd seen in the *Garden Island* news. It was a shot of a fisherman beside a record breaking ahi tuna that was dangling from a winch on the dock at Nawiliwili.

6

Lost and Found

Still in disbelief after Louie's announcement, Em deposited a tray of glasses at the end of the bar. Sophie paused in the middle of wiping the bar top free of sticky fruit syrup and grenadine, key ingredients in Louie's Liliko'i Lifesaver, the two-for-one drink of the night special.

Things had quieted down in the last two hours. The old boys had long ago given up their bar stools and tottered out. Except for a wedding party from Tucson, everyone had closed out their tabs and vacated the place. Louie and Marilyn slipped out together shortly after their big announcement.

Kimo popped his head in from the kitchen. "Hey, Em. The Maidens are holding an emergency meeting in the parking lot." That said, he disappeared again.

"Probably plotting Marilyn's demise," Em figured.

"Yeah. The engagement was a shock," Sophie agreed. "Did you know it was coming?"

Em didn't want to admit that she was hurt by the blindside.

"No idea. I mean, they've been together a lot lately, but Louie never ever talked about getting married again."

"Well, from what I hear, Marilyn makes a habit of it. What's this going to make? Six husbands?"

"I hate to ask."

"Maybe you should find out what happened to the rest of them."

Distracted, Em started dumping glasses into soapy water in the wash bin below the bar. "The rest of what?"

"The rest of her husbands. She's got tons of money. Maybe she's a Black Widow. Maybe she kills them and moves on."

This was no time to let her imagination run away with her. Em tried to focus on washing glasses while Sophie restocked the bar. Before they found the neighbor smoldering in the luau pit, Em would have dismissed the idea of a black widow going after Louie as crazy. Now she knew paradise wasn't all it was cracked up to be, if you looked behind the backdrop of palm trees, white sandy beaches and grass skirts.

"I hate to think she's only after Louie for this place. It would break his heart," Em said.

"I know Kiki suspects as much. I wasn't sure until . . ." Sophie looked over her shoulder and then walked closer to Em.

"Until what?"

"Until earlier tonight. Marilyn was super-friendly. She asked how business was going and said she was sure glad things had picked up lately. I just thought she was trying to make conversation. After their announcement, it got me thinking . . ."

"That she has plans for the Goddess."

"And probably not good plans. Maybe you should have your detective look into her background."

"I've told you, he's not my detective."

"But you wish."

Sometimes, Em thought, but she didn't want to admit it even to herself.

"He's got bigger fish to fry." Em dried her hands.

Kimo popped out of the kitchen again and walked over to join them at the bar. He picked up a bottle of beer and opened it.

"No more fish to fry. Kitchen's closed." He laughed at his own joke then said, "Em, you bettah get outside. Kiki's got some big *pilikia* going."

"*Pilikia?*" She tossed the towel down. She didn't know much Hawaiian, but she had heard the word tossed around the Goddess plenty when the late night crowd came in. *Pilikia* meant trouble. "Where are they?"

"Outside your office door in the back parking lot," he said.

"You got this, Sophie?"

The wedding party looked about ready to leave.

"Got it," Sophie assured her. "Better go see what they're plotting. I'd hate to have Louie's fiancée go missing so soon."

"Me, too," Kimo agreed. "If I ever get a call to bail Kiki out of jail, I'd be tempted to leave her there."

Em hurried through the small office in back. Just outside the door, Kiki and the Maidens were gathered in a tight knot in an empty parking stall.

Overhead, the stars appeared as thick as sand on the beach against the moonless sky. The one amber light in the parking lot cast the Maidens in jaundiced yellow. In a rainbow of vibrant muumuus now muted by the light, they were still wearing their huge sprays of fake orchids and ferns in their hair.

Em closed the door behind her without making a sound and heard Lillian say, "I didn't know there were restrictions. I thought anyone could join our group. Why, the day I ran into Suzi at Foodland, she said all I had to do was come to practice and start paying dues."

Kiki turned on Suzi. "I was *wondering* who said that. But right now our main concern is the Defector. I will not allow her to rejoin. No way. Nada."

"Did Marilyn actually ask to come back?" Big Estelle was leaning against the white van equipped to load her mother's Gad-About. Handicapped stickers and license plates were visible along with a small sign in the back window that originally said Baby on Board but had been altered to Babe on Board.

Little Estelle wasn't around. Em assumed she was already loaded in the van.

"She practically begged me to let her come back." Kiki pursed her lips. "She even squeezed out some fake tears."

"There's Em." Lillian saw her and waved. The rest of the women shifted around so she could join the circle.

"I suppose you knew all about the big engagement?" Kiki hated to be the last to hear anything.

"No. I'm as surprised as you." Em gazed around the circle of faces. "Sounds like Marilyn wants back in."

"She does, but she's not getting in," Kiki said.

"We have to vote on it," Big Estelle reminded her.

"Since when?" Kiki grabbed the sides of her head as if it were about to explode.

"Everyone should have a say." The minute Em voiced her opinion, Kiki turned on her.

"Everyone? Lillian barely knew Marilyn when she quit on us. And Flora? How is she supposed to vote?" Kiki indicated Flora with a wave of her hand. The woman was passed out across the trunk of the compact rental car parked beside them. "Trish isn't here. So this isn't a quorum."

"I say we give her a chance," Lillian suggested.

"Okay, then I vote no, no, and no." Kiki turned to Suzi. "And so do you, right?"

Suzi started to speak then thought better of it.

"What about aloha?" Lillian's voice quivered.

"What about a-NO-ha." Kiki started digging in her purse for her keys. "This meeting is over. I'll let the Defector know she's still out."

Just then the departing wedding party came around the corner. There were a dozen twenty-somethings, talking, singing and some of them weaving as they split up and got into their rental cars. A bridesmaid was complaining about having to be the designated driver as she pushed the car door remote and unlocked the doors. Two of the young couples got in without noticing there was a two-hundred-pound woman in a muumuu draped and drooling on the trunk lid.

"Big Estelle, wake up Flora before she ends up road kill. Put her in her car to sleep it off."

Big Estelle went to rouse Flora before the rental car pulled out. She deposited Flora in her SUV and then joined them again. "I'd better go back inside and get Mother," she said.

"I thought she was already in your van." Em rubbed the crease between her brows and wished she could rewind the day and start over.

"I left her in the bar."

"She's not in there."

"Maybe she fell asleep in the *lua*," Suzi suggested.

"She's not in the bathroom either," Em said.

"Well, she couldn't have gotten far. She's on the walker, not her scooter," Big Estelle looked around the parking lot.

"That's a relief," Lillian said.

"I'll go back inside and check, but I don't know how I could miss her," Em volunteered. "When you find her, come let me know."

Big Estelle, Suzi and Lillian ran off in all directions calling Little Estelle's name. Kiki fell into step beside Em as they headed back inside.

"Seriously, did you know about the engagement?" Kiki asked again.

Em stopped. "I told you. I had no idea."

"What are you going to do?"

"Right now I'm going to make sure Little Estelle is all right."

"Of course she's all right. She sneaks off all the time. We have a real emergency here. You can't let Louie marry that woman."

Just then Big Estelle raced out of the bar. "Mother's not inside anywhere!" She started weaving between parking stalls calling, "Mother? Mother!"

Em turned to Kiki. "Right now Louie's engagement isn't as important as finding Little Estelle."

Kiki sighed. "So you say. I'll toss my purse in the car and help look."

Em jogged a little ways up and down the highway calling for Little Estelle without any luck. She ran back and found Suzi pulling out of the driveway headed north. The realtor paused and rolled down the window.

"I'm going to head up to Princeville and look for Little Estelle along the way. Maybe she's walking home."

"You honestly think a ninety-two-year-old on a walker could get more than a couple of house lots away by now?"

Suzi rolled her eyes. "You never know."

"Where are the others?"

"Big Estelle is looking up and down the beach. Kiki went to search your house. Lillian is sitting in the parking lot sobbing."

They could hear David Letterman squawking his head off over at the house.

"Maybe I should call the police." Em thought of Mitchell Chambers dead in the taro patch.

"That's a good idea." Suzi drove off.

Em pulled out her cell phone and started to dial 911. On second thought she dialed Roland and told him Little Estelle had gone missing.

"Stop laughing," she had to add. "I'm serious."

"Okay." She heard him sigh. It was a second or two before he asked, "Where was she last seen?"

"In the bar."

"Before she scooted away?"

"She's on foot. Using a walker."

"You're kidding me, right?"

"I wish."

"I'll call it in and swing by on the way home."

Em hit the end button on her phone and started up the front steps of the Goddess. Before she reached the lanai, a yellow Jeep pulled in and screeched to a halt.

"Can you help me, lady?" A male tourist who looked to be in his mid-thirties, about Em's age, jumped out. He ran around to the passenger side door. Em started down the steps.

"Get out," he ordered someone in the Jeep.

"I can't get out on my own you nincompoop!"

When Em recognized Little Estelle's voice she ran around the car, and sure enough, there was Little Estelle, teetering on the edge of the passenger's seat.

"You got yourself in. Get yourself out." The man didn't make a move to help her climb out.

Em noticed that the front two button holes on his aloha shirt looked ragged. The buttons had been ripped off.

"What's going on here? What are you doing with her?" Em was afraid to find out.

"*She* attacked me." He kept his distance as he pointed at Little Estelle.

"So *you* say." Little Estelle pursed her lips and shook her head in disgust. "I'm a little old lady. Nobody's going to ever believe you."

Frustrated, the guy ran his fingers through his hair.

"Look, I'm not lying. I'm here on vacation from Nebraska. I stopped in to have a beer and then walked out of the bar and got into my rental car. I was almost to that beach, that place called Big Lumahai, when she popped up in the back seat, threw her arms around my neck and tried to *kiss* me. It was gross. I almost went off the road." He actually shivered.

"Is someone going to help me down?" Little Estelle was hanging from the handle at the top of the door frame by both hands. Her feet dangled above the ground.

Em turned to Little Estelle. "Is that true?"

"Of course not. He begged me to go with him."

"She's lying! I didn't even know she was in there until she lunged at me. Scared the poop out of me." He grabbed the front of his shirt. "She tried to tear my shirt off. She could have killed us both!"

"I wasn't going to kill you, honey. I was going to show you the time of your life. Bet you never did it with a real show girl before, and now you've lost your chance."

"This is gross." His expression was a mixture of sheer horror and panic.

"Please. Somebody get me down." Little Estelle was kicking her feet.

Em grabbed her around the waist and gently lowered her to the ground. The woman weighed little more than a box of Kleenex.

The man wiped his brow with the back of his arm. "Thanks, lady. Really. I owe you."

"I still don't understand how she got in there. She can barely walk." Em wondered if she should somehow stall the guy until Roland showed up.

"Ask her!" Little Estelle's victim hurried around the front of the Jeep and jumped in.

Little Estelle clung to the side view mirror for support until Em pried the woman's hands off the mirror. The tourist revved the engine and peeled out. Em stared at the license plate and repeated the number in her head just in case he was lying.

"Are you all right?" Em helped Little Estelle up the front steps to the Goddess lanai.

"Of course I'm all right. What a little pantywaist. I don't know what's wrong with you kids these days. You're all so darned serious."

"You climbed in there by yourself?"

"Well, I did have a little help from a couple that was leaving. I told them it was my daughter's car. They lifted me in."

"Where's your walker?"

"I ditched it in the parking lot before I snuck into the Jeep." Little Estelle pointed toward the mock orange hedge. Then she frowned and chewed on her lower lip. "Maybe we'd better not tell my daughter about this."

Just then Big Estelle came hurrying around the corner of the building.

"Mother! Where *were* you?"

Little Estelle started singing. "Got my motor runnin'. Lookin' for adventure . . . or whatever comes my way."

"Born to be wild? Really?" Em rolled her eyes.

"Gotta live it up. I may not have much time left," Little Estelle laughed.

"Where was she?" Big Estelle sounded more angry than relieved.

Behind her wire-framed glasses, Little Estelle's eyes pleaded for Em not to snitch.

Em leaned over and whispered, "Do I have your word you won't pull a stunt like that again? Next time you could end up in jail for tourist abuse."

Little Estelle thought for a minute and finally nodded yes.

"All that matters now is that she's back," Em gently prodded her toward Big Estelle. "Hang on to her, and I'll go get her walker."

7

A Close Encounter

By the time Roland pulled up followed by two white KPD police cruisers, the Maidens had cleared the parking lot, and all was quiet. Em assured him Little Estelle was no longer missing. Roland sent the cruisers on their way.

"So what happened?" Roland asked.

"You really don't want to know."

"You found her in a bush sleeping one off."

"No. Nothing like last time," Em said. "Are you hungry? There might be something left in the kitchen."

"Actually, I'm off duty. I'll take a Longboard."

"Sure." Em walked him into the bar. The place was empty except for Sophie, who was sitting on a barstool, elbow on the bar, her head on her hand. She looked exhausted.

"You can take off," Em told her. "I'll lock up."

Sophie looked Roland over. "Detective."

"Miss Chin."

"Thanks, Em. I think I will," Sophie said.

Em had given up trying to smooth things out between them. She walked around the bar, and Roland took over a barstool across from the beer taps. She filled a tall glass with Longboard, a local brew, and set it on the bar.

"Food?" Em asked.

"No, thanks. I had a big combo plate at L&L around six. I'm good." He smiled.

If she could let her guard down enough she just might find out how good he really was.

"Are we alone?" He took a sip of beer.

She glanced over her shoulder. The kitchen was dark. Kimo was gone. She hoped the dim light in the bar hid her blush.

"We're alone."

"Good. I've got some info on the gal in Mitchell's *halau*. Shari Kaui, the one who died."

"Oh." She should have known the case was the only thing on his mind. "You still think there's something suspicious going on?"

"I can't shake the feeling. Shari was a promising dancer. Mitchell didn't make it any secret that she would be the one to advance to *kumu* status one day. She was already his right hand, responsible for getting them grants and planning fundraisers. Quite the organizer as well as a talented dancer."

"So why would someone kill her if she was so vital to the group?"

"I'm thinking jealousy," he said.

"She was killed by someone who was attracted to Mitchell?"

"More like somebody who wanted Mitchell to elevate them instead. Now Chambers is dead along with Shari, so that kind of blows that theory."

"Why kill the *kumu* if the object was just to get Shari out of the way?"

"Right. I'll admit I don't know much of anything right now."

"It's just a feeling, right?"

"Yeah, just a feeling. Is Kiki going to enter the competition?"

Em was still thinking about Shari Kaui but finally nodded.

"She called in about registration. We're going into town to fill out the paperwork tomorrow. I volunteered to go along thinking maybe I'll hear something. I need some things from Costco anyway."

"I really appreciate this, Em."

"I just hope nothing turns up."

"I'm hoping there's nothing to it. The last thing I want is to put any of you in danger."

"Speaking of danger, Uncle Louie is engaged to Marilyn Lockhart."

"What's dangerous about that? A good marriage is a blessing."

She thought she must have heard wrong. "What?"

"A good marriage is a blessing. That's why I never got married yet. I'm waiting for the right woman to come along."

"Oh, really?" Having divorced her cheating ex, Em thought the fire-dancing detective sounded too good to be true.

"Really. So why aren't you happy about the engagement?"

"I'm worried Kiki will do something rash. She's worried Marilyn is after the Goddess. And then there's Marilyn herself. She's been married a whole lot of times, and I have no idea what happened to her previous husbands." She let the statement hang.

"What's a whole lot of times?"

"Rumor is four or five," she said.

"You want me to find out?"

"Payback is hell," she laughed. "But would you?"

"I'll see what I can do."

"Thanks, Roland."

"Just don't let Kiki pull any crazy stunts," he warned.

"With only a couple weeks to prepare, she's going to be completely focused on the competition number and their costumes for now. I think Marilyn's pretty safe."

"Other than Ms. Lockhart's track record, how do you feel about the engagement?" He was almost finished with his beer. Em found herself wishing he'd taken more time.

She sighed. "I want Louie to be happy, of course, but I don't want anyone taking advantage of him. Do you know how I ended up here?" On a small island like Kauai eventually everyone knew everything.

"I heard something about the Maidens sending for you."

"Kiki sent a letter and a one way ticket. The bar was always running in the red. They were convinced he was losing his mind and wanted me to know. I'm all the family he has."

"Now you've turned things around."

"We're doing better," she said.

"Do you regret the move?"

"No. But I'm not sure Louie's really losing it at all. I'm beginning to think Kiki was more worried about him losing the Goddess. Now this thing with Marilyn has her all wound up again." She picked up his empty glass. "Would you like another?"

"Nope. Driving. How about you lock up, and I'll walk you home?"

He waited while she turned off the lights and closed up and then walked her across the parking lot. The sound of the waves against the shore was intensified in the darkness. On a moonless night the white foam atop the surf was barely visible. A light that beamed out of the beach cottage spilled across the front lanai and over the sand. The palm trees lining the beach swayed in the trades, silent dancers silhouetted against the sky.

Em started up the steps, paused to say goodnight.

"Sorry I got you out here on a wild goose chase."

"No worries. I'm glad you found your runaway. Thanks for the beer."

"Anytime."

Standing a step below, he no longer towered over her. She could look directly into his eyes. Dangerous business.

"You need to be careful," he said.

"Careful?"

"Don't give yourself away while you're undercover."

"I don't plan to."

"You might not be able to help yourself. You started blushing when I asked if you were alone earlier."

Suddenly she was blushing again. Had he just moved closer?

Em cleared her throat and looked away. When she turned back he was still close.

"You're blushing again." He traced her cheek with his fingertip.

"You don't know that. It's too dark out here to tell."

"You're right. Maybe a closer look."

He leaned in and kissed her. His lips were cool. Up close he gave off the scent of coconut shampoo and trouble. His quick move was such a shock to her system that Em had to grab the screen door handle for support.

Inside, David Letterman let out shrill, earthshattering squawks.

"*Okole maluna!*" The bird shouted "Bottoms up!"

Roland winced.

"Louie's been spending too much time with Marilyn, which means Dave hasn't sampled any new drinks lately. He's pretty irritable."

"This could be parrot abuse," Roland said.

"Don't turn us in to the Humane Society."

"Don't tempt me."

She wished she wasn't so tempted to invite him in. There was no telling what would happen if she let her hormones take over.

Before she had time to give in his two-way radio went off. The voice on the other end said something about a stolen chicken.

"Gotta go," Roland had already cleared the first step. "Big emergency."

"A stolen chicken is an emergency?"

The island was over-run with wild fowl. Cars bumpers sported Take a Chicken to Lunch stickers. Colorful Kauai roosters were printed on T-shirts, coasters, coffee mugs, tote bags, notepaper and every kind of tourist trinket. Traps were sold at the feed stores, and dogs were trained to run them down. Usually no one cared when a wild chicken disappeared.

"Chicken *suit*. Not chicken."

"Someone stole a chicken suit?"

"You know the guy that jumps around in front of the chicken barbeque place in Kapa'a?"

"Don't tell me. Someone broke into their stand and stole the suit."

"No. The guy they hired ran off in it and disappeared."

8

Two Famous *Kumu*

The next morning Em left Sophie to run the bar while she rode into town with Kiki, who was still in a terrible mood from the night before.

"I called the Defector," she told Em. "First thing this morning. I think I heard Louie in the background. Did he spend the night with her?"

Em didn't think it was any of Kiki's business where Louie spent the night.

"He didn't come home, so I hope so."

"I still can't believe they're engaged. He must be crazier than I thought."

"He loves her, Kiki. She makes him happy."

Kiki snorted. "Happy my *okole*. I should tell him she's only after the bar." Kiki turned off onto the Kapa'a bypass, headed for Lihue. "Better yet, you should tell him. Maybe he'd believe you. He thinks she and I don't get along because we compete for wedding bookings."

Kiki had been the one and only wedding planner on the North Shore until Marilyn showed up.

"I'm not going to tell him any such thing without proof. She may not be after the bar at all."

After talking to Sophie last night Em wasn't sure what Marilyn was up to, but there was no way she was going to bad mouth the woman who might soon become Louie's wife. It suddenly occurred to Em that when they married, Marilyn might want to move out of her lovely home up in Princeville and live in the beach cottage. In that case, Em would be looking for a place of her own.

"You're going to do nothing?"

Kiki stopped at the traffic circle to yield to a Volkswagen bus. Then she started to pull out in front of it. Em yelled stop. Kiki stopped and waited until the road was clear. She missed the opening toward Lihue and ended up going around the entire circle before she was headed the right way again.

Em removed her clenched hand from the door handle. Thankfully there had only been three cars at the round-about.

Once her heart had stopped pounding she said, "I'm going to make the best of this and go along with Louie's wishes for the time being." She didn't dare admit she'd asked Roland to look into Marilyn's past.

"Maybe she'll just disappear," Kiki mumbled.

"What are you talking about?" Alarmed, Em wondered what Kiki was capable of.

"I'm just saying . . . maybe she'll leave the island. People do that, you know. They move over here and then decide island life is too slow and confining and take off again. We can only hope, eh?"

They did the usual errands, Costco, Walmart, the Humane Society Thrift Shop, then stopped at Kauai Pasta for lunch. Kiki downed a couple of three olive martinis while Em made the excuse of wanting to keep her wits about her and took over driving. On the way back to the North Shore they headed to Kapa'a and up the hill to the home of Kawika Palikekua, who had stepped in to take over Mitchell's *halau* as well as spearhead the Kukui Nut Festival's hula competition.

Kawika lived in a modest house painted sky blue with yellow trim. A baby goat was chained to a stake, happily munching on what was left of the grass in the front yard. Em followed Kiki into the front room of the sparsely decorated but neat home.

Kawika, a well-built man in his early forties, seemed surprised but more than happy to give Kiki entry forms along with a list of *halau* that had already signed up for the competition.

"Just fill the forms out and drop them off or mail them back to me by day after tomorrow," Kawika said. "I'm glad you're entering again, Kiki. It's been a while."

"We took some time off," Kiki said. "Took some time to tune up a bit."

As they talked, Em studied an impressive assortment of the hula competition trophies, *koa* wood bowls, and plaques on display around the room. There was a series of photos of Kawika performing solo and as a member of hula troupes from childhood until now.

Kiki pointed to a large group photo.

"That must be one of the last photos of Mitchell with the *halau*," she said.

Em moved closer to get a better look. Kawika pointed out Mitchell to her and then added, "And that's Shari Kaui. *Aw*. What a loss."

The thin, dark haired woman in a traditional costume was the hula dancer most mainlanders would imagine when they thought of Hawaii. Shari's smile was lovely, though she appeared frail.

"Who's your *kumu*?" Kawika asked Kiki.

Kiki hesitated and then laughed with a toss of her head. "We still don't have a *kumu*. We're looking for a teacher right now, not that we need one, but we could use a fresh eye and a bit of choreography help. We're a unique group."

Kawika glanced over at Em and then back to Kiki.

"Don't I know it," he laughed. "I'm sure whatever you come up with will be memorable."

"Thanks, Kawika." Kiki waved the paperwork. "I'll get these back in time. We'll see you at Mitchell's funeral. We're dancing."

Kawika was a little too slow at hiding his shock.

"Really?"

"Yes." Kiki nodded. "We've been on the program almost since the minute they found him. We might dance our Medley to Elvis, seeing as how Mitchell was almost as great at the King in his own right."

"That'll be out of the box." Kawika had the expression of someone who'd been hit between the eyes with a two by four. Protocol at the funeral had just flown out the window. "You know at the competition you'll get more points for songs in Hawaiian and also for songs written by Kauai composers. And for songs about Kauai."

"Thanks for the tip. I'll see what I can find."

Before they walked out, Em paused to indicate all of his trophies. "Looks like you've been dancing since you could walk, Kawika."

"Even before. My mother danced when she was *hapai* with me. I guess you could say I picked it up in her womb."

"How were you chosen to taken over for Mitchell?" She pretended to study a plaque on the wall trying to sound casually interested. The question was a valid one from a newcomer and a *haole*.

"Mitchell was training me become a *kumu hula* and have my own *halau* one day. So, I was the natural choice, of course. I've got some great ideas that Mitchell would never have approved, but I'll slowly integrate them into our dancing."

According to Roland, Shari Kaui would have taken over. With Mitchell and Shari both out of the way, Kawika had inherited the *halau* along with the prestige and the income that came with it.

"So, now you're in charge of the Kukui Nut Festival competition too?"

"Mitchell was getting so weak that the *halau* was already doing most of the work. I'm just trying to fill his slippers. I'll be the emcee. It's going to be some show. I've got lots of ideas I'd love to implement for next year, too."

"I'm sure it will be wonderful," Em said.

Kiki thanked him again. They said aloha and Em followed her out the door. They'd reached the sidewalk when a lowered, metallic silver Chevy truck slid up to the curb and parked behind Kiki's sedan. There was a huge *100% Local* decal in the back window.

"Oh, my gosh." Kiki shook her purse and started digging for her keys.

"Gosh what?"

"That's Jackie Loo Tong." There was more than a hint of reverence in Kiki's tone.

"Who's Jackie Loo Tong?" Em whispered because the man in question had just stepped out of the pickup. He was not much taller than Em. Close to five-seven maybe. His black hair was slicked back into a long waist-length braid. He wore a tight white sleeveless T-shirt that showed off well-honed biceps and the tribal tattoos banding them. His skin was a rich cocoa with a touch of gold.

He flashed a wide smile at Em as he walked over and gave Kiki an *aloha* hug and a kiss on the cheek.

"Miss Kiki! *Pehea 'oe.* How you stay? Long time no see."

"I'm good," Kiki was blushing from her hairline to her neck. "How are you doing, Jackie?"

"Great. Just got back from doing a little gambling in Las Vegas. Can't wait for the big competition, eh?" He glanced at the blue house. The baby goat was gnawing on the corner of the lowest wooden step. Jackie turned back to Kiki and pointed to the papers she was holding. "Are those entry forms? Are you putting your girls in the competition?"

Kiki's forehead was glowing with perspiration. "I am."

"Gee, you pretty brave . . . after what happened last time."

"They're much better dancers now," Em interjected. She didn't know Jackie Loo Tong, but already she didn't like him.

"And who are you, pretty *haole* lady?" Jackie gave her a wink and a sly smile. "Nothing I like better than a fine *haole wahine.*"

"This is Em Johnson. She's Louie Marshall's niece. She's managing the Goddess now."

"Wow. Long time since I been out the North Shore. I'll have to come in and check the place out sometime. You have Hawaiian entertainment?"

Em nodded. "Danny Cook and the Tiki Tones. The Hula Maidens dance for us nightly now."

"Oh." Obviously unimpressed, Jackie turned to Kiki again. "I'm glad to hear you girls are doing great. I can't *wait* to see your performance. I'm sure your ladies will really rock da house."

Em couldn't miss his sarcasm. Thankfully, Kiki did.

"Mahalo, Jackie. That means a lot coming from you." Kiki fingered her sunrise shell necklace and smiled.

"So, what about Mitchell? *Shock*-ing, eh?" Jackie shook his head.

"Really terrible," Kiki's voice fell.

Jackie shrugged. "I'm not surprised, though. He never took care, you know. He was in terrible health. I hear his *halau* is in upheaval now."

"Kawika took over, you know," Kiki said. "He seems to be doing great. Sounds like he has it all under control."

"Puh. Kawika. Good luck to them then. Him and his crazy ideas. I was pretty sure my dancers were going to take top honors this year and now that Mitchell's gone, I'm willing to bet big money on it. We would have won the overall championship last year if not for Mitchell's group. The judges aren't always fair, you know. They played favorites with Mitchell just 'cause he started the festival."

"Tell me about it," Kiki agreed.

Em studied Jackie Loo Tong and wondered how far he would go to win. She glanced at her watch. Kiki would gossip forever if they didn't get moving.

"It's nice to meet you Jackie," Em interrupted, "but I'd better get back to work. Kiki?"

Kiki bid Jackie Loo Tong aloha with another big hug and a kiss, and then she and Em climbed into the car.

"Here. Hang on to these." Kiki handed Em the papers and turned the key in the ignition. "He seemed pretty excited to hear the Maidens are competing again. Maybe this *is* a good idea."

Em was staring out of the passenger window thinking. When she got back to Haena she would call Roland first thing.

"People take these competitions pretty seriously, don't they?" she asked.

"Of course," Kiki said. "Hula is life."

Em thought about Jackie Loo Tong bragging about his own *halau* and his certainty of winning now that Mitchell was gone.

Hula might be life, but could it be the death of someone?

9

Back at the Bar

It was drizzling on the North Shore when Em returned. Kiki helped her unload her supplies at the house and left. By the time Em walked into the Goddess it was almost four, and the place was deserted except for Buzzy, the aging hippie who lived somewhere up the road. No one was really sure where he lived or even what is last name was. Folks saw him walking along the highway, and then he'd just disappear into the jungle. He'd been a fixture at the end of the road since the late 70's when an entire band of free love hippies built tree houses on the beach and named it Taylor Camp.

"Hey, Buzzy," Em waved. "You doing all right?"

Buzzy managed a nod and a vacant smile that was permanently in place. He was wearing a wide, black elastic band around his forehead with a battery operated light attached. The light was on, illuminating the Corona bottle on the table in front of him.

Em walked over to the bar. "It's not *that* dark in here," she said to Sophie.

"I told him he was running down his batteries. He said yeah, he'd been living on the edge for a long time." Sophie was prepping the divided container full of lime wedges, Maraschino cherries and olives. "How'd it go in town?"

"Not bad. Kiki got the entry forms. She said to give you this." Em handed her the competition line up sheet. "She thought you might recognize some of the groups they'll be competing against."

Sophie quickly scanned the list. Em noticed a slight tightening of her lips.

"What's wrong?"

"This is my mom's old *halau*." She pointed to one of the names on the list.

Em knew better than to question her. The girl didn't like to talk about her life on Oahu. She'd moved to Kauai to turn the page, and Em respected her wishes.

"Do you know any of the others?"

"I've heard of some of the other *kumu*. Looks like there are even a couple of groups coming all the way from Japan."

"Really?" Em glanced down at the list. "Wow."

"Yeah. Wow. One of the Japanese groups has an entry in the *Kupuna* division. They'll be up against the Maidens."

"Bad?"

"Terrible. Those Japanese dancers are like well-oiled machines. No mistakes."

"Sounds pretty scary."

"Yeah, I think the *kumu* beat them if they dance out of step."

"You're kidding, right?"

"Kind of."

"I met Kawika Palikekua, Mitchell's replacement, and we ran into Jackie Loo Tong."

"Jackie's one of the best."

"He thinks so too." Em reminded herself to call Roland ASAP. "Anything happen while I was gone?"

"We had a pretty good lunch crowd. Your uncle rolled in about one. He's pretty excited about the engagement. So excited he's working on a new drink recipe."

"Good. That parrot needs a drink in the worst way. Kiki's not happy about the engagement."

"To say the least." Sophie went over to the ice machine and scooped out a bucket of ice and lugged it over to the ice bin. "I hope she doesn't pull any stunts."

"You don't think she'd actually do anything to hurt Marilyn, do you?" "Physically?" Sophie thought about it for a minute. "No. But I'm sure Kiki can come up with plenty of ways to make the woman pretty miserable."

"Hopefully she'll be too focused on the competition to do anything."

Remembering the reactions of the two *kumu*, Em said, "I hope the Maidens don't embarrass themselves too badly."

"I've been on the phone during my breaks trying to find someone to coach them."

"Any success?"

"I'm close. I'm waiting for a friend to call me back."

"A coach? Not a *kumu*?"

"Actually I'm hoping more like a referee. There's not a *kumu* on island who will take them on. Wally Williams is here, and he said he'd be thrilled to help them with hair and makeup. He offered to design a costume."

"What about Kiki? Isn't that her territory?"

"I'm hoping they can work together."

"He'll be great. He was Fernando's stylist in Vegas long enough to learn about 'wow' factor and about what works on stage. When did he get back?"

"Last week. I called to see if he was on island and he picked up."

Wally Williams was the former partner of the late Fernando, a flamboyant pianist who had stepped into Liberace's shoes when they were still warm. Fernando recently met with an unpleasant end, but Wally was able to comfort himself by visiting their Kauai estate, one of many that Fernando had left him.

"I'm hoping to hear from my friend tonight," she added. "With any luck they'll both volunteer, and I'll have Kiki call a meeting of the Maidens in the morning."

"Speaking of calls, I need to make a couple. It'll just take a few minutes."

"No worries." Sophie picked some menus and headed for a knot of tourists hovering in hesitation on the threshold. "Come on in, folks. We don't bite. We've got the best Mai Tais in town and over forty-two tropical drinks on the menu. Each and every one is legendary."

Sophie waved them in and escorted them to a table on the opposite side of the room from Buzzy and his headlamp.

Em called Roland. He picked up on the first ring and said, "I haven't had time to look into Ms. Lockhart's background yet."

"No problem. I have some news for you."

Em cradled the phone to her ear and pulled Louie's battered leather chair out from behind the massive desk in the Goddess office. She'd just found a brief note from her uncle waiting for her.

I'll be home by six and won't be going out.

Gotta come up with a new recipe for a drink to commemorate my engagement.

Hopefully taste-testing would put David Letterman in a better mood.

"Already? What's up?" he asked.

"I went to town with Kiki today to pick up the registration forms, so it looks like they'll be dancing in the competition."

"Good work."

"And I met Kawika Palikekua. He's taken over Mitchell's *halau*, and he's not making a secret of the fact he's more than happy to be in charge. He said Mitchell was training him to be a *kumu*."

"Yet Shari Kaui was in line before him. Convenient she's gone, yeah?"

"That's what I was thinking. Kawika said he has lots of new ideas he can't wait to implement. And there's more."

"Pretty soon I'll have to put you on the payroll."

Em laughed. "I also met a *kumu* named Jackie Loo Tong."

"I know him. He likes to gamble."

"He said he's willing to bet his dancers will take the top prize now that Mitchell's gone. He wasn't mourning the loss of a fellow *kumu*, that's for sure, and he wasn't hiding the fact he was pissed about the way the judging went in recent years because the judges always favored Mitchell."

"Now the field is conveniently wide open."

"After meeting those two I think you might be on to something. No love lost between them all. Have you had any other intuitions?"

There was a slight pause before he said, "Just that I should come over after I'm off duty and keep you company now that Louie is spending his nights with his fiancée."

She fingered Louie's note, smiling.

"Sorry. He says he's worn out, and he'll be home tonight." Em laughed.

"What's so funny?"

"If you were really psychic, you'd have known that."

10

Bringing in Back Up

A handful of Maidens showed up at the bar to dance that night. Afterward Sophie asked Kiki to pass the word there would be an emergency meeting at ten the next morning.

"Why? What's it about?" Kiki wanted to know. "I can't just call and ask them to be here without an agenda."

Sophie knew better. If Kiki called a meeting anywhere, anytime, the others would show up no questions asked. But Kiki wanted to know why, and Sophie could tell by the panic on her face that she was not just on the edge. She was about to topple over it.

"I've lined up a couple of people to help you."

"Who?"

"You'll find out tomorrow."

"What if we don't approve?"

"Kiki, you don't have time to fart around and disapprove. Competition is less than two weeks away." Sophie hesitated a minute then added, "Should I call the Maidens or do you want to?"

"I'll call them," Kiki mumbled.

"Great. See you all in the morning."

Sophie watched Kiki weave her way through the room crowded with teetering cocktail tables full of drinks. She greeted locals and stopped to chat with curious tourists who asked about the intricate head *lei* of woven flowers and leaves that was Kiki's trademark adornment. As eccentric as Kiki could be, she was often a force to be reckoned with, but the woman had a heart of gold.

The Maidens were all there the next morning, not exactly bright-eyed, but they rolled in on time. Sophie had coffee and sweet rolls ready. Kiki asked for a shot of Bailey's in hers and everyone else wanted some.

"Coffee and rolls are free, but I'll have to charge you for the liquor," Sophie warned.

No one cared.

Flora was at the wide end of the banquet in a muumuu with the hems of her sweatpants sticking out beneath it. It was already in the high seventies outside but it was "fall weather" as far as the locals were concerned. Little Estelle had rolled in on her Gad-About and parked near the stage. She ignored them all, hidden behind the daily edition of the *Garden Island* news.

"Could you hurry it up with the coffee?" she barked at Sophie. "I can't read my paper without a cup of coffee."

"Ignore her," Big Estelle lowered her voice and leaned closer to Sophie when she passed by. "She's not reading the paper. Just the headlines."

"I *hear* you, Big Estelle." Her mother snapped the open pages and peered over them. "I have the hearing of a dog."

"And I have a property to show at eleven," Suzi Matamoto announced. "Can we get started?"

"Sophie called this meeting," Kiki said. All heads turned her way.

"Now that you all have your coffee, I have an announcement to make." Sophie replaced the pot in the coffee maker and then picked up the competition schedule. She walked back over to the tables where the Maidens were waiting and held it up. She waved the list.

"You ladies are facing some stiff competition at the Kukui Nut Festival."

Flora groaned and added some tequila from her plastic water bottle to her already spiked coffee.

"None of these women have handled anything stiff for years," Little Estelle chuckled from behind the newspaper.

"Mother!" Big Estelle rolled her eyes.

Sophie tried to ignore them.

"Not only are you competing with the *kupuna* from Mitchell's *halau*," she said, "which is now under the direction of Kawika Palikekua, but also Jackie Loo Tong's *halau*. And there are two coming over from Oahu and two from Japan."

"And you all know what *they're* like." Suzie stopped texting, put her phone in her purse and folded her hands on the table.

"They *breathe* in unison." Kiki's eyes flashed around the assemblage.

"They even weigh the same," Flora mumbled.

Trish Oakely, the photographer, had arrived late but had caught the conversation. She slid in beside Kiki. "None of them weigh over a hundred pounds," she said.

"Soaking wet," Big Estelle added.

"Is this conversation politically correct?" Suzi Matamoto glanced at her phone.

"You started it. But it *is* based on observation," Trish countered.

"What are we going to do? I think we're in over our heads." Lillian Smith had been silent up to now. She appeared to be suffering a sleep hangover. The sun streaming through the window was shining through her teased pink tinted hair. She glanced at Kiki and quickly away as she raised her hand. Her question was directed at Sophie.

"Lillian?" Sophie smiled encouragement. Poor Lil was wound tighter than a ukulele string about to pop.

"Maybe . . ." Lillian cleared her throat. "Maybe we should let Marilyn back into the group. She *is* a good dancer and . . ."

Sophie could feel Kiki starting to vibrate. She quickly cut Lil off before the fireworks started.

"I don't think that will be necessary," Sophie said.

"And I . . ." Kiki started to rise. She'd lost all color except for two bright spots of blush on her cheeks.

Sophie spoke over her. "The good news is that I've found you ladies some help. You all know Wally Williams." She waited while they nodded. "He'll be happy to help with your costuming."

Kiki nearly choked on a mouthful of Bailey's and coffee.

"I design the costumes," Kiki reminded them once she'd stopped wheezing.

Sophie took a slow, deep breath and smiled. "I think it would be great if you let Wally give you some input . . . just for the competition, of course."

"He *did* design for Fernando," Lillian reminded them. "Those jewel encrusted jackets Fernando always wore were to die for. I can help with bedazzling. I got a Bedazzler kit from QVC."

"I'm not wearing rhinestones in a competition," Kiki snapped. "That's *not* Hawaiian."

"I'm sure he'll come up with something that will win you high points." Sophie was beginning to doubt the wisdom of trying to help. It was going to be a long, rocky road to awards night at the Kukui Nut Festival.

"Fernando's costumes could rival anything you've ever come up with, Kiki." Trish got up and went over to the bar to get her own coffee.

"What about the silver lame shark gown complete with the fins for our heads?" Kiki was livid and had given up trying to hide it. "Or those anti-bellum *muumuus* with hoop skirts and parasols I designed for our Battle Hymn of the Republic Fourth of July medley?"

Little Estelle slammed the paper down on the tray clipped to the front of her Gad-About. "Ohforcrapsake, Kiki. Those skirts were so wide only two dancers fit on the stage at once."

Flora spoke up. "Yeah, and Lillian, Suzi and me got their hoops all tangled and were stuck in the car for twenty minutes outside Pizza Bowl the night we were supposed to dance at the bowling tourney. If the fire department hadn't brought the Jaws of Life we'd still be in there."

"Enough." Sophie crossed her arms. "Wally has volunteered, and I think he should at least consult on costumes. You'll certainly need more hands for sewing, hair, and makeup."

"Wow." Flora's coffee was gone. She took another sip of tequila straight out of her water bottle. "We're gonna have a pro do our make up?"

They all started talking at once. Afraid she was losing them, Sophie shouted, "I found you a coach."

Stillness settled over the bar until the only sounds in the room came from outside: rental cars passing by headed for the nearby snorkeling spots, birds chirping, roosters crowing back and forth.

"What do you mean a *coach*?" Kiki was gripping the edge of the table now. "Who?"

"Someone to help pull you together before the event."

"A *kumu*?"

"Not a *kumu*."

Kiki settled back into her chair. "A choreographer?"

"Not exactly."

"Another hula dancer?"

"No. Not exactly."

"Then *what* exactly?"

Just then a person appeared in the doorway. Sophie smiled and waved. "Come on in, Pat. Meet the Hula Maidens."

Pat strolled in. Lillian leaned closer to Suzi and whispered, "Is that a man or a woman?"

Suzi squinted at the new arrival and shrugged.

Sophie understood their confusion. Like her, Pat wore a spiked haircut, but that's where the similarity ended. The tails of a bright yellow aloha shirt with a pack of cigarettes in the pocket hung out over short denim cargo shorts. Pat wore no makeup and no jewelry other than a watch with a camouflage print band. She had on black cowboy boots with white socks sticking out over the tops.

Pat was not as beefy as a man or as curvy as a woman.

Sophie had never asked actually Pat's sexual orientation. Pat was just Pat. They met in the bar at CJ's up in Princeville where a group gathered every Monday for happy hour. Since Mondays was her day off, Sophie had started attending the happy hour "meetings" for a change of scenery and a chance to get to know people who didn't necessarily frequent the Goddess. Pat was a character who was fast becoming a no-nonsense friend. She told the truth and was happy to listen whenever Sophie needed to talk.

The minute Sophie decided the Maidens needed someone strong to pull them together for the competition, she thought of Pat.

"This is Pat Boggs, ladies. From now on Pat will be running your practices."

"But . . ." Kiki hunched in the banquet seat, frowning up at Pat.

"You'll still be in charge, Kiki," Sophie added, "but Pat's a former Army Drill Sergeant who has volunteered to keep order so you ladies can get it together. That's the only way you're going to be ready for the festival competition in time. I'll say again, Pat is a *volunteer,* so the less time you waste discussing this, the better." Sophie was thankful Kiki had backed down for the moment, but that didn't mean she wasn't brewing up trouble.

"Pat? Is there anything you'd like to say?" Sophie nodded to the former sergeant.

Pat Boggs eyeballed Lillian and then the others and drawled, "Yeah. First off, I'm a woman, not that that's anybody's damn bitness. Second, Sophie's right, I volunteered for this gig after she told me how y'all can't walk and chew gum at the same time, let alone dance your way out of a wet paper bag. I guess you're *still* plannin' to compete in the Kook-kooie—or whatever it is—Nut Festival. Looking at you all . . ." Pat hooked her thumbs in her pants pockets and eyed each Maiden in turn, "I'd say we got plenty of work to do and no time to waste. I may be tough, but I mean to do you all proud and get you whipped into shape. If you co-operate, you have my gar-un-tee that you won't walk out of that competition with your tails tucked between your sissy legs this year. Now," she turned to Kiki, "when and where is our first practice?"

Sophie watched Pat work the Maiden crowd control. The woman had more than once proven at a happy-hour-gone-wild that she could out shout anyone in a brawl and silence an unruly crowd. Pat could take a beer bottle to the head without flinching, so she wasn't going to back down in front of Kiki.

As far as Sophie was concerned, Pat Boggs was perfect for wrangling the Hula Maidens and keeping them in line.

11

Congratulations Are in Order

Em walked into the bar just as the Maidens' morning meeting was breaking up and found Kiki in deep conversation with a stranger by the front door. Em stopped Sophie, who was carrying a tray of refilled ketchup and soy sauce bottles to the tables.

"Who's that?"

"Her name's Pat. I asked her to coach the Maidens."

"Looks like she can handle them. How's Kiki with it all?"

"Going with it for now. She'll probably lay low and wait for Pat to slip up before she pounces."

"Hopefully that won't happen. They need all the help they can get."

"If anyone can handle them, it's Pat. How'd you know she was a chick?"

"How?" Em shrugged. "I'm from Southern California."

They both looked up as Uncle Louie's faded blue pickup truck rattled past the open window.

"Looks like he got away from Marilyn. Have you even had a chance to talk to him since the big announcement?"

"Not yet. He got in late last night and left early this morning. Left a note about going up to Foodland for some drink ingredients." Em glanced at her watch. It was nearly eleven. "It took him long enough."

"Probably grabbed a *loco moco* plate and stopped by for a quickie at Marilyn's."

"Please." Em shook her head picturing Marilyn's table littered with takeout cartons full of rice topped with egg, hamburger patties and gravy. "Don't go there. There's something about the image of my seventy-three-year-old uncle and his 'girlfriend' having a quickie after a *loco moco* that keeps me from wanting to go there."

"I hear you."

Em went back into the office to check the voice mail as Sophie continued to set up before the lunch crowd started to arrive. Em was barely in her chair when Louie breezed in the back door carrying a bag full of mangos and some mango nectar. Smiling and seemingly very carefree for a man his age, there was an old Hollywood personality air about him because of his perpetual tan, snappy Panama hat, and head of full of silver hair. He was a handsome man even when he wasn't smiling. His stunning smile was always genuine. Louie was warmhearted and cordial and made everyone feel at home in the Goddess—which was his key to holding on to the business for so many years.

"How's my favorite niece?" It was an old joke, but Louie always chuckled over it. Em was his only niece. In fact, she was his only relative.

"Good. I'm getting ready to call a list of people who want to book catering gigs. How are you?"

"Great! Still living the dream, that's for sure."

"By the way," she said, sobering, "I haven't officially congratulated you on your engagement."

He looked sheepish. "I'm sorry I didn't tell you ahead of time, but we wanted to surprise everyone."

Em wondered if *we* or Marilyn wanted it to be a big surprise so that no one could object.

"Have you set a wedding date?"

He shook his head with a smile as he sat down on the corner of the desk. "Not yet. It's going to take me a while to get used to being engaged."

Em was relieved. Anything could happen before Louie and Marilyn's marriage was a done deal. She still had time to find out about the woman's past.

"You're okay with it, aren't you?" His concern showed on his face. "I mean, I know Kiki and some of the other Maidens don't like Marilyn because she left their group, but she still cares about them. In fact, she was pretty upset when Kiki called and told her that she wouldn't be allowed to rejoin. I tried to convince her that she was too good for them. She's danced with some of the best, you know. She danced for Mitchell Chambers."

"So I hear. She must be upset about what happened to him."

"You bet. She's going to the funeral on Saturday. I told her I'd go with her."

"That'll be nice." Considering all the key *hula halau* players would be attending the funeral and the memorial luau afterward, Em decided she should go too; maybe she'd hear something of interest to Roland.

Louie shifted the bag of supplies. "I'd better get moving. I'm working on a new drink to commemorate the engagement. Marilyn loves champagne and mangos." His gaze drifted toward the ceiling; his voice took on a dreamy quality. "Why just the other night I was drizzling champagne over her . . ."

"My gosh!" Em jumped up, effectively cutting him off. "Look at the time. I've got to start making these calls, and there's still some planning to do for the art showing in two weeks."

"Pretty upscale stuff." He got a faraway look in his eye. "I wonder what Irene would think of an art show here at the Goddess?" He smiled as he always did when he spoke of his first wife.

"I think she would be pleased. Besides, it's not that upscale. The artist is a guy from over on the Po'ipu side who sculpts body parts out of bread dough."

Louie threw back his head and laughed. "Body parts? Is the show x-rated?"

Em frowned. "I hope not. I looked him up online. Most of the pieces were arms and legs and feet. Elbows. That kind of thing. Really lifelike. The heads have faces."

"Bread dough. Who knew?"

"Right."

"I hope no one ends up taking a bite out of an exhibit. Better keep an eye on Buzzy."

"Good idea," Em agreed.

Louie stood and shifted the bag of mangos.

"I'd better start experimenting with the new cocktail before the lunch rush starts." He headed for the door to the main barroom.

"I hope you're planning to take samples over to David Letterman. I think he's having the DT's."

"Yeah. He nearly bit my hand off this morning when I reached into his cage to refill his water dispenser."

"Do you have a name for the new cocktail?"

"Sure do. Two to Mango."

12

Mitchell's Big Send Off

Aloha Mitchell. We (heart) You Mitchell.

Handmade signs lined both sides of the highway. Weathered scraps of plywood, old surfboards, anything that could be painted had been lettered and propped up against telephone poles or fence posts by the locals to bid aloha to the revered *kumu.*

The number of signs multiplied until there was one every few feet as Em drove through Kapa'a and across the Wailua River Bridge. Balloons and bunches of ti leaves marked the entrance of the road to Lydgate Park where signs announced Mitchell's memorial luau.

Em turned left and wound her way along the road. She wasn't anywhere near the event pavilion yet, but she pulled in beside the car in front of her when it suddenly stopped. Better to take a space further back than be bogged in and have to make a U-turn in a crowd.

Like the parking area, the pavilion was jam-packed when she walked in. The din of five hundred voices resonated off the cement floor and the tin roof of the open air structure. One end was bordered by a tall lava rock wall and wide stage where a troupe of hula dancers swayed to the smooth sounds of a steel guitar accompanied by a dozen ukuleles and guitars.

Lovely in their matching *muumuus* and subtle floral hairpieces of waxy red anthuriums and vibrant green fern, the dancers seemed to float across the stage in perfect time to the music. They were definitely not the Hula Maidens.

Em got in line at a table set up near the entrance. It was customary to bring a card with money tucked inside for the family for occasions and celebrations of this sort. Em reached the table where a line of Hawaiian women of gracious ages lovingly called "aunties" nodded and smiled in thanks and welcome as she expressed her condolences, signed a guest book, and dropped her envelope into a wooden calabash filled with other donations.

At the end of the table, draped in leis made of precious *maile* vines from the forest high up on the mountains of Kokee on the West side of

Kauai, sat a hand carved *koa* wood box that had to be two feet wide and a foot high. Em watched as the guest in front of her paused, laid a hand on the lid of the box, bowed his head and closed his eyes. The nearly three hundred pound *kumu* had been reduced to ash and poured into the *koa* box.

Em paused before it when her turn came. She had no idea what to say. She hadn't known the man. She was here at Roland's urging. She sighed, closed her eyes and thought of Mitchell Chambers appearing in one last big gig in the sky. Before she moved on she whispered, "Break a leg, Mitchell."

Shuffling along with the newcomers around her, Em paused beside the last table in a long line of picnic tables running end to end down the length of a pavilion as long as half a football field. There were five identical rows set up to accommodate the huge crowd. She looked around and spotted Kimo at the back wall near the serving tables. He reached into an ice chest big enough to hold a dead elephant and then popped the ring on a cold Budweiser as she joined him.

"What a crowd." Em leaned close so he could hear her over the din.

"Plenty people here to honor da guy alright." Kimo took a long chug and drained half the can.

"Where are the girls?"

He nodded toward the stage. "Lined up on da right side."

"I'm glad I didn't miss them."

"They been standing there thirty minutes already. I hope they go on before I gotta get back and start the prep for dinner."

"I told Sophie to close up right after lunch if things got slow." Sophie and Tiny, Kimo's part time assistant chef, were the only ones holding down the fort.

Kiki had the Maidens assembled next to the steps to the right of the stage. For once they were modestly dressed in white ruffled muumuus with sprays of green ferns and white spider lilies in their hair. At least Kiki realized this wasn't the time or place to risk another wardrobe malfunction.

The dancers already performing completed their number with a lovely bow, turned as one and filed down the left stairway. Sparky Cloud, local radio personality and politician, was the volunteer emcee.

"Sparky is Mitchell's brother-in-law by his third wife's cousin," Kimo said.

"Ah." Em pretended to understand. Lineage on Kauai was always as complicated as a spider web. When she first arrived she'd tried keeping notes of who was related to who and how, but keeping everybody straight was impossible. She gave up early on.

Sparky, smooth as a game show host, thanked the retreating dancers and then started in on how Mitchell came from a long line of well-respected *kumu*. As Sparky went on, the musicians on stage waited patiently, some sipping beer, others staring off into space.

Em watched Kiki walk along the line of Maidens like a commander reviewing his troops, no doubt issuing orders to stand up straight and smile. When Sparky's rendition of Mitchell's qualifications finally ended, the emcee ignored the Maidens and announced Mitchell's own *halau*. The dancers had somehow managed to quietly slip up onto the opposite side of the stage and line up. Kiki and the Maidens watched in frustrated silence.

Under the direction of Kawika Palikekua, dancers dressed in traditional *pau* skirts, pantaloons, and strapless tops were ushered onto the stage. Kawika preened as proud as a peacock before he sat down cross-legged behind a tall *ipu heke*, the native double gourd drum used for chanting.

Even though Kiki was at the opposite end of the pavilion, Em could see the woman was livid. Lillian was ready to cry. Trish was busy snapping photos while diminutive Suzi Matamoto tried to hide her embarrassment. Flora was sipping on her Gatorade bottle.

The hypnotic beat of the *ipu heke* filled the pavilion with sound that harkened back to ancient times. Kawika began to chant, and then the dancers joined in. The air in the pavilion reverberated with the sound of his voice.

Apparently the Maidens weren't going to perform any time soon, so Em decided to go through the buffet line and then look for Louie. When she reached the serving table crowded with huge aluminum pans filled with familiar luau favorites, she noticed Marilyn was there dishing up rice.

Watching her plate fill with food as she passed by each server, Em finally reached Louie's fiancée. Marilyn smiled.

"Why hello, Em. Rice?" She gestured with the scoop in her hand.

Em shook her head. "No, thanks. There's already enough on this plate to fill a cargo plane. I'll save room for the good stuff."

The tall local woman beside Marilyn gave Em a look that clearly said *stupid haole*. Who didn't want rice? Em ignored her.

"Congratulations," Em told Marilyn. "I haven't seen you since the big announcement."

"Thank you, honey. I hope you're pleased."

Pleased for Louie, Em thought. "My uncle's really thrilled." She changed the subject. "It's nice of you to help out," she added.

Marilyn's eyes filled with tears. "It's the least I can do. I so loved the way Mitchell taught hula. He was so kind to me."

Em was holding everyone up. A young man in line beside her was shooting daggers.

"Where is my uncle?" Em asked Marilyn.

She scooted down to the next server and stared down into an

aluminum pan the size of a swimming pool. It was full of chicken *lu'au*, a dish that looked like a cross between creamed spinach and something that had already been eaten. Em nodded to the server that she'd have some. The mix of chicken pieces, taro leaves and coconut milk tasted a lot better than it looked.

"Louie is in the middle of the center table. You'll see his hat," Marilyn said.

Em made her way through the line, grabbed some chocolate cake and rice pudding off the dessert table and then spotted Louie right where Marilyn had said he'd be. He saw her too and waved her over to the empty spot beside him.

She maneuvered her leg over a long picnic bench—no small feat in a sundress while balancing a paper luau tray of food and a plastic cup of passion-orange-guava juice better known as POG. Her paper tray was so full it sagged on both sides.

Louie pulled chopsticks out of their paper wrapper, snapped them apart and rubbed them together to ward off stray splinters. Em had opted for a plastic fork. He stabbed the chopsticks into the massive pile of traditional *luau* food, took a big bite of the pork and then smiled.

"Delish. Dig in."

Em learned early on that Hawaiians really knew how to eat. They celebrated every occasion—births, deaths, anniversaries, weddings, birthdays, graduations, funerals, canoe races, rodeos and car wash openings—with mountains of food.

She'd just taken a bite of slippery chicken long rice when Louie partially rose off the bench to wave at someone.

"There she is." He sat back down. "Finally caught her eye."

"Marilyn?" Em looked around. Marilyn was still dipping up rice.

"No, Tiko Scott. We've been wanting you to meet her." Louie nodded toward a petite Asian woman with long dark hair that hung past her waist. She had lovely clear skin and bright black eyes. She was short, no older than early thirties, and very thin.

No wonder, Em thought. The woman was carrying a plate that only contained green salad.

Louie introduced them and scooted closer to Em so that Tiko could slip into a sliver of space on the bench beside him. She made the awkward squat and leg lift over the picnic bench appear graceful.

"Marilyn introduced us," Louie explained. "Tiki is the owner of Tiko's Tastee Tropicals."

"Nice to meet you," Em said. "Where's your place located?"

Tiko ignored her food and leaned across Louie to be heard over the chanting. "I don't really have shop yet. I've been selling my smoothies at craft fairs and festivals. I make all natural ingredients into powders to add to juices for organic smoothies and drinks. I'm hoping to eventually buy a cart or a wagon so I can be mobile."

"Marilyn turned me on to Tiko's smoothies. They're great, especially the Kauai Coffee and chocolate chip combo."

"I actually use carob instead of chocolate. I'm still trying to decide on a name for that one. Marilyn told me Louie is an expert at inventing names for drinks."

"And legends to go with them." He turned his megawatt smile Em's way. "I was thinking that it would be great to offer some of Tiko's drinks at the Goddess. Smoothies are big sellers and we've got blenders." Louie laughed. "I could come up with some socko descriptions."

Tiko's smile was hard to resist. She reminded Em of an exotic jungle fairy. She had the healthy glow of a vegetarian and seemed like a sweet person. But experience warned Em to be wary—and Marilyn had introduced Tiko to Louie.

The Goddess was a potential gold mine, and Marilyn was smart enough to see that. Em was inclined to heed Kiki's warnings and be wary of the black widow.

"How do you know Marilyn?" Em ate a forkful of chicken lu'au.

"I used to dance with Mitchell's *halau*," Tiko's smile faded. "I met her there. But since I grow all organic ingredients, I needed to devote more time to my garden and getting the business off the ground. So I quit hula six months ago. Being in a serious *halau* takes a huge time commitment. It's a way of life, not just dancing. I really miss it, though."

A glance at the stage confirmed as much. The men and women under Kawika's direction were still chanting and were seated on their knees performing near impossible backbends. Their heads touched the floor behind them as their arms waved in the air.

Waiting on the floor beside the stage, the Maidens stared in awe. Em hoped Kiki wouldn't get it in her head to have the women try squatting or backbends or they'd have to call in a backhoe operator to get them up off the floor.

Tiko toyed with her lettuce as Louie demolished most of the pile on his plate. Em dug into the huge glob of sugary rice pudding and promised herself she would swim an extra twenty minutes tomorrow.

"Marilyn has been so supportive," Tiko said. "She's always buying my mixes. Even though she's not dancing with them anymore, she makes shakes for the *halau* when she's in town on class day."

"So what do you think?" Louie leaned closer to Em. "I'd like to buy a couple of cartons of Tiko's mixes and feature them on the Goddess menu for kids and non-drinkers."

"We can certainly think about it."

She'd also been thinking about Louie copyrighting his drink menu because, according to their new next door neighbor, a television script writer, Louie's recipes were original, inventive, and worthy of publication. Tropical drink recipe books were popular staples for tourists to take back to the mainland. If he planned to write descriptions for the smoothies, she'd have to look into the rights to them, and she reminded herself to see about copyrighting the Goddess drink menu.

"I'll have a booth at the Kukui Nut Festival," Tiko said. "Stop by and sample some of the smoothies if you're there."

"Sounds good," Em nodded, anxious to talk to Tiko a bit longer. Though Tiko had left Mitchell's *halau* months before Shari Kaui died, she might have some insight into what—if anything—was going on.

Wild applause filled the pavilion. Em couldn't decide whether the audience was truly appreciative or just thankful Mitchell's former *halau* was finally finished.

Louie excused himself, gathered up Em and Tiko's empty plates and headed for the trash cans surrounding the pavilion. The jovial Sparky was at the mic again.

"Mahalo, mahalo, Kawika. What a tribute to Mitchell, to know that his dances and choreography will live on under your guidance and aloha."

There was more clapping and hooting and shouts of "*Hana hou!*" a complimentary ovation from the audience for the performers to "work harder" and do another number. A smiling Kawika took the mic from the emcee.

He waited until there was complete silence before he spoke. Even from across the huge venue, she could see the tears welling in his eyes. "I am so *honored* to teach this fine group of dancers. Of course, I wish Mitchell were still here. And we all know that our beloved Shari Kaui is the one who really should be standing here before you accepting all this applause. She's the one who should be *kumu* now, but *Ke Auka* has seen fit to take them both . . ."

With a dramatic pause, Kawika mournfully swung his gaze heavenward for a moment. When he looked out at the crowd again, he appeared to have to force himself to smile through his sorrow. "But . . . the show *must* go on, and so *I* vow to do *my* very best to live up to the standards Mitchell instilled in us. *Mahalo* again, and again, and again for your support. Oh, and anyone who cares to donate to our *halau* fund for the perpetuation of hula just go to our website, dubya dubya dubya dot hulahalauolalaula dot org. We've got photos and calendars and handmade hula implements for sale too. Just click on gift shop." He started to hand the mic back to Sparky, stopped and added one more, "*Mahalo* again."

Beside Em, Tiko wiped away tears.

"This must be hard for you," Em whispered.

Tiko nodded. "My heart will always be with my hula brothers and sisters. Mitchell was a wonderful man and a gifted teacher."

Em waited a moment before she made like a curious *haole*. "The Shari that Kawika just mentioned? Who was she?"

Tiko sighed. "Shari should have been the next *kumu*, but she was very ill and passed a few months ago. So terrible."

Em fished for a way to work Jackie Loo Tong into the conversation and get Tiko's take on the man. Was Tiko at all suspicious of the two deaths so close together?

13

The Honk-In

Before Em figured out how to bring up the rival *kumu's* name, Kawika's dancers began to leave the stage.

Kiki and the Maidens perked up expectantly. Most of them anyway. The chanting had put Flora in a hula coma, face down, butt up, draped over the edge of the stage. Trish handed her camera off to someone sitting in front then shook Flora on the shoulder and roused her. Suzi waved at someone in the crowd. Big Estelle stood at the end of the line glaring down at Little Estelle, who'd parked her scooter next to the stage. Mother and daughter were arguing as usual. Flora finally stood up, yanked on the neckline of her *muumuu*, blinking around in a daze.

Em suddenly noticed another *halau* was slipping into position near the stairs across the stage from the Maidens. She held her breath and watched Kiki's face go from painted on blush to livid purple.

"And now," Sparky Cloud shouted into the mic, "the *reknowned* Oahu *halau* from Kaimuki would like to . . ."

Em expected Kiki to rush the emcee, but before Kiki could move, Little Estelle laid on the horn on her Gad-About. The shrill toot toot tooooooooooooot echoed around the pavilion.

Sparky paused with his mouth open behind the mic as Little Estelle executed figure eights on the scooter while she blared the horn.

Folks in the food line turned to stare. Servers paused with tongs of pork and noodles and slotted spoons dripping with *lomi lomi* salmon and long rice. Even the silent men gathered around the coffin sized coolers turned to see what was going on.

Sparky Cloud turned and slowly faced Kiki. His smile faltered for half a second then he recovered and shrugged apologetically to the dancers from Kaimuki. He nodded to Kiki, and she began to lead the Maidens on stage.

Big Estelle broke rank long enough to shush her mother. Little Estelle parked right below center stage. Her voice echoed in the silence.

"About time! My bladder won't hold forever."

Sparky waited until Kiki and the Maidens lined up. Compared to the stage at the Goddess, the Lydgate Pavilion was immense.

Kiki mouthed, "Spread out!"

No one moved. There was ample room for them all, but they clumped together in terror. Lillian had paled as white as her *muumuu*. Standing before some of the top dancers in the islands, the Maidens had lost their starch, which didn't bode well for their Kukui Nut Festival competition appearance.

"So, right now we have a little change of pace, folks." Sparky's megawatt smile was once again anchored in place. "*All* the way from the North Shore—as if you couldn't guess, eh?—we have *Kiki Godwin* and the *Hula Maidens.*"

Everyone understood his crack about the North Shore, also known as Haolewood. He could afford to be snide since the area wasn't exactly his voting base. And as far as the rest of the *kumu* and other dancers were concerned, the Hula Maidens were not *real* hula dancers, they were just women who danced hula.

If it hadn't been for Little Estelle's honk-in, Sparky would have overlooked and left the Maidens lined up until the end of the program.

Kiki ran over to start the CD on their boom box. Em crossed her fingers beneath the table. Two awkward minutes of silence crawled by as Kiki fiddled with the CD player. The flower arrangement she'd pinned in her hair was beginning to sag. Her face glowed with sweat. Something was definitely wrong.

Finally she pushed the play button and ran over to get in line. When "Tiny Bubbles" came blaring out of the speakers, Em flinched. All around the open air pavilion, folks stared in disbelief as the Maidens, most of them anyway, began to dance. Lillian stood frozen in fear. Flora, instead of executing steps, swayed back and forth with a vacant smile.

"Tiny bubbles . . . in the wine . . ." crooned the late Don Ho. Little Estelle sang along at the top of her lungs.

The tourist favorite was not exactly the anthem for a memorial. While the Maidens limped through the dance, the audience thankfully turned its attention elsewhere. It was too much for Em to watch but she did out of a sense of loyalty mingled with horror.

When the song finally ended, Kiki ran to the boom box, pushed stop and unplugged the cord. The rest of the Maidens watched in dismay and then after some not so quiet whispers and gesturing, filed off stage.

Sparky watched them go with almost too much glee.

"Wow. That was some tribute to Mitchell, eh folks? Tiny Bubbles. I haven't heard that one in ages. I thought it had been retired in the nineties, but I guess not. Thanks, Kiki. Seeing you and your ladies dance always brings tears to my eyes." He paused and gave the audience a melodramatic wink. "In a good way, yeah?"

As the next *halau* took the stage, Kiki wound up the boom box cord and shot Sparky Cloud a dark glare, then marched past him with head high, shoulders straight. A long piece of fern dangled off the side of her head and hung down near her left shoulder.

Most of the Maidens had already disappeared into the buffet line. Kiki marched over to where Em and Louie were sitting. She toted a small Igloo cooler.

"Scooch together. I need a seat," she told them.

Em scooched. Kiki wadded up the ruffle on her *muumuu*, wrestled her legs over the bench and sat down. She slammed the cooler on the table, opened it and pulled out a huge plastic balloon wine glass and proceeded to fill it to the brim with white wine.

They shared the table with locals, folks with Solo cups of fruit punch and cans of beer. Kiki's was the only wine glass, and after the Tiny Bubbles fiasco Em would have wanted to fade away. Not Kiki. Em didn't bother her until the woman had made a dent in the wine.

"Are you okay?" Em finally ventured to ask.

Kiki growled. "I brought the wrong CD. Right case, wrong CD inside. None of our serious songs on it. Had to go with Tiny Bubbles." She took another long swallow. "Only other choice was *Mele Kalikimaka,* and Christmas is two months."

"It wasn't that bad," Em tried to encourage. "The girls all seemed composed. No one fell over."

"They were scared spitless. They barely moved." Kiki refilled her glass. "Can you imagine them competing? Nothing good will happen."

"Try to stay positive. It's a good sign that Sophie found help."

"Maybe. We'll see." Kiki finally noticed the young woman beside Em. "I know you from somewhere," she said.

"I'm sorry," Em apologized. "I should have introduced you. This is Tiko Scott. Louie's thinking about adding some of Tiko's smoothies to the menu."

"Ah, yeah. The smoothie lady. That's how I know you. From the Farmer's Market. I hear your stuff is great." Kiki stared at Tiko a moment. "Didn't you used to dance for Mitchell?"

Suddenly shy, Tiko nodded. "Yes. For a long time."

"I *thought* I knew you from somewhere other than the smoothies. You're not with them anymore?"

"No." Tiko explained how she was too focused on growing her business to hula.

"Why don't you join the Maidens? We'd love to have someone with your experience."

"It's not too late to dance in the competition," Em added.

"She's too young for that," Kiki clarified. "We're in the *Kupuna* division, remember? Old farts only. But we'd love to have you dance with us at our other gigs."

"I just can't make that commitment right now," Tiko said.

"But that's the beauty of our group," Kiki pressed. "We're not like a real serious *halau*. We don't commune with the land. We don't get up at dawn to bathe in the ocean before performances. Why, none of us is ever up at dawn. We're sleeping off the night before. We dance for the joy of it. You can dance with us and still have a life. We're the party *halau*." Kiki held up her wine glass in a salute. Folks around them turned to stare for a minute then quickly looked away.

On stage, Jackie Loo Tong was going on and on about Mitchell and what a great and talented *kumu* he'd been and what a great loss the community had suffered.

"He's sure an interesting guy," Em hoped Tiko would comment.

Kiki said, "Yeah. Probably thanking his lucky stars that Mitchell is gone. Now Jackie's group will have a chance at the competitions."

Tiko leaned closer and lowered her voice. "There's always been friction between Mitchell and Jackie, but Kawika is more than qualified to take over. He's got some fresh ideas. Mitchell's dancers will work extra hard for him."

"Too bad they lost two strong leaders in a row," Em prodded.

"Pretty rotten break if you ask me. Downright weird in fact," Kiki said.

"Very odd," Em added.

Tiko disagreed. "Shari was ill for years. She hid it well, though. Mitchell's death was a shock, but he was warned he hadn't long to live. No one wanted to believe that, most of all Mitchell, so he went on as if he were healthy. I tried to get him on a good solid nutritional program, but he wouldn't give up all that rich Hawaiian food. And he loved sweets." She shook her head sadly. "There wasn't much anyone could do but try to cheer him up. The dancers he went out with the night of his death said he was so depressed. He'd been to the doctor that day and wasn't very optimistic."

Em was beginning to think Roland was no more psychic than the bench they were sitting on until she heard Jackie Loo Tong say, "We all know how much Mitchell loved his dancers, and I know he'd only want the best for them. If any of you are interested, we are opening up membership in our *halau* this week."

"Unbelievable," Kiki's eyes bulged. "He's recruiting Mitchell's dancers right in front of Kawika. In front of the whole audience. Right here at Mitchell's memorial, and the man isn't even cold in his grave. That takes some balls."

"Technically he's not cold in his box." Em quickly scanned the room. It was suddenly so quiet you could almost hear cockroach footsteps in the pavilion. Kawika was in back at the welcome table, one hand resting on the *koa* wood box that held Mitchell's ashes and one pressed against his heart. His mouth hung open in shock, but there was cold black fury in his eyes. Em was pretty sure he was contemplating doing major damage to Jackie Loo Tong.

If he noticed Kawika's anger, Jackie right went on as if couldn't care less. "Because we run the *halau* in the true Hawaiian spirit of aloha, we don't have a website. We are not looking to make a profit spreading the Hawaiian culture. We just want to dance and to excel at it. If you're interested, find me later and I'll be happy to give you my phone number and the details."

"Well," Tiko said, straightening her already perfect posture. "That was not *pono*. *Kumu* should behave better. Where's the aloha?"

Kiki emptied the wine bottle into her glass. "Wow. That was something. I'm glad I stayed long enough to see it."

Tiko asked Em for the time. When she found out it was almost four she said, "I've got to go."

"Why don't you call the Goddess this week and set up a time to come by with some samples, and we can talk?" Em suggested.

"Unfortunately my car isn't always working," Tiko told her. "But I'll try."

Tiko reminded Em of Sophie, who drove a rusted, beater Honda. Both young women were trying to make ends meet on an island where everything was overpriced and jobs hard to find. The ones who needed dependable cars the most were the least able to afford them.

"So where's Miss Marilyn?" Kiki asked Em. "I saw Louie get up and head for the back of the room."

Em looked around. "She was helping in the food line. Oh, there she is. She's sitting at the welcome table behind the calabash."

"I hope someone's watching the money envelopes."

"Kiki, she's not all that bad. She's been helping out all afternoon, and she's not even a member of the *halau* anymore."

"She's helping so people will notice and think that she's great. That's all it is."

"Still."

"You'll never convince me she's on the level."

Em noticed Kimo off to the side of the pavilion. "Kimo's waving, trying to get your attention," she told Kiki.

"Probably ready to leave."

"Aren't you going to eat something?"

Kiki polished off the rest of her wine. "No. After the Tiny Bubbles fiasco I can't get out of here soon enough."

After Kiki left, Em found Louie and told him goodbye. He promised he'd head back to the Goddess in time to lead the customers in The Tiki Goddess song. She was unlocking her car when her cell phone went off.

Caller ID showed it was Roland.

She found herself hiding a smile and warned herself to look out. Detective Mr. Sharpe and his oiled up, fire-knife-dancing-self meant nothing but trouble as far as she was concerned.

"Where are you?" he wanted to know.

"Hi. Nice to talk to you too."

"Sorry. I'm not used to making chit chat."

"Chit chat? *Hello* is chit chat?"

He was silent on the other end.

"I hear you breathing," she said. Okay, so he wasn't into chit chat, but there was plenty that was right about him. She pictured him oiled up and ready to fire dance on the beach.

"I'm at Lydgate just leaving the memorial."

"Is it over?"

"Not by a long shot, but I'm tired of sitting on a picnic bench, and I need to get back to the bar. Sophie has been on her own all afternoon."

"So it's up to you and Sophie to run the place tonight?"

"Kimo and Kiki are headed back. She won't pass up the chance to dance solo while the rest of them are still here at the luau."

"You have time to grab a bite?"

"Are you asking me out to dinner?" She burped up kalua pork and the combination of foods warring for space in her stomach.

"I'm going to Scotty's to have a late lunch/early dinner. Just wondering if you had any info. We could talk."

So, Em heard it loud and clear. He wasn't asking her out to dinner.

"I'm too full to eat, but I picked up something at the luau."

"Then you can watch while I eat. I'll buy you a drink."

She sighed. "I work in a bar. A drink is the last thing I want."

"If you want something else, I'd be happy to help you out there, too."

Was he actually flirting? She looked at the caller ID again. "Who are you, and how did you get Roland's phone?"

"I'll meet you at Scotty's in Kapa'a," he said.

"Why not?" What the heck, she thought. It was on the way to Hanalei.

14

Not Officially a Date

Scotty's was one of the few restaurants with an ocean view, and Roland had scored a table beside the wide wall of windows outfitted with a bank of garage doors that stayed rolled up when the place was open.

"I've already ordered." Roland pulled out a chair for her. Once Em was seated, he sat down across from her. "You change your mind about eating?"

Considering all the pork, chicken, heavy coconut laced dishes, warm, creamy rice pudding, various noodles and baked hunks of taro she'd eaten, she shook her head no.

"Nothing, thanks. But I could use a club soda."

The waitress came over and left him a salad, and he ordered Em's club soda.

"So," he mixed extra Caesar dressing into the greens. "How was it?"

"Well, for starters, Kiki and the Maidens danced Tiny Bubbles."

Roland choked.

"You need the hinnie-lick maneuver?"

He choked harder.

"Sorry, that's Louie's joke. Sorry." Her cheeks were blazing.

She was about to run around behind him and grab him around the diaphragm, but he finally swallowed and took a drink of water.

"Are you all right?"

"I'm okay. Tell me you're kidding about Tiny Bubbles."

"It was that or *Mele Kalikimaka*. It was pretty embarrassing. All the big name *kumu* and their *halau* were there. Even Kiki realized it was a terrible choice, but she'd taken the wrong CD, and Little Estelle had stopped the show with a honk-in . . ."

He held up his hand. "I get the picture. Please, no more."

The waitress brought Em's club soda and promised she'd be right back with Roland's entrée. The tall coco palms outside the windows were blowing in the trades. White caps danced in the water. Em scanned the ocean. Dark blue water stretched out to the horizon. It was too early for whales to make their annual migration past Kauai, otherwise they'd be putting on a show.

"Kawika was there. He said all the right things, but he seemed more delighted than mournful to have taken over Mitchell's *halau*. You think he could have killed Mitchell just to step into his flip flops?"
"Slippers, not flip flops."

"Whatever. Do you think he'd kill to be in charge?"

Roland shrugged. "It does seem pretty extreme."

"The *halau* has its own website now. Sounds like a real moneymaker."

He paused. The waitress arrived and set down his plate. Em stared at his grilled *mahi* sandwich and cole slaw. It looked great.

He noticed. "Hungry?"

"If I eat one more bite I'll throw up."

"Thanks for that. Back to Mitchell's *halau* website, I can't imagine it makes enough to want to kill for it."

She shrugged. "Who knows? Something else, could be nothing, though."

He took a healthy bite out of the mahi sandwich and waited for her to go on.

"Jackie Loo Tong openly tried to recruit Mitchell's dancers as soon as he got on the stage today."

"What did Kawika do?"

"Nothing, but if looks could kill, Jackie would be dead. Do you think Tong killed Mitchell so he could have his students?"

Roland thought for a minute before he said, "Pretty drastic."

"Has anything like that ever happened before?"

"You asking if anyone has ever murdered a rival *kumu*?"

"No. I'm asking if people ever move from one teacher to another."

"Sure. Dancers have been known to change *halau* . . ."

"Like Marilyn." Em pictured Louie happily drizzling mango juice into champagne.

"You know how mad she made Kiki and her merry band when she left them."

"Speaking of Marilyn . . ."

"I heard from a contact, a friend of a friend in California who checked on a few data bases for me."

"Wow. That was fast."

"That's the mainland for you. She's been married four times, never divorced. She's had bad luck with husbands."

Em shook off a chill. "They all died?"

He nodded. "Nothing suspicious. Seems she goes for older men. Each of them fell ill and died."

"Of the same thing?"

"No, all different causes. She always ended up with money, though."

"No kids? She told Louie she never had any."

"Nope. None anyone knows of."

He took huge bites. One minute the sandwich was there, and then it was gone.

"Want to split a dessert?"

"No thanks," she said.

"They have this thing called a puffasada."

"Puffawhata?"

"Puffasada. They stuff pineapple and berries into dough, roll it in panko crumbs and fry it."

"Naturally."

"Then it's topped with whipped cream."

"Why not just stab yourself in the heart?"

"Hey, I'm in great shape. My doc says so."

Anyone with two eyes could see he was in great shape on the outside.

"I'm tempted," she admitted, "but I really need to get back to the Goddess."

"Thanks for attending the memorial. You came back with food for thought. Sorry you had to take off work."

"It was nice to get out, and I connected with a woman named Tiko Scott. Cute. Asian. She has a smoothie business. Marilyn introduced her to Louie because Marilyn's hot on the smoothies and suggested they go on our menu. Do you know Tiko?"

He shook his head no. "I think I've heard the name, but I don't know her."

"She seems nice. Used to dance with Mitchell, but she left the *halau* months ago. I tried to get her to talk about how Mitchell and Kawika got along. She explained the deaths about the same as you did. Shari Kaui was very ill before she died, and Mitchell's heart was bad, and he didn't take care of his health."

"Pretty much why no one is suspicious."

"Maybe you're wrong. Maybe they just died."

"Maybe, but then why is my big toe bothering me?"

"Your big toe? Seriously?"

"Yeah. It hurts whenever I get a hunch."

"Kind of like gout, only different? Is that what happened to your psychic grandma? Her toe ached when she had a premonition?"

He signaled to the waitress to bring the check. "Hey, don't throw rocks. My *tutu was* psychic."

"And so is your toe."

His two-way radio on the table beeped. He turned it up just enough to hear what sounded like gibberish to Em.

"Gotta go." He stood up, took some bills out of his wallet and left them on the table. "I'll walk you to the car."

"Emergency?"

"Somebody in a chicken suit just robbed the convenience store at the Shell station by Brick Oven Pizza."

"Let me guess. The runaway chicken guy."

"You got it."

"Hope you catch him soon and toss him in the coop."

15

Sarge Boggs Takes Over

Two mornings later a light mist was falling. Inside the Goddess, Kiki paced the back of the barroom as the Maidens trickled in with as much speed as the rain dripping off the roof outside. They ordered coffee and drinks from Sophie and sat down along the banquette. Big Estelle was last to arrive.

"I'd have been here sooner," Big Estelle rolled her eyes, "but mother insisted on finishing her Zumba DVD first."

Little Estelle came riding in on her Gad-About.

"How can she do Zumba?" Lillian threaded a finger through her bouffant to scratch her scalp.

"She doesn't. She just likes to watch the buff guys in spandex." Big Estelle tossed her purse on the vinyl banquette and headed for the bar.

"Tightest butts in the world. Nothing bulges like Spandex. Gets my motor running." Little Estelle gave her horn a toot for good measure. She yelled to Kiki, "What are we waiting for?"

Pained, Kiki took a long swallow of her drink and wished martini glasses were bigger. Sophie tried to dissuade her from hitting the hard stuff so early, so she promised to have only one. She needed a swift kick in the keester to raise her spirits. After what happened at the memorial, she was convinced she'd made a grave error in entering the Maidens in the competition.

"We're waiting for that . . . *person* to get here," she said.

"Pat." Sophie stuck a tall celery stalk in two Shark Attacks and handed the drinks to Big Estelle. "Her name is Pat."

"Pat is running the class today," Kiki reminded them. With someone else in charge, she planned to spend the next two hours thinking up ways to get them out of the competition.

"What song did you choose? Are we learning something new?" Suzi stopped texting long enough to look up and ask.

Kiki ate one of the three olives that had been marinating in her drink. "The number Sophie choreographed for the shave ice truck blessing. Not that many people have seen it. That way we won't have to start from scratch, just add some finesse."

"Good idea." Trish walked through the door, set down her camera and started braiding her red hair. "Sorry, Kiki. I had to shoot a wedding at the Nawiliwili Yacht Club last night, and I got home late."

"Don't worry. You haven't missed anything." Kiki made sure the boom box on the stage was cued up and ready to go. For the past two days she'd made triplicate copies of their CD's. She stashed one in each of her and Kimo's cars and taped another set to the back of the boom box. There was no way she'd ever be caught without all their music again.

Someone was making a clunking racket outside the front door. All eyes turned in time to see Pat Boggs walk in carrying a snare drum and drum sticks. Wearing jeans and pair of red cowboy boots topped off with a wild, neon green aloha shirt, she clumped straight to the stage and set the drum down before she scanned the room.

After one look in her direction, the Maidens went back to talking among themselves. Pat picked up a drumstick.

BOOM. BOOM.

Lillian covered her ears. Flora woke up. Big Estelle, Trish and Suzi jumped to their feet. Sophie turned around to hide a smile. Kiki glared. If Pat noticed, she didn't let it bother her.

"Line up on stage, you pussy toads," Pat shouted. "We got no time to waste."

Little Estelle tossed aside her morning copy of the *Garden Island* news and clapped her hands.

"Whoohoo!" she shoved a fist in the air. "That's what I'm talking about. Like she said, line up, you pussy toads. The party's over!"

Pat turned on her faster than a starving gecko on a slow termite. "Look, old lady, *ap-pair-adently* you think I need help. What part of 'I'm in charge here' don't you understand? You just roll your little self back to the table and read your paper. I kin handle this."

"Pat, do you ever senior-sit?" Big Estelle was smiling from ear to ear. "If so, I need your number."

Pat planted her feet shoulder width apart. Hands on hips, she stared at the lineup of women. Kiki had purposely stalled and was still beside the bar.

"Miss Kiki," Pat stared across the room, "you plan on dancing in the competition?"

Kiki felt her face go purple. It wouldn't do anyone any good if she fell over with a stroke right there in the Goddess. She refused to end up as gossip fodder for the whole North Shore.

"Of course I'm dancing in the competition."

"Then I suggest you get your sorry butt on the stage and dance!" Pat waved a drum stick.

"That woman has just sealed her own fate," Kiki mumbled to Sophie. "I don't have to take this."

"You want to win?" Sophie grabbed Kiki's empty glass and shoved it into a bin of soapy water.

"She's not even a dancer," Kiki whispered.

"She's a former drill sergeant. I couldn't think of anyone better to whip you all into shape in two weeks. Give it a try."

Kiki stomped onto the stage and took her position front and center.

"Is the music ready?" Pat asked her.

Kiki nodded. "Just push play." She prayed everyone would remember the steps the first time through.

"Sophie went over the dance with me in private," Boggs shouted. Either she wanted to make an impression, or she was stone deaf. "So I know what it's *supposed* to look like. I'm gonna push play on that boom box of yours, and you all are going to show me what you got."

Kiki glanced over at Lillian. On a good day Lil could *almost* dance in time with the beat. Right now she could only stare bug-eyed at Pat Boggs. Her lower lip quivered.

"So help me, Lillian," Kiki whispered, "if you start crying, I'm going to pull out what's left of your fuzzy pink hair one strand at a time. Focus!"

Pat punched play. The music started. The right half of the line went left, the left half went right and they collided. Dwarfed by Flora, Suzi was smashed between the two halves of the line and spurted forward. She would have sailed over the edge of the stage if Pat hadn't thrown up her hands to stop her. She shoved Suzi back into place and pushed the stop button on the boom box. The room fell deathly quiet.

"Fall in again, ladies," Pat shouted. "We're gonna give this a try without music. You're gonna walk through the steps while I beat this here drum to keep time. You think you can handle that?"

No one said a word. Pat pounded the drum with each word she yelled.

"DO YOU THINK YOU CAN HANDLE THAT? If you can, say yes ma'am."

"Yes, ma'am."

"I can't HEAR you."

"YES, MA'AM!"

Pat started beating the drum and shouting, "One, two, three, four and one, two, three, four and . . ."

Kiki made a mental note to herself to ask Kimo for the phone number of his old Samoan friend, a huge *moke* with a name that sounded like Fall-offa-sofa. She didn't care how much he would charge to squash the stuffing out of Pat Boggs and make her disappear before the end of the week.

16

A Thoughtful Defector

They cowered and danced through close to two hours of practice before Sophie, bless her heart, stepped in and suggested to Pat that the ladies had had enough for the day. It was hard to admit, but their timing was actually improved after all the shouting and drumming. Pat Boggs was an immovable force who wasn't cowed by anything Kiki tried, and Kiki had to give the woman credit; even Lillian was executing the steps with a little finesse.

"I will see all of you ladies in the mornin'," Pat shoved the drumsticks in her back pocket and picked up the drum. "I suggest you go home and practice on your own. I'm gonna be harder on you tomorrow than I was tuh-day."

She stomped out of the room the way she came in with boot heels pounding and her ring of keys jingling at her waist. A moment or two passed before the Maidens, suffering from shock and exhaustion, finally climbed off the stage.

They'd no sooner stumbled into their seats then Marilyn Lockhart came breezing into the room carefully balancing a low sided box full of tall Styrofoam cups lined up in neat rows.

"I'm so glad you're all still here!" She called out. "I've brought you all a treat."

"This day just gets better and better." Kiki ignored her and walked over to the end of the bar. "Sophie, I need a vodka martini." She watched as Marilyn handed out cups to all of the girls. "Make it a double," she added.

"You got it." Sophie took a martini glass from the shelf behind the bar.

"Here you go, Kiki. You'll love this." Marilyn set a tall cup down next to her elbow.

"What is it?" Kiki pulled off the plastic lid and stared into the cup of fluffy opaque substance. "I have a rule not to drink anything blue," she said.

"It's an energy smoothie, from Tiko Scott."

Kiki stared at her.

"You know. Tiko's Tastee Tropicals. Louie is going to feature her smoothie packets on the menu. When he told me you were all practicing I made these for you. I added my own personal touch too."

Kiki sniffed hers. Some of the others were already downing the smoothies while Flora added tequila to hers.

"Try it," Marilyn encouraged. "I hear Mitchell's *halau* loves them."

Kiki shrugged. She'd been too upset to have breakfast and after the long hard session she was famished. She picked up the smoothie, tasted it, and polished off half before she set it down on the bar again. If the smoothies were good enough for dearly departed Mitchell's *halau* then it was good for her.

"Not bad," she admitted. "What did you say it has in it?" She picked up the cup and had some more.

"Acai berries and Tiko's flavored powder packets." She leaned closer to Kiki. "I brought them as a little peace offering. I didn't mean to put you on the spot by asking you to take me back into the group."

"What are those little white chunks?"

"Hawaiian seasonings I learned to make when I was one of Mitchell's students." Marilyn beamed. "Besides, I spoke to Jackie Loo Tong at the Memorial, and he said he'd love to have me join his *halau* so no hard feelings. When I told him that Louie and I were engaged, he congratulated me and said that he'd look forward to coming up here to the North Shore and having his dancers appear at the Goddess sometime."

Kiki's throat contracted and she hacked up smoothie into her cup. "Jackie Tong wants his group to dance at the Goddess?"

"If it's all right with Em and Louie, of course." Marilyn took a look at Kiki's face and stepped back. "Sometime. In the future, that is."

Kiki started banging her forehead on the bar.

"Maybe you'd better take off," Sophie suggested to Marilyn.

"I was only trying to show her I'm not upset. One door closes and another always opens, right?" Marilyn spread her arms wide as if to embrace the world. "Right?"

"That's right," Lillian agreed. "When life gives you lemonade . . ."

"Make smoothies." Big Estelle raised her empty cup.

"I'll drink to that." Flora upended her cup and tried to slurp out the last few drops.

Kiki kept her head down until she heard Marilyn's slippers slap the floor as she crossed the room. Then Kiki lifted her head and had some more smoothie just to make sure she wasn't really missing something.

"That was disgusting," she whispered.

"I don't know," Sophie looked around the room at the others. "They all sucked those down pretty fast for disgusting."

"Not the smoothies." Kiki glared at Marilyn who was collecting cups and lids and accepting thanks from the others. "That woman. Trying to make peace. Bragging that she's dancing with Jackie Loo Tong and that they're going to horn in on our one and only gig. This place is sacred to us. He can't bring his dancers here."

"If Louie and Em don't mind he can. So can anyone else."

Kiki's eyes suddenly welled up. "Good God. I think I'm channeling Lillian." She batted her eyes to clear them.

Across the room, Suzi gathered up her purse. "I have to go. I'm supposed to show a house in forty-five minutes." She got to her feet, took a step and stopped. She braced her hands on the table and closed her eyes. "Whoa."

"Are you all right?" Trish reached for her.

Suzi shook her head. "I feel weird. My stomach is . . ."

"Rumbling." Big Estelle was on her feet, clutching her middle, staring across the room at the restroom door. "I'm not gonna make it to the *lua*."

"Run!" Suzi was right behind her. "Cause I gotta go too."

The two women ran to the bathroom. Stall doors banged against the wall. The others left in the room looked around frantically.

"Men's room!" Trish shouted. She took off with Lillian right behind her.

Little Estelle started driving the Gad-About around in circles shouting, "Hurry! Hurry! Somebody come outta there! I gotta go!"

"What in the heck?" Sophie turned wide-eyed to Kiki.

Kiki couldn't even look at her empty smoothie cup. Her intestines were bubbling like a nuclear reactor on the verge of a meltdown. She grabbed her gut and doubled over. Her eyes watered from the pain of holding it all in.

She looked up at Sophie and gasped, "Help!"

Sophie pointed to the back. "Use the toilet in Em's office."

"Damn you, Marilyn!" Kiki hunched over and ran into the office yelling, "You've poisoned us all!"

17

Too Much of a Good Thing

"I haven't cried this hard since my third husband died!" Marilyn howled and buried her face against the front of Louie's aloha shirt, a reproduction 1940's print covered with cavorting beach boys and hula dancers.

Across the living room of the beach house she shared with her uncle, Em watched Louie pat Marilyn on the back. It was bad enough that Em had been dealing with a near comatose parrot all morning. They woke up to find David Letterman sprawled out on the littered newspaper in the bottom of his cage. Never knowing if he'd actually taken his last drink and keeled over or if he was just passed out, things were always a little tense until Louie found Dave's pulse and declared the bird merely a casualty of excessive samples of various versions of the new Two to Mango champagne cocktail.

"What's the matter?" Em had been trying to get to the bottom of Marilyn's distress since the woman had burst through the door wailing. She had a feeling Kiki was behind the tsunami of tears.

Marilyn's head came up off Louie's chest with the imprint of a coconut button on her right cheek.

"I . . . I was ooo . . . only trrr . . . trying to do something nnn . . . nice for them."

"Who? The Maidens?" Em crossed the room and sat on the edge of the rattan coffee table near the sofa. She looked at Louie who merely shrugged.

"Y . . . yes. I brought them all sm . . . smoothies."

The screen door banged open, and Kiki barged in. "She's poisoned us all! She tried to kill us!"

Marilyn's entire demeanor changed. Gone was the always composed, always refined woman they'd known up to now. She pushed off of Louie and jumped up, squaring off with Kiki.

"You bitch. I did not! I was doing a *good* thing. I was trying to be nice to all of you."

"Good? You call that a good thing?" Kiki pointed in the direction of the Goddess. "We've all got the runs. Kimo's afraid the septic tank is going to back up, and they'll have to shut down the place until they get it pumped. What did you give us? What's the antidote?"

Kiki lunged at Marilyn, but Em jumped up and grabbed Kiki's hands a second before they could clamp around Marilyn's neck.

"Whoa. Take it easy, Kiki." Em had to admit Kiki was an odd shade of green.

"I brought them all smoothies made from Tiko's acai berry powder. There was nothing wrong with them."

"Then why the heck are all the Maidens stuck in the *lua*? They've got the runs worse than the lava flow at the Kilauea crater. What did you give us? And why, Marilyn? Why? Are you that devious? If you think we'll ever change our minds and let you come back now, you're crazier than I thought."

Marilyn turned to Em. "Call her. Call Tiko. She'll tell you. I didn't do anything on purpose. Her number is 822 . . ."

"Wait." Em pulled her cell phone out of her shorts pocket. Maybe Tiko did have an explanation. Maybe Marilyn had mixed the powder up incorrectly. "Okay. Go."

Marilyn gave her the number, and she punched it in. Tiko answered on the second ring.

"Hi ,Tiko. This is Em Johnson, we met a couple of days ago. Yes, from the Goddess. Yeah, I'm fine. Listen, I'm calling because we've got a little problem here. Marilyn brought the girls some acai berry smoothies made with your powder . . . yes . . . I'm sure that is one of your best sellers . . . but . . . okay that's great . . ."

Kiki, Louie and Marilyn stared while Em waited for Tiko to finish touting the popularity of the berry smoothie powder.

"Well, that's wonderful. The trouble is some of the girls are having a little problem now that they've finished drinking them."

Kiki cupped her hands and yelled at the phone in Em's hand. "It's not a little problem. We're dying! We've got the runs! Our intestines have been liquefied. I think I'm going to need a whole new colon."

Em listened for a second and then turned to Marilyn. "Tiko wants to know if you added anything to the powder."

Kiki wrapped her arms around her midriff. "She said she added some seasoning."

Marilyn blinked her lashes a couple of times as if trying to bring the room into focus.

"Did I add something?" she whispered.

"You admitted you did," Kiki shouted. "You said it when you passed them out."

Em held the phone against her heart. "Settle down, Kiki." Then she put the phone to her ear again. "Just a minute, Tiko. Marilyn, did you add anything to the smoothies?"

"Why, yes." She suddenly began to blink as if coming out of a fog. "Yes, I did. We learned to make a special Hawaiian seasoning in Mitchell's *halau. Inamona.* It's made from *kukui* nuts."

Kiki grabbed her head. "*Inamona?* You put *inamona* in those things?"

Em had never actually seen anyone tear at their hair before, but Kiki was doing a fine job of it.

Marilyn nodded. "I wanted it to be special. I thought . . ."

Em still had the phone to her ear. Tiko said, "Did she say she put *inamona* in the smoothies?"

"She did," Em said.

"That could be trouble," Tiko said.

"Big trouble," Em told her. "They all have the runs."

"She put in too much." Tiko was silent for a second then said, "Sounds like she used way too much."

Em turned to Marilyn, "Tiko says you used too much."

"You *think?*" Kiki squeezed her eyes shut and held her breath for a second. When she opened them she pinned Marilyn with a hard stare. "*Inamona* is used in very small amounts to season *poke,* Marilyn. You know, the *pupu* made from fish? If it's not cooked thoroughly, or you use too much, causes diarrhea. Very *bad* diarrhea."

Louie unfortunately chose that moment to chuckle. Kiki turned on him.

"What's so funny, mister? We're probably going to lose a day of practice tomorrow from dehydration. Little Estelle and Suzi are so small that their systems can't handle it. Suzi called her sister to come pick her up, so word is out. By now this is story is probably all over town. You'll be lucky if one of us doesn't sue you!"

"What did I do? I didn't do anything!" Lawsuits terrified Louie.

"*You,*" Kiki tapped him on the chest with her finger, "are *engaged* to her."

"Hello? Hello?" Tiko's voice came out of the phone.

Em nearly forgot she was still on the line.

"I'm here," Em said, wishing she was anywhere but here.

"Does this mean you won't be buying any of my products for the bar?" Tiko sounded despondent.

"Actually, I was going to set up a meeting with you today," Em said.

"Maybe you could come by this afternoon? I'd love to show you around my garden and my kitchen, too. I have approval from the health department to use my kitchen."

Em jumped at the chance to leave the chaos, especially if there was going to be a problem with the septic. She couldn't bear the stench when the "honey wagon" came to pump out the poo. She told Tiko she'd try to be there before three-thirty and ended the call.

Marilyn was still sniffling. Em had never seen the woman in such a state. Her straight shoulder length blond hair was completely mussed. It stood out like a nimbus, and her mascara was smeared around her eyes and tracking down her face. Her nose looked like a wet strawberry.

Kiki didn't look any better. Her long hair was loose and straggling down the sides of her face in clumps. Her skin was the color of sticky rice.

"I'm so sorry, Kiki," Marilyn apologized again.

Kiki was shaking as she plopped down in the closest chair and rested her forehead on her hand.

"She meant it as a peace offering," Louie reminded Kiki. "You'll get over it."

"Get over it?" Kiki heaved a heavy sigh. "It's always something. Why can't we just be normal?" Her eyes mushroomed to the size of golf balls. "Sorry, I gotta . . ." She jumped up and ran down the hall toward the bathroom.

If everyone else wasn't so distraught, not to mention the sight of the unconscious parrot across the room, Em would have laughed. Normal had taken a hike years ago.

"I hope this doesn't ruin Tiko's chances to have you feature her smoothies." Marilyn looked around and then grabbed the hem of Louie's shirt and wiped her nose with it. "This isn't her fault. That poor girl needs a break."

"There are parts of you I'd like to break," Kiki hobbled back in. "You think anyone is going to order one of those things when this gets out?"

"I can call them killah smoothies," Louie laughed.

"That's not funny," Marilyn's lower lip shot out in a pout.

Louie wrapped his arm around her shoulder and pulled her close. "How about I take you home, honey. You can freshen up."

"What about my car?" she sighed.

"You're too upset to drive. I'll hang around your place until you feel like coming down to get it again."

"Okay." She smiled up into his eyes. "That would be nice."

As they left together holding hands, Em breathed in the moment of blessed silence. She walked over to Letterman's cage to check on him. The bird was still on the floor. She stared at him until she saw his chest rise and fall. He loved mango, and Louie's new cocktail had plenty of mango syrup, but Dave had disapproved of every sample of every version Louie had concocted last night.

"That bird is going to have some hangover." Kiki was standing at Em's shoulder.

"You look drawn. Maybe you should go home and lie down," Em suggested.

"Yeah. I've probably lost thirty pounds. You know how much gunk is stored in the average intestinal tract?"

"No, and I don't want to."

Kiki walked over to the sofa, flopped down on her back and crossed her ankles.

"You'll never convince me that woman didn't try to kill us. Or at the very least, keep us out of the competition."

"Wouldn't she have waited until closer to the event?"

"Maybe this was a test run."

"Maybe she just wanted to show off the fact that she learned how to make that *kukui* nut seasoning," Em said.

"She showed us all right." Kiki closed her eyes a second then snapped them open again. "She's joined yet another *halau*."

"Not Mitchell's? She didn't go back to them?" Em's mind snagged on the idea that maybe Marilyn went back to Mitchell's *halau* because Mitchell was gone. Conveniently gone. Where had Marilyn been the night Mitchell died? She made a mental note to find out.

"Jackie Loo Tong's. Can you believe it? She's going to dance with him. She even went so far as to suggest they'll all come perform at the Goddess."

"Do you think they would?" Em wondered.

"You'd really want them here?" Kiki misunderstood and looked like she was about to burst into tears.

"I meant, would they just invite themselves like that?"

Kiki shrugged. "Why not? We would."

18

Tiko's Tropical Paradise

Tiko's small cottage was located on a three acre parcel not far from the Wailua Country Store. As Em pulled into the long, gravel-lined drive, she had to veer right to let a red convertible Mustang pass her on its way out. The driver was a young local woman who gave Em a big smile and a wave as she passed by.

Em couldn't help but admire the lush variety of plants that filled the front yard. Various colorful gingers lined one border while there were hedges and exotic flowering trees of all kinds, not to mention limes, orange and lemon trees. An old mango tree had a trunk big enough to house a couple of toddlers.

Tiko was waiting on the front lanai.

"Your place is fabulous." There was beauty at every turn. Em didn't know where to look. "I can see how this takes you hours of work."

"Wait until you see my herb and vegetable gardens out back. Thank you so much for coming, especially after what happened to the Maidens. I feel just terrible."

"Don't let it worry you. They're always embroiled in some kind of mess, usually of their own making."

Em took another look around the front yard and garden before they went inside. "I'm in awe of the beauty of this place. I love those torch gingers."

"*Mahalo.* They seem to love it here."

"And what are those?" Em pointed to a huge bush covered with blossoms that looked like white bells.

"I don't know the official name. Most people call them angel's trumpets."

"They're stunning." Everywhere she looked Em saw something beautiful. "Did you plant all of this yourself?"

Tiko shook her head. "This land has been in my family for years. My grandmother started the flower and herb gardens. She knew a lot about Hawaiian herbs, which ones could heal, which were dangerous. So many secrets were lost over time when the old ones pass on. That was my cousin in the convertible. Our *tutu* raised us both in this house. Charlotte moved back to Kauai from the mainland a little while ago."

They walked through the compact but neatly appointed home. Tiko's furnishings were modest, the sofa and chairs draped with colorful *pareau*. Everything was in its place, and there was an absence of clutter. The house was situated so that the trade winds blew through and kept it cool.

Photos of Tiko dancing were on display. They filled one wall along with implements that were used for certain dances, dried seed leis, and even a dried ti leaf skirt had been spread out and pinned on the wall.

Scented candles and soft sounds of recorded flute music added to the tranquility.

"I'm glad you don't blame what happened this morning on my smoothie mix."

"At first I wondered if one of the ingredients might have spoiled, but then Marilyn admitted to adding the seasoning she'd made up."

"I'm sure she didn't mean any harm. I remember Marilyn was excited about learning to make *inamona* and all the Hawaiian crafts we tried. She didn't mean to harm the ladies with her addition to the smoothies. She was always such a lady when she was in Mitchell's *halau*."

"I think maybe she wanted to show off some of the knowledge she'd gained while dancing under such a renowned *kumu*," Em said. "She didn't realize too much of good thing could be so harmful. But Kiki will never believe it wasn't sabotage."

"They're all right, though?"

"It hit some of the ladies harder than others, but they're all on the mend. You can't keep a good Hula Maiden down."

They walked into a light and airy, well organized kitchen. Tiko opened an old fashioned cookie jar, a white ceramic dog with red trim. She pulled out what appeared to be a handful of small, individually wrapped candies.

"These are my homemade ginger chews. They settle the stomach, but if you love ginger you'll enjoy munching on them. They're completely organic."

Em thanked her and tucked the chews into her pocket.

She showed Em the set up in the kitchen where she dehydrated all of her fruit and prepared the smoothie powders. "I grow most of my own ingredients, weigh and measure and package everything right here."

Unassembled boxes with her colorful label were stacked along one wall. There were also boxes of zip lock bags in various sizes which were also labeled. She explained to Em how long it took her to make each flavored powder supply. Her goal was to have enough for her smoothie stand at the Kukui Nut Festival and extras for Louie, should Em decide to place an order.

Tiko paused by the back door. "If you have time, let's go out back, and I'll show you the garden."

They stepped outside the back door. Wind chimes lined the overhang of the small back lanai. The breeze set them all singing. Em looked out over the gently rolling back yard and let her gaze sweep up the backside of Sleeping Giant mountain known for its distinctive shape of a giant lying on his back.

An extensive garden plot ran down the property parallel to a wire fence. They walked toward the garden together.

"This is where I grow all my own vegetables, and I send extra produce to the farmer's market with my neighbor." They passed by thriving sections of long beans, kale, arugula, carrots and cucumbers. There was an area with three neat rows of papaya trees. "Those are all sunrise papayas," Tiko pointed out.

"The ones that are bright orange inside? Do you make smoothie powder from those?"

"I do."

"I'd really like to carry some papaya. And I hear the acai berry is really popular among the health food crowd."

"That's right. Though I doubt the Hula Maidens will be very enthusiastic about them now."

"They'll get behind anything that will keep the Goddess operating in the black," Em assured her.

They moved on, working their way around the garden.

"Is that all your land up there?" Em pointed to the land beyond the fence that rolled up the hillside.

"Not all of it. Most is forestry land. There are hiking trails up there, but most of what grows there are weeds."

By the time they reached the back of the house again, Em was ready for the glass of ice cold lemonade Tiko offered.

"I can see now why you're not dancing hula anymore," Em said. "This is quite an operation. I can't believe you manage it alone."

"It's my passion," Tiko told her.

"Does your cousin help you?"

"No, only when I need someone at a big craft fair. If she can get off work, that is."

Em took in the neat cottage with its creamy yellow siding and ivory trim. Set against the many shades of green and various coconut palms scattered across the rolling landscape, it looked like a tropical doll house on a picture postcard. Em loved it.

"Do you live up here all alone?"

Tiko's smile faltered for a minute. "Since my *tutu* died of a heart attack three years ago. She was ninety-nine."

"No significant other in your life?" Em couldn't believe someone with Tiko's looks and personality was still single.

Tiko's gaze roamed over the land and then toward the Sleeping Giant. She shook her head no.

"Not at the moment." She paused a moment more before she turned to Em with a smile. "I haven't much time to devote to anyone or anything else right now."

Em finished her lemonade. "If you can spare some product before the festival, why don't you pack up three dozen packets each of your best sellers. I'll have Louie write up some fun descriptions of the mixes for us to use on the Goddess menu."

"Nothing R rated, right? I'm trying to build an organic, healthy image."

"Definitely all PG. We could use a few more choices like that at the Goddess. Tourists love to bring the kids in for the show. This will give them something to enjoy while their parents are swilling down Mai Tai's."

"If you like, you can wait out here while I go in and get some boxes ready for you. I'll send you an invoice later."

The wind chimes were singing in the breeze as a passing cloud misted the garden. Em couldn't have found a better place to relax for a few minutes.

"You sure? That would be great."

Tiko not only packed up the smoothie packets but she also cut an armful of tropical, torch ginger, crab claw heliconia and pink gingers and helped Em load them into her car.

"Will you be going to the Kukui Nut Festival?" Tiko asked.

Em opened her car door. "I'm going along to support the Maidens."

"I hope they do well," Tiko said. "They seem like a fun group."

"You should think about dancing with them if you ever have time. They only have one rule," Em said.

"What's that?"

"Don't fall over."

Tiko laughed. "If I ever have time again, I'll think about it."

Em pulled into the Goddess driveway and parked by the back door to the office.

She called out to Sophie to let her know she was back. A handful of tables were filled with tourists enjoying early happy hour. Em went back to unload the boxes and stack them against the wall in the small space she thought of as Grand Central. When she went back outside to move her car she noticed their neighbor, Nat Clark, unloading groceries from the back of his SUV. He saw her just as he pulled out a huge cardboard box full of Costco items.

"How've you been?" he called out.

She crossed the parking lot rather than shout. Nat rested the box on the tailgate and waited. A successful television writer who lived in the refurbished cottage he'd recently purchased, Nat was handsome in a bookish way behind his thick tortoise shell glasses. He'd bought the beach house next door as a retreat from the hectic life he lived in both Honolulu and L.A. His only regret was that he couldn't spend more time on Kauai.

"I thought you wouldn't be back for another three weeks," Em said.

Nat had left her the spare keys to the house in case there were any weather disasters or he needed something.

"We wrapped early and then found out the show was cancelled for next season."

"That's a bummer. I'm sorry," she said. "I liked watching *Crime Doesn't Pay: Hawaii*."

"Yeah. Well, right now it's not paying for me." He shoved his glasses up his nose. "My agent already has a line on another show, and until I hear anything, I'm ready for some R&R. Everything looks great around here, as always."

"We've had good rain, so everything is green. I haven't smelled any gas leak or seen any water gushing out of your pipes. No one has walked out with your 60 inch TV, either."

"Great. Thanks for keeping an eye on the place. Everything else all right? What's going on at the Goddess?"

"Nothing out of the usual. Poor David Letterman is in a champagne-induced coma, the Maidens are gearing up for a hula competition—if they can recover from a case of unintentional intestinal poisoning—and Uncle Louie just announced his engagement to Marilyn Lockhart."

"That's why I hate to leave this place."

"I'll bet."

"No, really. My agent is shopping me to a big cable network where I'd be working on reality TV concept development."

"You mean you'll have to come up with shows like the ones where little people save pit bulls or moms dress toddlers up like show girls to win rhinestone tiaras?"

"Exactly. There are enough situations percolating in your Uncle's bar to keep me in ideas for years." He hoisted the box. "I've got some stuff in here I need to put in the freezer. You have time to come in for a drink? I'll pick your brain."

Sophie would be nudging her to take him up on it. He was charming, he had three homes, and he seemed like a genuinely nice guy. But thanks to her ex, she was still leery of men.

"I need to pick yours too, about your suggestion for us to publish *Louie's Booze Bible* of tropical drinks. We don't even know where to start, but I've got a mountain of things piled up in the office." She thought of Sophie urging her on and added, "But I'll take a rain check."

"Anytime." He gave her a broad smile and picked up the box again.

He was good looking for sure, but he couldn't twirl flaming fire knives.

19

Kiki Switches Course

"What do you mean you've decided on a different dance for the competition?"

Wally Williams—long-time partner of the late world-renowned pianist Fernando—tossed a handful of costume sketches on the table in front of him and threw his hands in the air. The sketches scattered, some drifted to the floor.

Sophie walked out from behind the bar as soon as she realized trouble was brewing. She hurried across the room to position herself between Wally and Kiki. She watched a bead of sweat escape Wally's artfully coiffed hair. It looked like he'd cloned Donald Trump's do.

The rest of the Maidens huddled in silence around the table. No way was anyone going to speak up. Even their new "Sarge" Pat Boggs waited for Wally and Kiki to sort things out.

Kiki leaned around Sophie to get into Wally's face, "I have decided against the Elvis Medley, that's what I mean."

"You can't switch songs this late in the game. I've put too much time into costume designs."

"I don't want to wear a muumuu version of Elvis's white jumpsuit, that's all I'm saying. He'd rock and roll over in his grave if he saw your designs."

"I worked in Las Vegas, remember? I *knew* Elvis. *You*, madam, did not."

"What does that have to do with the price of *poi?*" Kiki wanted to know.

Pat Boggs beat the snare drum to get their attention. "Kiki, did you just drive in from the far side of stupid? You can't change the darned song this late in the game. Y'all barely remember the one you already learned. Y'all got memories as long as my dick, and I don't have one." She hit the drum hard once to make a point.

Kiki's lower lip jutted. Her fingers curled into fists at her side. "If you don't stop beating that thing . . ."

Sophie braced herself and wished Em would walk in. "How about we all cool off and *listen* to each other. Kiki, why change the song now?"

"I woke up in the middle of the night and I remembered Kawika told me they give extra points for songs in Hawaiian, for songs written by Kauai composers, and songs about Kauai. I remembered one of my neighbors wrote a song about the Hanalei *taro* fields in Hawaiian, and so I went over early this morning and woke her up and I have permission to use the music."

She turned away long enough to fish through her purse and then held up a CD. "It's only got three verses, and we can learn it in no time."

"What about choreography?" Sophie was worried about Wally. He was sweating and panting as if he'd just run a marathon.

The Maidens waited to hear what Kiki had to say, all but Little Estelle, who had opted to stay home and watch a twenty-four hour Zumba marathon on the Fitness Channel.

Kiki took a deep breath before she turned to Sophie. "I have most of it worked out, but I was hoping you could help me polish."

"This is going to put you behind schedule," Sophie warned. "I really don't have time to devote helping you with new choreography right now."

"With the Kauai composer's song we'll earn a whole lot of points before we even hit the stage."

Wally lost steam and sank into the banquette beside Lillian, who had been one of Fernando's biggest fans.

"I've worked for days on these designs." Wally indicated the pages on the table and the floor with a limp wave. "Do you know how many episodes of *Project Runway* I had to sit through to come up with all of this?"

"I really don't care," Kiki sniped. "There was nothing Hawaiian about them except for the shape of the muumuu."

"And I'd have made them white jumpsuits if you'd agreed. And what on earth is wrong with rhinestones and chiffon?"

"We are not drag queens, that's what."

"Hey!" Pat hit the drum. "None of that. Be civil, lady."

Kiki turned on Pat. "I warned you."

Before anyone could stop her, Kiki sidestepped the table, grabbed Pat's drum and heaved it out the open window.

"What were you thinking?" Pat knelt on the banquette and hung her head out, looking down the gravel driveway. "You busted it!" she yelled. "You owe me a new drum."

Just then Louie's truck pulled in off the highway, headed for the house.

"Oh no! Hell no!" Pat shouted and waved to Louie, but he didn't hear her. There was a loud thud and crunching noises as he ran right over the drum and drove on.

"Yes!" Kiki clapped her hands. "He killed it."

All of the Maidens started talking at once after Pat ran out the front door.

"That's it!" Sophie shouted. The room went silent. "Kiki, you'll have to replace that drum."

"It was worth it."

"You have a point about helping raise your scores, but I think it's really late to start a new dance." Sophie turned to Wally. The women were giving her a headache. "Can you design a dress with a taro patch theme?"

"Taro grows in mud," he grumbled. "How can I create with that image? My mind is a blank."

"Well, I can certainly come up with something," Kiki announced. "No problem. How about you just help us with makeup on the day of the performance?"

Wally sniffed. "I suppose that would be all right. Designing won't be any fun anyway if you don't use the Elvis routine."

"Well, I'm not going to, so get over it."

"How long is it gonna take you to have the song ready to teach?" Sophie asked.

"A couple of days, if you'll help me."

Kiki had put her on the spot. Sophie looked around. The Maidens were waiting for her answer. She couldn't let them down, not after the way they'd banded together to help prove her innocence a few months ago. She sighed and shook her head.

"I must be crazy, but all right. I'll help you with the new song. How about we work on it together tomorrow morning and see how it goes?"

"Anytime," Kiki agreed. "In the meantime I'll make notes and have as much done as I can for your approval."

Sophie heard a mournful tapping sound and looked outside. Pat was in the driveway holding her drum. The drumhead was torn off, the rim flattened. She tapped the drumstick against broken wooden shell and mournfully marched through the lot toward her van.

"I say we adjourn and go into Hanalei for lunch," Kiki suggested.

Looking forward to some peace and quiet, Sophie didn't try to talk them into the pulled pork special. Five minutes after they left, Em walked in from the office with a stack of clean dishtowels.

"What's up, Sophie? You look so down even your spikes are drooping."

Sophie ran her hand over the gelled points of her hair. They were still standing at attention.

"Just kidding," Em said.

"Nothing but chaos over here this morning. Kiki's changed the performance number, and Wally's been taken off of costume design and demoted to sewing and makeup."

"I knew that was coming. Where are they?"

"They all went to lunch in Hanalei."

"Good."

"My thoughts exactly. I need a Maiden break."

A van load of tourists wearing "John Family Reunion" T-shirts followed the male driver inside and lined up behind him in the doorway. Sophie grabbed a pile of menus.

"Is this where we sign up for Snorkel-O-Rama?"

"The trip up the Na Pali?" Sophie pointed left. "You have to drive back to Hanalei town, and you'll see some tour boat offices on the highway."

"We never passed a town."

Em winked at Sophie. "You did," she said. "It's small. A couple blocks of stores and a post office."

"I'm hungry," one of the kids whined.

"Me, too!" Three more shouted.

The wife looked around the room and pursed her lips. "I'd rather eat at the hotel." She sounded just like the whiny kid.

"If they serve lunch we can eat here. Do you serve lunch?" The man asked.

"Sure. We have a great *mahi mahi* sandwich special today," Sophie said. "And pulled pork."

A teenager with ear buds pretended to gag. "I hate fish!"

"We hate fish." The younger kids took up the cry.

The whole group turned and walked out without a word.

"Aloha. Thanks for coming." Sophie put the menus back on the bar.

"Can't win them all," Em said. "Is it really going that bad with the Maidens?"

"Time is running out, Kiki wants to choreograph a whole new song and have the Maidens learn that instead of perfecting an old one."

"Any way she'll listen to reason?"

"No. She's on a tear. She not only demoted Wally, she tossed Pat's drum out the window."

"Oh, no."

"Then Louie ran over it."

"He didn't say anything about it when he came in."

"He probably doesn't even know he did it."

"He's at home mixing up a new drink in honor of the Maidens' performance at the competition. Trying to make up for Marilyn's smoothie incident."

"Hoping to smoothie the waters?" Sophie went back to the bar.

"Nicely put."

"If I'm going to help Kiki with the dance this week and go to the competition, you need to think about hiring part time help."

Sophie left Em alone to mull it over and went to get a bucket of ice out of the ice machine. By the time she returned and dumped ice in the deep bin beneath the bar, Em had a suggestion.

"What about Buzzy? He's always here. He's stood in once or twice in an emergency and seems capable of handling his handyman work. He'd probably fill in once in a while for free beer."

"How will you keep him from drinking while he's behind the bar? Besides, the last time he was in he told me he was dating a dolphin."

Em laughed. "It sounded like you said he was dating a dolphin."

"I did. He is. Or so he claims. She lives at Tunnels. They commune telepathically."

"Please tell me he's not having sex with her."

"Not yet. She wants to get to know him better."

20

I Spy a Rat Close By

Two days later Kiki felt like the dance was ready and called the Maidens together for a morning practice.

She refused to call Pat Boggs but Sophie had. Kiki put Pat to work running the boom box and keeping the girls in step, which freed Kiki up to fine tune the movements. Suffering the loss of her drum, Pat improvised with an empty Crisco can that Kimo had in the kitchen.

As the music played, Pat would occasionally yell, "Freeze!" and stop the CD player. The dancers froze, and Kiki would run around between them and adjust their arms and hands to the correct positions.

Wally sat at a table in the far back corner with Little Estelle. The pair was busy cutting taro leaves out of two three foot stacks of green felt squares. Kiki's plan was to sew each of them onto silver and aqua colored muumuus to represent *taro* patches. The felt leaves would flutter as the Maidens moved.

"Hit it," Kiki said.

Pat hit play on the boom box. The Maidens started dancing. Sophie worked behind the bar but was on call in case Kiki needed her. Wally and Little Estelle were busy whispering about the dancers and cutting out leaves. Kiki was in shock; for the moment, all was right in her world.

They danced for another twenty minutes, stopping, starting, adjusting. Everyone but Lillian was making headway. A tall Hawaiian in a tank top, shorts and rubber slippers walked through the door with a bulging black Hefty bag slung over his shoulder. Kiki asked Pat to stop the music.

"Hi, Benny."

He dropped the bag on the floor. "Here you go, Kiki. A t'ousand *kukui* leaves. Is Kimo in da back?"

"For sure. He's got a big pan of *ahi poke* for you. *Mahalo* for these." She opened the bag and peeked inside. A pan of seasoned raw *ahi* tuna was a small price to pay for the leaves she needed.

Benny smiled and waved at all the Maidens as he went toward the kitchen.

"Take a break everybody. Gather round." Kiki pulled a handful of leaves out of the bag. "These are *kukui* leaves. We're going to make head *lei* out of them for the competition."

"They're gonna wilt by then." Flora picked up a five pointed leaf and rubbed it between her fingers.

"We're making one *lei* each this afternoon for practice and another the night before the competition."

"What?" Suzi stopped texting and looked up from her phone. "Two head *lei* workshops? Why? I can't do anything this afternoon. I have a meeting."

"I want everyone at my house this afternoon for the mandatory workshop," Kiki said.

"I need some notice ahead of time, Kiki. I have a job, you know," Suzi said.

"Making adornments is part of the competition."

"I'll make it for her," Trish volunteered. "I don't have to work until I shoot a wedding tonight at Hanalei Colony."

"That's not the point." Kiki took a deep breath. "All of you need the experience of making your head *lei*."

"I hate crafts," Big Estelle said.

"I gotta get home. I'm having the shakes," Little Estelle called out.

"Then put those scissors down before you cut off a finger," Wally warned.

"I'm having Zumba withdrawals," she said.

"Can't we pay someone to make our head *lei*?" Suzi wasn't going to give up.

"Bunch of pussy toad whiners." Pat tapped out a rat-a-tat-tat on the can.

As the women argued among themselves, Kiki bent over to tie a knot in the *kukui* leaf bag. When she straightened up, she noticed the office door was open about an inch. A red glowing dot inside the otherwise shadowy room caught her eye. It reminded her of the way a rat's eyes lit up when hit by a beam of light.

But if there was a rat in the office, its eye was a good five feet above the floor.

She was looking at one big rat of the two-legged variety.

With as much nonchalance as she could muster, Kiki strolled over to the bar.

"Sophie, did you say Em was in town?"

"Yeah. Louie, too. They went to pick up some extra stuff for the art show tonight. The bread dough artist is coming in later to set up so you all can't be here too long."

Kiki let her gaze flick over to the office door for a beat and then continued to make her way along the bar, moving casually. She was able to approach the door without being seen.

She was creeping along with her back pressed against the wall beside the door when Pat suddenly noticed. Kiki put her finger to her lips, but it was too late.

"What in the world are you doing, Kiki?" Pat asked.

Cover blown, Kiki gave a Ninja shout, raised her foot and kicked the door all the way open. There was a cry and a crash behind it. Kiki rushed in and found Marilyn spread-eagled on the floor on her back. A camera lay a few feet away.

"I knew it!" Kiki cried. "I saw someone spying on us." She planted her hands on her hips. "You. You are beyond despicable, Marilyn Lockhart."

"I am not!"

There was a stampede to the office door. Everyone but Wally crowded around. He kept right on cutting out felt taro leaves.

"I can't see! I can't see!" Stuck behind them all, Little Estelle started tooting the Gad-About horn.

As the Maidens flanked Kiki, she grabbed Marilyn's camera and waited for the woman to pick herself up off the floor. A trickle of blood slid out of her nose. Marilyn wiped it off, looked at her hand and whimpered.

"You could have *killed* me!"

"She was filming the practice through a crack in the door," Kiki explained.

Marilyn tried to grab the camera. "I was not."

"The camera light was glowing like the eye of a big fat rat!"

"You're crazy," Marilyn sniffed. "You've finally lost it, Kiki."

Kiki held up the camera for all to see.

"*Me? I'm* crazy? I don't think so." She turned the camera over and fiddled with it for a minute then handed it to Trish. "Can you work this thing?"

"Probably." Trish studied the buttons.

"It's broken," Marilyn sniffed.

"You wish," Kiki said.

Flora, in a muumuu that made her look like a rainbow had exploded on her, drifted away from the group and sat down on one of the carved tiki bar stools. She tried to order a burger and fries, but Sophie told her to hold on a second.

"Got it." Trish started the playback on the video. The women pressed closer. Kiki smiled triumphantly as the proof unfolded before their eyes.

"Oh, Marilyn," Trish didn't hide her disappointment. "I didn't want to believe it."

"Did she?" Big Estelle wanted to know. "Did she film our dance?"
Trish nodded. "She did."

"Everybody move. I'll run 'er down," Little Estelle yelled.

"How could you?" Big Estelle asked Marilyn.

Little Estelle thought her daughter was talking to her. "It's easy. I'll just put the Gad-About in drive and floor it."

"I'm going to be late for my appointment." Suzi walked back to her table to get her notebook and purse and then suddenly stopped. "Someone promise to call me if Kiki kills her."

"I will," Trish promised.

Kiki grabbed Marilyn's arm and started tugging her toward the bar. Marilyn started bawling and shouted, "No! Let me go."

Before Kiki knew it, Sophie and Pat Boggs had flanked her.

"Let her go, Kiki," Sophie ordered.

"No! We have to deal with this. Call 911. Let's tie her to a chair until the police get here."

"Tie her to the back of the Gad-About, and I'll drag her around the parking lot!" Little Estelle clapped with glee.

Sophie put her hand on Kiki's arm. "What are you *doing?*"

"She has to pay! She could have ruined our chances to redeem ourselves."

Pat smiled and hooked her thumbs into her pockets. "When's the last time y'all hung somebody in this town?"

"This isn't just a bar, this is a restaurant, and we'll be serving lunch soon. We can't have this mob hysteria going on in here," Sophie warned. "Now let her go." She turned to Marilyn. "You owe Kiki and these ladies an apology, and then you need to leave."

"She's not getting away with this!" Kiki felt her eyes start to bulge. They were actually throbbing in their sockets, and she was trembling uncontrollably.

Sophie turned to Trish. "Erase the video of Kiki's choreography."

Trish pushed buttons, waited, then nodded. "Done."

"Now give Marilyn her camera," Sophie said. Trish did.

Kiki was about to blow. "Who were you filming for? Jackie Boo Song? I mean . . . Jackie Loo Tong?"

"I didn't think it would matter," Marilyn shrugged.

"Then why hide in the office like the *rat* you are. Why not come in, sit down, and say you wanted to film us? Because *you* knew it was wrong. You were *spying* for your new *kumu.*"

Marilyn remained stubbornly mute and stared daggers at Kiki.

"That choreography belongs to me and Sophie." Kiki was nose to nose with Marilyn now. "It's against every rule of hula and ethics to tape someone else's dance and copy it. Even if you didn't know that, Jackie Too Long certainly does. I mean Jackie Loo Tong."

Marilyn looked like she might burst into tears, but the way she was glaring, Kiki knew they were fake. There was no apology coming either. Then again, rats never apologized.

21

Speaking in Tongues

Em walked into the bar with Louie right behind her. They'd made a quick trip to town and unloaded the car. It had been a pleasant, normal experience. She should have known that bliss would be shattered the minute she saw the Maidens' cars in the lot.

"What's wrong, Marilyn honey?" Louie hurried to her side and tried to get Marilyn to look at him.

"Your precious fiancée here was filming our competition dance for her new *kumu*, *that's* what," Kiki said.

Louie's jaw dropped. "That can't be true." He turned to Marilyn again. "Can it?"

A strangled cry that sounded like an immature rooster's first crow burst out of Marilyn before she shoved Louie aside, pushed past Em, and ran out the back door.

Louie ran out after her, his aloha shirt flapping.

Suddenly Kiki reached for Em and grabbed onto her arm. Her mouth opened and closed like a grouper, then she started panting. It looked like she was trying to say something, but her mouth wasn't working.

"Calm down, Kiki," Em told her. "No harm done, right? How about we get you a drink?" She turned to Sophie. "Medicinal martini. Quick."

Kiki sputtered. "Sthgudbeita. Kakapatazila."

Pat slapped herself in the forehead. "Holy crap. She's speaking in tongues."

Everyone was staring.

"Pull yourself together, Kiki," Em urged.

"Yeah, calm down," Pat advised. "If you killed Marilyn, the worst that could happen is that you'd end up in jail, but a stroke will ruin your dancing."

"The Defector isn't worth jail or a stroke," Little Estelle said.

"You think we're still going to have to make those leis today?" Big Estelle asked no one in particular. "If not, I'm taking mother home."

Em could tell Kiki was still seething.

"Plumuffcaditpla!" Kiki suddenly yelled. Her eyes were wide and panicked as she slapped her palm over her mouth.

"Seeing as how Kiki can't string a sentence together at the moment, I say you're all *dis*-missed." Pat saluted. Everyone but Trish collected their things and ran.

Em lead Kiki over to the bar and helped her onto a barstool beside Flora.

"I'm going to leave you right here for a minute. Sophie will get you a double martini with extra olives while I go tell Kimo he needs to take you home."

Kiki tried to protest but only managed, "Bulahlapopa."

Em watched Sophie fill a martini glass with ice to chill it down for Kiki's drink.

"You're sending Kimo home?" Sophie didn't try to hide her panic. "It's almost time for the lunch crowd. There may be a cruise ship van coming in."

"We can't let her drive in this condition. She can't even talk." Em leaned over the bar and whispered, "Do you think we should call 911?"

"N . . . ne . . . no!" Kiki shook her head. "No neen on on."

"I'll drive her home," Trish volunteered. "She'll be all right. This happened one other time when we were performing at a party in somebody's driveway, and it started to pour rain. Kiki ran to save the boom box, and when she pulled the plug there was an electrical arc, and she was thrown clear across the driveway. Only spoke gibberish then too. It wore off in a few minutes, and she was fine."

Sophie set a very full martini on the bar. Kiki slid it toward herself and sucked down half the glass without lifting it. She closed her eyes and sighed.

"Bebba. Mooch bebba."

Sophie started frantically clicking the stud in her tongue and turned around. Em made sure Trish had Kiki under control then she ran through the office and out the back door. She found Louie with Marilyn beside her car.

"I thought you loved me," Marilyn cried.

"I do, but right now I don't know who you are." Louie was glummer than Em had ever seen him. His arms hung limp at his sides, his head was bowed.

"Those women hate me." Marilyn reached up and played with the top button on his aloha shirt, but Louie didn't touch her. "I don't know why, but they do. I've tried being nice, but nothing works, so when my new *kumu* asked if I would help him out, I agreed. I didn't know it was wrong."

Em wondered how Jackie Loo Tong could see the Hula Maidens as competition. Just how far would the man go to win? She hoped she hadn't urged Kiki to enter the Maidens in a competition that might literally prove to be dangerous.

She could see Louie weakening.

"You'd better leave, Marilyn," she said. "Let everyone cool off a bit."

Marilyn turned to Louie. "Honey? Do you really want me to go like this?"

Louie's shoulders sagged. "It's probably the best thing to do right now . . . maybe . . ." He glanced at Em. She turned away but wasn't about to leave him alone with Marilyn. "Maybe we should call off the engagement. Just for now. Until things settle down."

"But . . ." Marilyn started sobbing into her hands.

Louie looked like he might give in and invite Marilyn over. Em ached for him but didn't mind playing the heavy. There was no telling what Kiki would do if she ran into Marilyn right away.

"I think you'd better go, Marilyn. Please," Em said. "Louie needs some time to think this through."

Still crying, Marilyn took her car keys out of her pocket and got into her Lexus. Louie gave her a forlorn wave as she backed out of the parking stall, but she didn't look at him. She was pulling onto the highway when Sophie popped her head out of the back door.

"You better get in here, Em. The bread art guy just showed up and so did your cop. Kiki wants Marilyn arrested."

"Are you all right?" Em asked Louie.

"Sure." He shrugged and shoved his hands into the pockets of his baggy linen shorts. "Go ahead. I'll go to the house and work on a new drink. Take my mind off of things."

"Take it easy on Dave. Not too many samples for either of you, okay?"

"Right. I'll be over in a bit."

"No hurry." She hustled back over to the bar where she found Roland cornered by Kiki. The usual spray of flowers in her hair was quivering. Her *pareau* was drifting dangerously south and needed a good tug up over her breasts. If Roland noticed, he didn't let on. He kept his focus on the small notebook in his hand as Kiki waved her arms and opened her mouth.

"S . . . hehehe . . . neeeeeds . . . gooooo . . . jaaaaaail."

"You want to press charges?" Roland tried to take a step back but was up against a table. Em hurried across the room.

"What happened?" He looked at Em the way a drowning man eyes a life ring floating toward him.

Em let Sophie explain the situation in as few words as possible. When she was finished Roland shook his head.

"Really, Kiki?" The corner of his mouth lifted. "You want me to jail someone for videotaping a hula?"

"Yesssssss. Yessssss." Cobra like, Kiki slowly swung her head back and forth then up and down hissing the word. "Law ginst. Against. It. Stealing."

"I don't think there's an actual law on the books against it, but I can understand why you'd be upset. How about I swing by Ms. Lockart's place and give her a stern warning?"

"Not . . . good . . . enough." Kiki shook her head no.

"I'm afraid it's going to have to be. I'll give her a stern warning, and you concentrate on getting your ladies ready for the competition."

Em helped Kiki to a booth closer to the kitchen and went to talk to Kimo, who assured her his wife would be fine as soon as she calmed down. He wasn't going anywhere.

When Em returned to the bar, Roland was still on the threshold.

"I've got to run," he said.

"Sorry you can't stay. I owe you a lunch for this."

"All in a day's work."

Just then Marco the bread artist came up the steps with an armload of boxes. Em introduced them and then told Marco he could put the boxes in her office. He went on through.

Em turned to Roland again. "This competition is driving the Maidens crazy."

"How can you tell? They always seem crazy to me."

"Good point." She thought he seemed hesitant to leave. "You sure you don't want to stay for lunch?"

"I do, but I can't."

She caught herself staring until Marco walked back out of the bar.

"I'm going to need some help," he told her. "I've got a right hand and a couple of heads left to bring in."

Em looked up at Roland again. "Go," she said. "Around here insanity is infectious."

22

Practice Makes Perfect

The lobby of the Island Holidays Resort was filled with carefully placed columns and potted palms, perfect hiding places for Kiki to avoid the Maidens. Earlier they'd come straggling into the hotel toting all of their hula gear like a lost tribe. As soon as they were all settled in their rooms they started assailing her with questions.

She peeked around the column. None of the girls were in the lobby, so Kiki darted to a potted palm then made a run for the bar in the Island Fantasy lounge. She spotted an empty chair and plopped.

"There you are! I've been looking all over for you!"

Kiki groaned. Lillian was suddenly standing over her, clutching the front of her *pareau.*

"What is it, Lillian?"

"Aren't we supposed to be in line to go into our rehearsal on the stage by now?"

Kiki looked at the clock on the wall behind the bar. "*You* are supposed to be in line. I have twenty minutes." Time for a cocktail or two if she chugged them.

"They said we get badges. Where are the badges? And how about passes? I bought a pass for MyBob, and he'll need it to get into the competition. Do you have them? Do you have the programs? I thought we were getting programs."

"And what about T-shirts?" Suzi appeared beside Lillian waving a piece of cardboard around. "I heard we get complementary T-shirts. Do you have them? I'm going to have everyone put their room numbers on this chart so we'll know where to find them. What's your room number, Kiki?"

"I was first." Lillian's lower lip quivered.

Kiki rubbed her temples and sighed. "When I get the packets, you'll get your stinking badges, Lillian."

Lillian snuffled and scurried away.

"That was cold, Kiki." Suzi watched Lillian leave.

"You are all driving me crazy." Her head was splitting. "I don't think I can do this."

Suzi sat in the empty chair next to Kiki's, her room chart momentarily forgotten. "Is there anything I can do to help?"

"Order me a drink, and tell me why we're doing this again."

Suzi waved to the waitress.

"We're here to repair our reputation. You have to admit, since the Marilyn smoothie debacle, things have been going great. We have three coolers full of flowers, and we know what to do with them, thanks to you and Wally and your *lei* making workshop. And so far, Pat's backed you up and has been keeping the peace. Lillian's only cried four times. Who knew Wally would be so good at weaving *haku leis*? And he helped you sew all those felt leaves on the dresses."

"By the time we finished I was thinking Spandex Elvis jumpsuits covered in rhinestones would have been simpler," Kiki mumbled.

She'd made the aqua taro patch gowns for Suzi, Flora, Trish, Lillian, Big Estelle and herself. She'd crafted a *ke kepa*, for Pat Boggs to tie over her shirt and an extra dress for Little Estelle after she threw a fit and threatened to disrupt the performance if she didn't get one.

"They all look great," Suzi assured her. "All those green felt leaves flapping on that aqua material. Genius."

"You think?"

Suzi nodded. "Well, I've never seen anything like them before."

Kiki sighed. "*Mahalo* for that."

The waitress arrived to take her order. Kiki glanced at the clock.

"I don't have time for a drink right now," Kiki decided. "Sorry." She turned to Suzi. "Time to face the music."

She and Suzi walked together through the lobby past booth after booth of craft fair vendors. Across the open lobby, she saw the Maidens all lined up waiting outside the door of the huge hotel ballroom. They were all wearing their matching *pareau* for rehearsal as she instructed. Lillian's face mirrored sheer terror. Even Little Estelle had a somber expression.

Kiki walked up to Lillian and reached into her purse.

"I forgot to give you this double sided tape. Use this, and you can stop holding your *pareau* up like a soggy bath towel."

"Will it work?" Lillian eyed the tape doubtfully.

"It works for JLo, and she's got chichi's." Flora was smiling like a cat in an empty bird's nest.

Kiki leaned toward Trish. "What's with Flora? I asked all of you to keep her from drinking until rehearsal's over."

"She's just happy because her crocheted toilet paper covers are selling like crazy at her friend's crap fair booth," Trish said.

"So are Tiko's smoothies," Kiki added. "I noticed she has a line a mile long. I can't even think about having another one."

Just then Sophie and Pat came rushing over with Wally in tow. When the Maidens crowded around, Pat shushed them and made them line up single file again.

"Why aren't you ladies in your gowns for dress rehearsal?" Wally looked askance at their sarongs.

"No one wears their costumes until the competition performance," Kiki informed him. "We get points for those too."

"Well, I can't wait to see how they look."

"Where's Em? She said she'd be here." Trish looked around the fair. "Didn't she come with you, Wally?"

"She dropped us off and went to park the car," Sophie said. "She'll be here in a minute."

Little Estelle piped up. "She should have valeted."

23

Rehearsal Before the Last Rehearsal

I should have valet parked.

Em jogged up the hotel driveway. They left the North Shore late because she had to show Louie how to make the new smoothies. For a man who could concoct countless cocktails without looking more than once at a recipe book, he was hopeless at opening a simple smoothie package and adding the right amount of water.

Sophie was right; they needed a part-time bartender.

Em entered the lobby. The signs on the walls were confusing. She asked a bell hop which way to the ballroom, and she headed in the direction in which he'd pointed and turned down a long carpeted hallway. Within a few yards she heard voices raised in anger and thought she recognized Jackie Loo Tong. No way could she pass up the opportunity to eavesdrop on a *kumu* throw down.

She turned to face the twin elevators on the wall beside her and pretended to be waiting for one to open.

"You t'ink you can steal my *haumana* and get away with it?"

Em realized Kawika Palikekua was the one shouting at Jackie Loo Tong.

"They aren't your students," Jackie fired back. "They were Mitchell's, and he's gone. They can go anywhere they want, and if they want to come to me, then I'll take 'em."

"Don't piss me off," Kawika warned. "You don't want to go there."

Jackie shot back, "You don't scare me, brah. Pretty soon I'll have all of Mitchell's students. You'll see."

"You can't handle a big *halau*."

"You're not going to be around dat long anyway. Mark my words," Jackie warned.

"Go to hell, Jackie."

"Oh, a*lo*ha, Kawika. See *you* there. You'll get there first."

Em peered around the corner of the elevator alcove. Sure enough, there was Jackie Loo Tong looking smug as he watched Kawika walk into

Island Fantasy Bar. Jackie started toward the elevators with his head down in concentration. Em slipped down the hall and didn't breathe until she heard the elevator bell ping.

"Don't piss me off." Or what? Kawika sounded dead serious when he warned Jackie not to push him.

"Soon I'll have all of Mitchell's students. You're not going to be around dat long anyway." Another warning from Jackie. Anxious to report in to Roland, she realized she was already late for the stage rehearsal, and she'd promised Sophie and Kiki she would be there so she put off calling him.

As Em walked into the craft fair and passed the first booth, she noticed Tiko had a long double line at her smoothie table.

"Hi, Tiko." Em walked to the front of the line.

"Tell the Maidens good luck from me," Tiko said.

"Where are they?"

Tiko pointed over her head. "Lined up for the rehearsal. By the ballroom doors."

Em hurried over. The Hula Maidens were so nervous they were not even harping at each other as they stared wide-eyed at the craft vendors. They barely acknowledged Em when she gave each of them a hug. Danny Cook's trio had just arrived, and Kiki tore into them for being late though rehearsals were running behind schedule.

Drumless, Pat Boggs marched up and down the line of Maidens like General Patton.

"Okay you pussy toads, this is it. This here is almost the real deal. This here is the rehearsal before the rehearsal before the show. I've sneaked a peek at the competition, and there's little childrens who dance better than you all, but if you put your feeble minds to it, you just might not fall over and embarrass yourselves."

"She's right." Little Estelle rolled along on Pat's heels. "Get it together. Keep it together. Get it together. Keep it together."

Pat suddenly stopped and almost fell over the Gad-About. She leaned over until she was nose to nose with Little Estelle.

"Grannie, my question is what part of 'I am in charge here' don't you understand?"

Little Estelle shot back, "I told you more than once I am not your grannie. If any of my offspring ever gave birth to something like you, I'd have made them leave you on a rock in the desert. You act like you were raised by a pack of wild dogs."

"Gators. It was a bunch o' gators."

One of the double doors to the ballroom opened, and a regal looking Hawaiian woman wearing a floor length vintage muumuu and close to ten strands of rare shell *lei* crafted on the forbidden island of Ni'ihau stepped out to greet them.

She waited until Pat fell silent, and all the Maidens, including Kiki, were waiting for her to speak. First she glanced down at the clipboard in her hands then slowly stared at each of the terrified, speechless *haole* women in their *pareau*.

"I am Auntie Gloria. Are you the Hula Maidens?"

"We are," Kiki said.

She looked them up and down. "Are you here to rehearse or are you ready for an afternoon by the pool?"

"Rehearse," Sophie told her.

"Then you're up next. Follow me, ladies."

Auntie Gloria led them into a ballroom filled with a sea of empty folding chairs. A papier-mâché rock waterfall filled the far corner from floor to ceiling. Dusty plastic ferns stuck out of its fake lava crevices. The huge empty stage had ten times the room the Maidens were used to at the Goddess. On the opposite wall a scaffold with risers held the sound technicians behind a light and sound control board. Behind them was a bank of windows that overlooked the hotel entrance with its circular drive.

The sky was picture perfect blue. Tall coco palms swayed on the gentle trades.

As the Maidens listened first to Kiki and then to Pat give them last minute instructions on entering and exiting the stage, Em realized this was serious big time hula. Big time. She was as nervous for the Maidens as they were.

She sat down in the first row and watched Pat pace in front of the stage. Sophie lined the women up, short dancers in front, taller dancers in back. She made certain Suzi was in the center front as the petite realtor had a better memory than the others.

"Okay, hit it Danny," Sophie called out.

The Tiki Tones started playing the original song written by Kiki's neighbor. Em didn't understand the Hawaiian words, but as she watched the Maidens dance, their motions explained the lyrics. The women bowed as low as they could, miming the planting of *taro* in the muddy fields. They pulled hard to imitate pulling the *taro* roots out when they matured. They waded through mud, paused to wipe their brows as they toiled beneath the hot sun. They sashayed back and forth carrying heavy bags on their back and then proceeded to pound the *taro* into *poi*.

Lillian fell out of step and threw off the entire back line.

Sophie yelled, "Cut!" The band stopped.

"I'll do better!" Lillian cried. "Don't throw me out of the show."

"Move over beside Flora." Sophie pointed out Lillian's new position. When she was inebriated, Flora was steady as a rock and never missed a step . . . until she passed out.

The adjustment helped, but the group still looked stiff and scared.

"*Aka'aka*," Sophie pointed to her face, reminding them to smile.

Half of them attempted a smile but wound up grimacing.

The rest of the rehearsal went on without a hitch. When it was over, Auntie Gloria escorted them out without a word. Once they were in the craft fair area again, Tiko came running over.

"Ladies, I have complimentary smoothies for you. Please stop by the booth. They're my bestselling chocolate chip and Kauai coffee bean combos," she said.

Kiki made a prune face. "Sorry, but I don't think I can stomach one."

"Oh, please. I'd like to make up for what happened last time," Tiko urged.

"Has Marilyn been anywhere near the booth?" Kiki asked.

Tiko's smile faded. "No. Not at all. I promise."

"Where is Marilyn?" Kiki asked Em.

"I have no idea. Hopefully she won't stop by and see Louie at the bar to 'help' him out while Sophie and I are both here."

"I hope you have a business left when you get home. I wouldn't put it past her to steal the day's take."

They all walked over to Tiko's table where the line was fifteen people deep. Her cousin Charlotte was chatting and taking orders. Tiko had some all lidded and ready for the Maidens.

"We really wish you'd join our group, Tiko," Kiki pressed.

"I'll think about it," Tiko promised. "*Maybe*. In a couple of months."

"Really! That would be so great." Kiki was ecstatic.

"No smoothie for you Kiki?" Tiko watched Charlotte pour soy milk into the blender.

"Sorry, but there's a seat in the bar with my name on it. I heard some of the musicians will be there jamming after rehearsals." Kiki told them all goodbye and walked away.

Em watched her head toward Island Fantasy. The other Maidens finished off their smoothies in record time and then fled to the bar after Kiki. Em walked out of the craft fair with Sophie.

"Look over there," she said, trying to be discrete as she nodded toward one of the wide pillars in the center of the room. "See the woman in the huge black hat and sunglasses?"

"Is that who I think it is?"

"Marilyn."

"Still spying for Jackie?" Sophie rolled her eyes.

"Looks like it. I hope that's all she's doing here. At least she's not at the Goddess with Louie." Em tried not to stare at Marilyn. "So, how do you think rehearsal went?" she asked Sophie.

Sophie, who had dyed her spikes neon lavender for the occasion, was clicking her tongue stud against her teeth. She stopped long enough to smile at a handsome local who sauntered by carrying a guitar case toward the bar.

"Honestly, they were so scared they looked like a bunch of zombies who just learned to walk."

"Maybe you should let them drink before the show," Em suggested.

"Great. Drunken dancing zombies. You think?"

"Sounds like a good name for one of Louie's concoctions." Em sighed. "I hope I didn't make a mistake talking them into this."

Sophie eyed her carefully. "You know, I still can't figure out why you wanted them in this competition so bad. It's no day at the beach."

"So I see now. This is serious stuff. I just thought it would be great if they made a better showing than last time."

Em almost admitted Roland had wanted someone here with eyes and ears on Mitchell's *halau*. But Sophie had stepped up and taken on the Maidens at the last minute, and she had enough on her plate without having to worry about a potential murderer in their midst.

"I'll just be glad when it's over," Sophie said.

"Me too. Believe me."

"How about we join the girls at the bar? I'll buy us both a Lava Flow."

"I've never seen you drink." Em was shocked. She had never asked why because she figured it was none of her business. What she did know of Sophie's past wasn't pretty.

"I've never needed one so bad. I just never drink at work."

"You go ahead. I need to make a couple of phone calls. Besides, I'm full of smoothie right now," Em said.

24

Em Reports In

With everyone occupied in the bar, Em went outside to the pool area. The Island Holiday Hotel was on the beach between the Wailua River and Hanamaulu, surrounded by what used to be cane fields but were now fields of waving weeds. Every so often a field mysteriously caught fire but no one seemed too concerned.

There was an artificial grotto with a wall of water thundering down, three pools, a swim up bar, a restaurant on the beach, and the required sixty foot coconut palms swaying in the trade winds. *Cue the tourists*, Em thought as she gazed around.

She pulled out her phone, called Louie.

"Are you doing all right?"

"Sure. I've been running this place since before you were born. I haven't left the top off the blender once. The smoothies are a hit by the way, but I've been adding a shot of rum to them, though. Otherwise they're kinda bland."

"You're not putting rum in kids' orders, are you?"

"What?" he yelled.

The place had to be crowded. She could barely hear him over the background noise. Glancing over her shoulder she checked to see if anyone was near. The last thing they needed was the liquor commissioner coming down on them.

She cupped the cell phone. "You're not putting rum in kids' drinks, are you?"

"Just a minute." He called out, "Lady, get those naked kids off the windowsill. We don't allow diving into the parking lot puddles." There was another pause. "What did you say, Em?"

"*Stop* putting rum in the smoothies."

"That's no fun."

"I mean it. Stop. Sophie will be on her way in a few minutes."

"How is it going there?"

"Fine. Rehearsal went fine."

112

"Good. Tell the gals hello from me. And Marilyn sends her love," he added.

Yeah right. "Was she there?" Em thought she had stopped by to see him before coming to the festival.

"No, she couldn't make it. It's just me and Kimo. Hey, did you hear Buzzy's thinking of getting married?"

"What?"

"Buzzy's thinking about getting married," he yelled over the noise. "He was just talking about an underwater ceremony. His fiancée must be a diver."

Em hung up and walked into the grotto as she hit Roland's number. Cooling mist sprayed off the waterfall. She stood at the end of the walk inside the fake cave where she could see the ocean a short distance away.

"Em." He answered on the first ring.

"Hi. I'm at the hotel."

"What's up?" His voice seemed to surround her.

"Where are you? I'm hearing an echo."

"Turn around."

She turned. He was three feet behind her with his phone to his ear.

"What are you doing here?" She shut off her cell.

"I thought I'd stop to see how it's going. I'm also checking out the space in the ballroom. When I dance for the closing ceremonies I don't want the ballroom to go up in flames."

"Good idea."

"So what's up?"

"For one thing, a guy named Buzzy might be engaged to a dolphin." She tried not to smile.

"Buzzy the hippie handyman on the North Shore?"

She nodded.

"It'll never last."

Em laughed. "Nothing gets to you, does it?"

"I've seen too much to let a guy marrying a dolphin get to me. Gotta hang loose, as we say. So, you were calling about what?"

She glanced around to make certain no one was nearby. She hoped the sound of the waterfall would muffle her words then she said, "Let's walk on the beach."

They walked past the beach bar and grill where a couple of locals greeted Roland with waves and smiles. Then they crossed a grassy lawn area to the sandy beach. The trades were blowing across the water. In the distance she saw an inter-island jet bank and begin a landing at Lihue airport. Across the water to the southeast, too far to be seen, was the island of Oahu with its crowded freeways and tourist mecca of Waikiki.

"I overheard Kawika and Jackie Loo Tong arguing in the hallway between the bar and the elevators when they thought they were alone."

"You're sure they were arguing?"

"I know a threat when I hear one. It was about stealing dancers. Kawika asked Jackie if he thought he could get away with stealing his students. Then Jackie fired back with, 'You're not going to be around that long anyway. Mark my words.'"

"That sounds like more than a threat."

"You don't think one of them would try anything this weekend to ruin the festival, do you?"

"Maybe. If it upset the competition and they could win the top prize."

"What kind of prizes are we talking here?"

"A trophy, two hundred dollars and a year's supply of pepperoni flavored pig jerky sticks."

"You're kidding, right?"

"We don't kid about pepperoni pig jerky."

"For this people kill each other?"

"This is really about the *kumu*'s reputation," Roland said. "And money. I checked out the *halau* website and pulled Mitchell's tax records. For a non-profit his *halau* is making a boatload of money. I'm guessing they weren't reporting much of it."

Em took in the view down the beach, then across the land toward the mountains in the distance.

"Everywhere you look on this island there's something beautiful." When she turned toward Roland again he was staring down at her.

"You're right about that."

"I wasn't fishing for a compliment."

"I already know you better than that. You be careful, okay?"

"I've got the easy job," she said. "I just have to snoop. I don't have to toss flaming knives or chase guys in chicken suits."

"Back to what you heard . . ."

"Kawika warned Jackie to stop taking his students. Jackie said that the dancers could go anywhere they wanted."

Roland turned and headed back toward the hotel grounds. "Want a hamburger?"

"No, thanks. How many of those do you eat a week?"

"Enough that I should buy stock in ground beef and quit my day job. How was the bread art show?"

Em sighed.

"That bad?"

"Not entirely. Louie's new drink, Two to Mango, was a hit. We served them in plastic champagne flutes and everything. Real classy for the

Goddess. There wasn't much room to display the art pieces. I didn't know Marco had brought so many. There were lifelike hands and feet, elbows, knees, calves, shoulders. You name it."

"*Ule?*" He side-eyed her.

She'd lived there long enough to know what *that* meant.

"I told him no penises. We draped all the cocktail tables with black fabric. Everything was fine until a woman walked in and sat down at the bar. Unfortunately someone had moved a head over to the bar. There it was, grinning at her beside her elbow. She took one look, passed out, fell off the tiki stool and hit her head on the bar going down. Louie was terrified she'd sue."

"Did she?"

"Not after he gave her free luau tickets for life."

25

Away We Go

Day one of the Kauai Kukui Nut Festival Hula Competition started with Kawika Palikekua welcoming everyone on behalf of the *halau* he'd inherited from the late Mitchell Chambers. Opening ceremonies began with presentation of people from the community representing the disposed Hawaiian royal court, followed by a lengthy *oli*, a chant in Hawaiian, and then a traditional *pule* or prayer.

"I hope everyone will refrain from taking their own videos and photos. We have an official photographer in the back with printed photos for sale after each group performs. And you can purchase videos later too. No take photos from your seats, eh? Our friendly bouncers are standing by to toss you out. Gently of course." He laughed and preened. "Okay, so now we can start."

Kiki found a seat near the front row on the bar side of the huge ballroom and settled in to watch the children compete in the Keiki Division of the contest. The children were all adorable. As usual she found herself wishing that she'd started dancing hula as a kid.

Her mind wandered as group after group of young dancers did their thing. Their families and the rest of the audience roared with approval as if the contest was scored on applause and not by a panel of judges.

It was hard to concentrate while plagued by doubts about the Maidens' taro patch number. The song was about Kauai, written by a Kauai musician, in Hawaiian. But would the judges like it? She had no idea if the Hawaiian language usage was acceptable or if they'd like the melody.

Wally grudgingly admitted he thought her design for the muumuus was good, but then what did Wally know, really? Dressing the flamboyant Fernando for Las Vegas had been one thing, but the man had no idea how to design for a bunch of over-the-hill dancers like the Maidens. All she could hope for was that they didn't look like decrepit show girls by the time he finished with their hair and makeup tomorrow night.

After an hour of sitting through the kiddie competition, Kiki had worked herself into a stew of anxiety and decided to get a drink and wander out to the foyer, check out the crap fair, and find some of her cohorts.

When she saw Tiko at the smoothie table she stopped to chat her up, determined not to rest until Tiko committed to join the Maidens.

"Do you get any time off to step in and watch the performances?" Kiki asked once she had Tiko's attention.

"Not really." Tiko introduced Kiki to her cousin, Charlotte Anara, who had stepped in to help her keep the line moving. Charlotte was younger than Tiko with long waving black hair that fell past her waist.

"She's beautiful." Kiki took a sip of a vodka tonic she'd sneaked out of the bar. "Is she a dancer, too?"

Tiko had filled two smoothie cups and was reaching for plastic lids. As she snapped them in place she nodded. "Charlotte has danced hula before, and she's great at it. Working for Garden Island Vacation Rentals she has fairly regular hours. You'd probably have more luck recruiting her than me."

There was a break in the crowd so Kiki introduced herself to Charlotte.

"You should join the Hula Maidens. Our group isn't all *kupuna*, though most of us are over fifty." *Way over*, Kiki thought as she smiled at Charlotte. "We're always looking for young talent. If we had a wider age range we could enter more competition divisions. We practice at the Tiki Goddess out on the North Shore. You're always welcome to join us."

"I'll think about it," Charlotte said. "*Mahalo* for asking."

Em came walking over to join them and said hi to Tiko, then Kiki introduced her to Charlotte.

"She might join the Hula Maidens." Kiki couldn't wait to tell Sophie.

They stood by while Tiko used a marking pen to identify two smoothie cups and then handed them over to Charlotte.

"These are for Jackie and Kawika. I wrote Kawika's name and put stars on it so you won't mix them up. He hates chocolate. I just put coffee bean chips in his."

Charlotte picked up the smoothies and left the booth.

"I've been giving all the *kumu* complimentary smoothies. Are you sure you don't want one yet, Kiki?"

"I'm sure. The septic tank at the Goddess still hasn't recovered from the last smoothie episode."

"You're sure doing well," Em commented.

"I'm featuring a variety of healthy additions. I've even got some kava, an old Hawaiian relaxant." She handed them each a smoothie menu from a pile of copies on the table.

Kiki and Em read over the list of probiotics, immunity boosters, antioxidants, kava for anti-anxiety, caffeine boosts, conjugated acids and vitamin supplements.

Kiki set the menu down and raised her glass. "I irrigate my intestines with cocktails to keep them lubed. Thanks, though."

The double doors to the main room opened, and a good portion of the audience filtered, some headed for the bathrooms and others for the crafters tables. Tiko's line started to back up, and she had no time to spare, so Kiki looked around for some of the Maidens.

"There's Sophie and Pat," she told Em. "They're coming out of the ballroom and headed this way."

"How'd you like the performances?" Kiki rattled the ice in her glass.

"Adorable," Sophie said.

"I'm sorry I missed them," Em said.

"Where were you anyway?" Kiki wanted to know.

"Out by the pool. I wanted to call Louie."

"Has Marilyn ruined the place yet?" Kiki smirked.

Em ignored the comment. "It actually sounded pretty crowded."

"You all will have to go some to whip them kids," Pat frowned.

"We don't have to compete with the kids. Just other *kupuna*," Kiki clarified.

Pat sniffed. "I'm just sayin'. So how come y'all don't have a solo dancer? They're up next."

"The only one we would stand a chance of placing with is Flora because she's Hawaiian," Kiki said.

Pat wouldn't drop it. "Then how come you didn't enter her?"

"Because," Kiki set her empty rocks glass on a nearby table, "last time she danced solo, we had to pay someone to watch her all day long."

"Watch her?"

"To keep her from swilling out of that Gatorade bottle she carries around."

Pat Boggs' eyes bulged. "You mean that's not Gatorade?"

"Not by a long shot."

"I thought she'd had a stroke or som'p'in. I didn't know she's always drunk as Cooter Brown," Pat shook her head.

Sophie laughed and turned to Em, "I'd better head back to the Goddess."

"I told Louie you'd be on the way."

Everyone had to hug Sophie goodbye.

"Ready to go in? Intermission's almost over." Kiki checked to make certain the festival badge around her neck was turned the right way. "I like to sit up front."

They started to head back into the ballroom. Kiki looked for some of the others and then stopped dead still. Pat ran into her and cussed.

"Damn, Kiki. Get a brake light or somethin'."

"What's wrong?" Em followed Kiki's gaze.

"Don't look over there," Kiki warned.

Em and Pat looked anyway.

"What are we looking at?" Pat said.

"Defector alert." Kiki tilted her head to the right. "Over there near the windows. She's hiding next to that rack of hand painted T-shirts. She's got on a big black hat and sunglasses. She looks ridiculous."

"Do you think no one will recognize her?" Pat wondered.

"She's still spying," Kiki said.

"At least she's not at the Goddess hounding Louie to forgive her." Em sounded relieved.

"She's up to something." Kiki was sure of it. "And whatever it is, it isn't good."

26

Another One Bites the Dust

Em followed Kiki as they moved with a sea of spectators being funneled through the ballroom doors. Kiki hurried down front and claimed seats off to the left side of the stage. They were no sooner seated than the lights dimmed and Kawika came back on stage. He stepped up to the podium and smiled at the crowd, but his smile was short-lived. He shuffled through a pile of notes on the stand, then tapped on the mic to see if it was on.

A hush fell over the ballroom as everyone waited in anticipation for him to announce solo portion of the competition open.

"Aloooooha," Kawika said.

"Alooooha," the audience responded.

"Welcome back to the second portion of our . . . completion . . . I mean . . . competition . . . the solo dancers." The newly appointed *kumu* wiped his brow with the back of his hand and blinked as he looked up into the bank of bright overhead spotlights. "Our first con . . . contestant in this division comes all the way . . ." Kawika paused. His hands tightened on the podium.

Em whispered to Kiki, "Does he look pale, or is it just the lights?"

Kiki leaned forward in her seat. "Something's wrong."

Kawika struggled to continue. ". . . all the way from Tokyo, Japan." He swayed to his left, then to his right, then took a step back, threw up, and passed out cold.

An audible gasp filled the room. For a moment everyone was frozen in shock, and then members of Kawika's *halau*—formerly Mitchell's—rushed the stage and knelt around their fallen leader.

The audience remained spellbound. A few visiting *kumu* joined the *halau* on stage. Some people in back precariously climbed onto their seats to get a better view. The less curious went to the no host bar for refills. On stage, someone started to chant. Soon others joined in.

Em shivered. "That gives me chicken skin," she said. "Has anyone called 911? What about CPR? Chanting isn't going to save Kawika if he's having a heart attack."

She fished her cell phone out of her purse and punched in the emergency number. She was informed that the lines were full.

"Everyone in the room with a phone is calling in." She looked around and spotted help on the stage. "Thank heaven, there's Roland."

Dressed, or rather mostly undressed, in the *malo* he wore during his fire knife dance, Roland came on stage and parted the male and female dancers huddled round Kawika. Two uniformed officers who were working the event joined him. One was on the two-way radio, the other standing with his hands on his hips watching the crowd.

Within two minutes they heard a fire truck and ambulance coming up the highway. The glow from spinning red lights whirled around the ballroom walls when the emergency vehicles pulled up in the driveway right outside the windows.

Cell phone in hand, Kiki said, "I'll text the Maidens and let them know what's happening."

Em glanced around the room. Unlike the Maidens, most of the other *halau* sat together to watch competitions. The Japanese were dressed in matching hot pink T-shirts and *pau* skirts made of yards of cloth. They took up eight rows and were all on their feet, holding hands.

As the EMTs came running up the center aisle wheeling a stretcher, Kiki said, "Can you believe it? If Kawika croaks, this will be the third member of Mitchell's *halau* to wind up dead."

Even though it was happening right before her eyes, Em couldn't believe what she was seeing.

But as she listened to the chanting and watched the EMTs labor over the fallen *kumu*, she had to admit Roland's hunch might have been spot on. Maybe his toe was psychic. Someone could very well be systematically killing off the upper echelon of Kauai's top *halau*.

When Kiki tried to clamber up onto the seat of her folding chair, Em grabbed her arm and tugged her down.

"Do you want to break your leg?"

"I just got a text from Suzi. She's in the room somewhere. She's putting this all on Facebook." Kiki was headed toward the aisle. "Anyone want anything from the bar?"

Em shook her head no. She kept hearing Jackie Loo Tong's voice as he argued with Kawika: "*You're not going to be around that long anyway. Mark my words.*"

"Nothing for me," Em told Kiki.

She paused to watch Roland on stage. Naked from the waist up, he folded his beefy arms across his bare chest and watched the EMTs work while uniformed KPD officers on opposite ends of the stage kept an eye on the crowd. Though very few people had left the ballroom, the festival organizers and security were in the aisles ready to direct people out in an orderly fashion.

Em scanned the room. Jackie's *halau* was gathered together and dressed in black *halau* T-shirts. A few dancers were in their seats watching with concerned expressions. Some were on their feet, talking to one another, and others were taking photos with their phones. Em left her seat and walked up the aisle to the back of the room and then moved closer to Jackie's section. She didn't see him anywhere, so she walked along the far wall, checking up and down each row. He wasn't near the photograph or video sale tables or across the room at the bar.

There was no sign of him anywhere.

As she wandered along the back wall, Em caught a glimpse of Marilyn trying to slip off in the opposite direction. Marilyn had longer legs, and she was in a hurry. Em practically had to jog to catch up.

"Marilyn!" Em touched the woman's shoulder.

Marilyn jumped and turned with a wavering smile. "Oh hi, Em."

"What's with the hat and glasses?"

Marilyn's hand flew up to her oversized sunglasses as if she'd forgotten she was wearing them. She pulled them off.

"I was afraid if Kiki recognized me there would be trouble."

"Sophie and I saw you earlier today in the lobby."

"Well, look who's here." Kiki walked up holding a drink. She looked Marilyn up and down. "Been serving smoothies again? Did'ja just give one to Kawika?"

Em studied Marilyn to gauge her reaction.

"Did you?" she asked. "Did you give Kawika anything that would make him ill?"

"Of course not! What are you two insinuating? I just came to see the show. Why on earth would I want to hurt Kawika? I adore that man."

"Why do you do anything you do?" Kiki asked.

"Where is your new *kumu*?" Em asked Marilyn.

"Do you mean Jackie?"

"Yes. Jackie," Em said.

"Or did you already defect from his *halau* too?" Kiki asked.

"How would I know where he is? Ask one of his dancers." Marilyn turned to Kiki. "I'm not officially a member until after the competition."

Suddenly the crowd collectively held its breath. Em glanced toward the stage and watched as the EMTs shifted Kawika onto the gurney and raised it. There was an oxygen mask strapped to his face. They wheeled him off into the wings and took him out the back way.

Roland and the other officers followed them out. A janitor with a mop and bucket walked on stage.

"Glad I'm not on barf detail," Kiki muttered.

The microphone squealed when a young male dancer tapped the mic. He blew into it and then softly said, "Is this on? Can you hear me?"

"Louder!" someone in the back row yelled.

"Can you hear me now?"

There was some scattered applause.

"If everyone would please stand and join hands we'll say a *pule* for Kawika."

A man's voice shouted, "Is he *make*?"

"No. He's not dead. They're taking him to Wilcox."

"Who is that on the mic?" Em whispered to Kiki.

"I don't remember his name, but I recognize him. He's been one of Mitchell's dancers for years. I've seen him dance for his mom's musical group too. They entertain at restaurants and bars sometimes. I think their last name is Leahe."

The room fell silent. Everyone bowed their heads as the young man led the audience in a prayer for Kawika who was in route to Wilcox Hospital, a short distance away in Lihue. He asked for blessings for Kawika, the EMTs, the doctors waiting at the hospital, everyone present, the dancer waiting in the wings, those at home who couldn't be there, the firemen of the KFD, the police, and the festival committee. Before he finished he even asked for blessings for the tires on the ambulance.

Finally everyone said, "*Amene.*"

The new M.C. paused to confer with Kawika's troupe, who had remained gathered in a tight knot of eerily calm hysteria on stage. The young male dancer who led the prayer was in a hushed argument with them. He tried handing the mic off, but no one would take it.

Looking flustered, he returned to the podium and focused on the crowd again.

"The last thing Kawika said before they took him away was . . ."

"We can't *hear* you," a man shouted.

The new emcee spoke up. "He said that the show must go on. So . . . if the musicians playing for the solo dancer from Tokyo will take their places, and all of you will take your seats, the solo competition will begin."

Hoping Roland was still in the hotel, Em was anxious to find him. She turned to Kiki, whose head was on a swivel.

"Hey. Where'd Marilyn go?" Kiki wondered.

There was no sign of Marilyn anywhere.

"She can't be far." Em was amazed at how fast Marilyn disappeared.

"Maybe she got rid of Kawika so Jackie can steal more of students."

"Before tonight I would have said no, but I don't know what to think anymore."

"Well, I think you should tell Roland. He won't believe me."

"I was just going to look for him."

"Good. Maybe we can be rid of her once and for all." Kiki turned back toward the stage. The lights went low, and the Japanese solo dancer took her place. The hum of a slide guitar blended with a ukulele and acoustic guitars. The spotlight found the dancer, who was poised and ready.

"I'm going up front again," Kiki whispered.

"I'm going to find Roland."

"Yeah, maybe now he'll arrest Marilyn."

Em thought Jackie Loo Tong, given his absence, was the more likely suspect as she headed for the exit. But the double doors were closed; no one was allowed to go in or out during a performance.

Em scooted back out of the way, hugging the wall like the rest of the folks waiting to get out. She watched the solo dancer on stage. The woman from Tokyo was a far cry better than any of the Maidens. Maybe it would have been best for her friends if the show hadn't gone on after Kawika hit the floor. She was hoping the dance would end soon when she spotted Tiko standing near the exit.

Em crossed the open space between them and slipped into an empty spot against wall. Tiko looked anxious to get out.

"Did you leave the booth unmanned?" Em asked.

"No, Charlotte's there. I got caught inside when I came to see what the commotion was," Tiko said. She continued to watch the dancer on stage.

Em studied her profile and asked, "Do you remember Marilyn buying a smoothie from you earlier?"

Tiko turned. "Marilyn? I don't think so. I've been there most of the afternoon."

"Shh!" An older woman next to Em shushed them. They fell silent until the performance ended and the lights went up again, then Em moved with the crowd to the craft fair area and followed Tiko to her booth where her cousin was still busy.

"Kawika collapsed?" Charlotte poured soy milk into the blender and added a variety of juices with barely a glance.

"How did you know?" Tiko stepped behind the table and tied on her Tiko's Tropical Smoothie apron.

"That's all everyone out here is talking about," Charlotte said.

Em stood off to the side and watched the cousins take orders as fast as they could. Their efficient moves back and forth in the small space were as choreographed as any dance.

"Does Charlotte know Marilyn?" Em waited until Tiko shut off the blender and was reaching for a cup.

"I don't think they've ever had an opportunity to meet."

"Meet who?" Charlotte wanted to know as she made change for a man with two kids.

"A *haole* lady," Em said. "In her sixties. I was wondering if she ordered a smoothie in the last couple hours. She's blond, but she had on a huge black hat that covered her hair and big sunglasses. You couldn't have missed her."

"I kind of remember waiting on somebody like that. Why?" Charlotte paused to ask a young hippie mom with a baby in a tie-dyed sling what she wanted to order.

"Just curious," Em said.

No use getting Tiko upset about Marilyn. Em still doubted the woman had anything to do with Kawika's collapse since Jackie Loo Tong was still the number one suspect in Em's mind. But if Marilyn was dangerous, she had to be stopped.

There was no sign of Roland in the fair area. Em was about to leave when Charlotte asked Tiko, "Who took over for Kawika?"

Em paused, picturing the soft spoken male dancer at the microphone.

"His name is Raymond Leahe," Tiko said.

"Do I know him?" Charlotte asked.

"Maybe you'd recognize him. He's a great dancer. Mitchell was going to elevate both Shari and Kawika to *kumu* status but Mitchell never noticed what a fabulous hula dancer Raymond is. Raymond never got angry about it, but in my opinion he *so* deserves to lead that *halau*."

Em said goodbye and went to look for Roland. As she walked through the craft fair and out to the lobby, she found herself wondering if Raymond Leahe might have finally gotten angry enough to get rid of the only dancer left in his way.

27

Suspicious Suspects

Kiki found Trish and Suzi in the ballroom and crawled over the laps and legs of spectators as she made her way along the row to the empty seat beside them. She splashed vodka on the head of a bald man sitting in the row in front of them, lifted the hem of her *pareau* and wiped it off.

"Aloooooha!" He smiled over his shoulder.

"Aloha handsome. Where you from?" Kiki batted her false eyelashes, certain he was a tourist. He was too pale to be from Kauai. There were five empty Budweiser bottles on the floor by his chair. Obviously like everyone in the room he was high on Hawaiian music, hula, and witnessing Kawika's collapse.

"Seattle."

"Seattle," Kiki laughed. "Home of the palest *haoles* in the world." She figured she'd spread enough aloha to make up for the splash and sat down.

Trish leaned over Suzi. "Did you hear?"

"About Kawika? I saw him go down."

"Not that. Pat is out looking for Flora. She and Little Estelle stayed in the bar too long and wound up dancing for the crowd."

"Dancing what?"

"They thought it was hula. Flora was dancing. Little Estelle sat on the Gad-About and waved her arms around. The bouncer tossed them out when Little Estelle offered to strip for donations. Flora wanted to leave by then anyway. She thinks she was scheduled to dance in the solo competition like last time. They went to put on her makeup and do her hair."

Kiki's shock turned to relief. "Then she's probably in her room. If Pat's smart she'll lock them in."

"We looked. They aren't there, and we don't know where they are," Trish said. "We got tired of searching and split. Little Estelle can be very cagey."

"Someone ought to take that scooter away from her."

"I just hope Pat finds them before Flora somehow makes it to the stage," Trish said.

"I think we should go help," Suzi added.

"Sergeantoggs wants to be in charge, then let her." Kiki glanced at the stage and mumbled, "I wonder what the holdup is?"

So far the new Master of Ceremonies hadn't appeared to announce the next dancer.

"You know, I saw Marilyn earlier," Kiki told them. "I'm betting she gave Kawika one of her doctored smoothies."

Suzi quickly checked her cell phone and then shut it down again. "Really, Kiki, that's nuts. Why would she?"

Kiki leaned over Trish and tapped her temple. "*Think* about it, Suzi. Without Kawika, Jackie can talk more of Mitchell's students into defecting. Maybe all of them."

"Wow," Trish stared at Kiki. "You might be right."

"I didn't just fall off the taro truck like some people around here." Kiki set her empty glass on the carpet beneath her chair.

When Raymond Leahe finally re-appeared, he was still sweating like a pig without a mud hole.

"And now," he looked everywhere but directly at the crowd, "from the island known as the Gathering Place, Oahu, Miss Kelani Lin."

"Look at him," Kiki whispered to Trish. "He's quaking so hard he might wack himself with that mic and get a fat lip."

"Maybe he's going to pass out. Maybe he's got what Kawika has."

"Depends on whether or not Marilyn gave him one of her doctored up smoothies."

28

Em Snoops Around

Em wished Sophie was there as she searched the hotel for Roland until one of the security guards told her that he was backstage. After convincing the man she had important information for the detective, he called the guard at the backstage entry point and told him to let her through.

She followed the scent of coconut oil along the corridor. It led her straight to Roland, who was still greased up and ready to perform his fire knife dance. He'd covered up with an aloha shirt but hadn't buttoned it. His bare legs were exposed. Practically everything was exposed since he was wearing a *malo*, which barely covered his important parts.

Roland was on the phone but held up a hand to acknowledge her. At a pause in the conversation he gave her a quick smile and mouthed hi.

"Are you still going on tonight?" she asked.

"I'm calling a replacement right now."

Her gaze kept slipping to his open shirt and the bare brown skin beneath.

"See anything you like?"

"Ha ha." She looked away. Her cheeks lit up hot as his flaming knives.

"I feel ridiculous conducting an investigation in this get up." He went back to making arrangements for a replacement over the phone. When he ended the call he automatically started to put the cell in his back pocket. He looked down at his *malo* and sighed.

"Have you heard anything from the hospital?" Em asked.

"Kawika is in critical condition. He's got diarrhea, vomiting, abdominal cramps and electrolyte imbalance. Symptoms that could mean anything. He's been under a lot of stress after Mitchell's death and taking over the organization of the festival. It could be food poisoning or something worse. They don't know yet. I asked for the doctor to run extensive toxicology tests."

"Do you think he was poisoned?" She pictured Marilyn skulking around in her ridiculous oversized hat and glasses. He shrugged. "I hope not, but now I'm sure it's more than coincidence that he's the third one to go down in the same *halau*."

"Kiki is still convinced Marilyn is behind this."

"But you're not."

"It's just so crazy. Are you starting to suspect her?"

"Why take out Mitchell's *halau*?" he speculated. "What's in it for her? Why not just poison Kiki and end the feud?"

"She did *accidentally* give all the girls violent diarrhea, remember?"

They stood in a narrow hallway behind the stage area. A long expanse of linoleum tiled floors and exposed pipes on the ceiling led to the huge ballroom kitchen area. The sound of hushed voices reached them, and then one of the visiting *kumu* from Oahu appeared in the hall escorting his solo dancer to wait her turn.

Em looked around. "I have other information, but I really don't feel comfortable discussing it here."

"Me, either." Roland picked up his fire knives and held them out to Em.

"What do you want me to do with those?"

"Carry them. Please." He pointed to the lamp oil bottle on the floor not far away. "I'll take the accelerant."

Em took the long thin poles. Each had a knife on one end and a foam ball on the other. She imagined lighting them on fire, twirling them around and tossing them in the air.

"Want to give it a try sometime?"

"Did your toe just talk to you? Maybe you are psychic." She glanced up at him as they walked down the hall. "I was *just* wondering how long it would take for my hair to grow back once it was singed off. Where are we going?"

"I want you to check out the dressing area for me. See if Jackie Loo Tong is in there."

"I haven't seen him anywhere. He wasn't in the ballroom when Kawika collapsed." She followed him through the back passageways of the hotel, through double glass doors into the spa registration area off the main lobby. A huge empty area in back had been partitioned off with poles draped with curtains for walls. The names of the various *halau* and their *kumu* were pinned to the curtain doorways.

As they passed Jackie's assigned space, Roland nodded on his way toward a sign that read *Sharpe*. Em hung back and stopped at Jackie Tong's dressing area. She took a deep breath and slightly pushed open the curtain. Inside, two local women were getting Jackie's solo dancer ready to perform. One was putting on her makeup while the other was busy arranging flowers on an intricate hairdo. Both of them turned to look at Em. There was no sign of Jackie.

"So sorry," Em shrugged and smiled. "Wrong room." She noticed a space down the way for the Hula Maidens. She stopped outside Roland's dressing area.

"Should I come in?" she asked.

"Sure."

She pulled the curtain back. He was standing in the middle of the small space taking his *haku* ti leaf *lei* off his head.

"Jackie wasn't there," she mouthed.

Roland put the *lei* in a cooler against the far wall.

"Do you make those yourself for every performance?" she asked.

"My auntie is retired. She likes to make them for me. Keeps her busy."

"She could make plenty of money making adornments for the Maidens."

"She's not senile enough yet."

Em laughed. When he looked like he was about to untie his *malo* right in front of her, she turned and grabbed the curtain. "I'll wait out in the lobby."

"I'm not shy."

"I am." Too tempted to stay and watch, she hurried out.

The spa reception area was deserted. Em sat down in a chair to wait, picked up a Yoga magazine and wondered if all the women who were into Yoga were long and lean to begin with, or they were into it because they already looked good in Spandex tights and tank tops.

She'd signed up for a Yoga class in Hanalei once without knowing it was for advanced students. At five-four she felt like a dwarf surrounded by Amazons. It was Bikram Yoga where the temperature in the room was, for some mystical reason, cranked up to 100 degrees. She was dehydrated and seeing stars by the time it ended and barely able to crawl to her car.

Before she had time to thumb through more than half the magazine, Roland appeared in his aloha shirt, shorts, and rubber slippahs. He was carrying his small black spiral notebook. Em tossed the magazine back on the table.

"Let's go talk by the pool. It should be nice and quiet out there right now."

"Perfect," Em said. A little peace and quiet didn't seem like much to ask for.

29

More Insanity

They wandered down the winding cement path through lush, landscaped gardens full of palms, ginger and heliconia. Hawaiian music drifted on the trades, muted by the rush of the wide waterfall that cascaded into the pool and the sound of the waves hitting the beach. A handful of people were strolling outdoors, but most were inside at the fair or in the ballroom.

The small cabana that served food for the pool area was closed and shuttered for the evening. They sat down at one of the metal and glass tables closest to the beach beneath a black night sky spattered with bright stars.

"Nice outside," he said.

"What's it like going from one crisis to another?" Em watched him set his phone on the table atop his notebook.

"Kind of like you knowing the Hula Maidens."

She laughed. "Hey, you got me into this one. If I wasn't here right now I'd be at the Goddess, and the only thing I'd have to worry about is running out of rum."

"When Kawika collapsed I thought about the conversation you overheard. We haven't located Loo Tong anywhere. He's not in his room, and he's not with his *halau.*"

"Or with his solo dancer," she added. "He wasn't in the ballroom when Kawika passed out either. I looked all over and didn't see him there anywhere."

"His car isn't in the parking lot. As soon as one of the patrol cars spots it, I'll get a call."

"It can't be hard to miss." She recalled the low slung, souped up classic truck covered with window decals. "You can't arrest him just on suspicion, can you?" Em hoped she hadn't jumped to conclusions, but she was certain she'd heard the exchange between *kumu* correctly.

"You did hear him threaten Kawika."

"I know. But maybe someone else wanted Kawika, Shari and Mitchell out of the way."

"Like who?" He sat back in the chair and propped his ankle on his opposite knee, leaned back and waited.

"Raymond. The dancer who took over as M.C."

"The nervous guy?"

"Right. He's in Mitchell's *halau*."

Roland nodded for her to go on.

"According to Tiko, he's a great dancer, but Mitchell always overlooked him when it came to grooming the next *kumu*. Shari was close to Mitchell and running *halau* business. Kawika was next in line for *kumu*. Tiko thinks Raymond deserved to be elevated, but he was always in the background."

"But did he want it bad enough to get rid of the others? Was he jealous of Kawika?"

Em quickly shook her head. "Tiko just mentioned she felt bad for him. He wasn't treated fairly."

Roland tapped out a Tahitian drum rhythm with his fingers against the edge of the table. Em could see that he was deep in thought. She wondered if his toe was talking to him.

"The guy looked nervous on stage," he said.

"Very."

Just then his cell phone beeped. He answered, gave a few curt replies and ended the call.

"They found Jackie at the Lelani Motel in Lihue. He checked in with one of the dancers from Oahu earlier this evening. Seems they were having a little practice session, and it didn't involve hula."

"So he has an alibi." Em was disappointed. She so wanted the lead suspect not to be Marilyn.

"That doesn't mean he couldn't have given Kawika something before he left. Something that wouldn't kick in until he was long gone," Roland speculated. "When the officers told him what happened to Kawika, Tong was in shock. He admitted he hated Mitchell's success, but he'd never hurt him or Kawika—other than to spread gossip."

"So what is your toe telling you now?"

"My toe is silent. But I'm thinking that until we find out what's wrong with Kawika we might just be barking up the wrong coconut tree." He paused to study her for a moment then leaned closer. "Right now, seeing you in the torchlight is tempting me to think about something other than murder."

"What is it about you and fire?"

"Some like it hot."

"I'll bet you say that to all your volunteer P.I.s."

Suddenly a shout echoed from the faux cavern and waterfall area. The surf behind them and the roaring waterfall made it hard to distinguish the words. They both jumped at once to see what was happening.

"Stay behind me," Roland advised.

As they neared the cave at the pools, Em tried to see around him. "Oh, no," she groaned.

"What?" He held her back.

"That sounds like Pat Boggs."

"Who?"

"Someone Sophie brought in to help with the Maidens."

Just then strains of "Blue Hawaii" came pouring out of the cavern accompanied by a beeping horn.

"Let me guess," Roland shook his head and let go of Em's arm.

"Little Estelle."

They ran around the edge of the larger of three pools and into the cavern where the wall of water fell twenty-four-seven. Little Estelle was parked at the edge of the smallest pool facing the falls. Her Gad-About headlight illuminated the center of the cascade.

On a ledge behind the falling water, a fleshy hulk swayed back and forth. At the edge of the pool, Pat Boggs took off the heavy key chain dangling from her hip pocket and slipped off her worn black cowboy boots. She was still dressed when she dropped into the waist-deep water and waded across the kiddie pool.

"Oh, good grief." Em slapped her forehead and squinted at the falls.

"That's Flora dancing on the ledge behind the falls, and she's stark naked."

Not far from Em at the edge of the pool, Little Estelle honked out a four count beat on the scooter horn. The Maidens' boom box was balanced on the steering bar and "Blue Hawaii" was still blaring, Elvis's voice carried loud and clear over the water.

Em reached over and tried to hit the stop button and said, "Stop the music, Little Estelle. Please."

"No, she can't dance without it."

"We've got to get her down off that ledge." Em tried to turn off the boom box again.

Little Estelle whipped the Gad-About sideways to shield the box from Em's reach. Elvis crooned louder, *"The night is heavenly . . ."*

"Flora! Get your sorry ass down off that ledge!" Pat yelled. "Don't *make* me come up there and drag you down or you'll live to regret it. You hear me?"

Roland stepped to the edge of the pool and called out to Pat. "Stop right there. I'll get hotel security to handle this."

"She's butt nekked," Pat yelled back. "It's *my* job to take care of these old women."

"Not on hotel property. Let it go," Roland's voice echoed in the cavern. A second later, he was on his phone.

Em found Flora's *muumuu* draped over a lounge chair near the pool. She tossed it to Roland. When Little Estelle dropped her guard and glanced over at him, Em quickly slapped the stop button on the boom box and then successfully wrestled it away from Little Estelle.

When Em looked up again, three locals wearing black hotel security T-shirts were running toward them. In their mid to late twenties all three were burly enough to throw some hefty weight around.

"Oh man," one of them groaned when he saw what was happening. "Brah, you got to be kidding me."

"I got this one." The youngest cupped his hands around his mouth and yelled, "Auntie Flora! Wat you 'tink? You going get hurt. Get down."

Flora's arms waved in circles over her head, and her heavy breasts started to bang together like pendulums. The cellulite on her hips and thighs wobbled like Jello in plastic sacks.

Pat was still in the water off to one side of the falls. She shouted, "Come out of there Flora 'fore you slip and kill yourself. You'll screw up the line up tomorrow night if you can't dance."

Little Estelle started to chant, "Jump! Jump! Jump!"

The security guard who knew Flora handed his short wave radio and black baseball cap to one of the others. He stripped off his security T-shirt and got into the water in his black jeans.

"Wait." Roland tossed him the *muumuu*.

The security guard waded to the falls and in one quick move pulled himself onto the slippery ledge and joined Flora behind the curtain of water.

"Can you hear what he's saying?" Em asked Roland.

"I hate to guess."

"You're not going to the rescue?"

"Things like this are better left in the hands of experts. Hotel security deals with nutcases on a regular basis," he said.

"And you don't?"

"If I went in right now I'd leave a coconut oil slick on the water."

"Speaking of nuts," Em pulled out her cell and speed dialed Kiki. "I need you by the pool," was all she had to say before she ended the call. One thing about the Maidens—they always showed up in an emergency.

The security guard was still negotiating with Flora behind the falls when Kiki, Trish and Suzi came running across the pool deck into the cavern. They were followed by Lillian and MyBob.

"What's happening?" Kiki squinted across the faux cave lit by wavering tiki torches. "Is that Flora? Is she . . ."

"Naked," Trish finished.

"Stark naked," Em nodded.

"Gross," Suzi said.

"Look, Mom!"

"Oh, no." Em saw a tourist with twin boys about seven or eight years old. The mother was trying to cover their eyes but didn't have enough hands. One of them started stripping.

"Timmy! Put your clothes back on."

Lillian's Bob was running around on the deck. "Is there a ladder around here? Maybe Flora needs a ladder."

One of the beefy security guards shrugged. "She got up there. She can get her fat ass down."

By now both of the twins were naked, and one was already in the pool.

"Mom!" the twin still scrambling to get in the water yelled. "The man said ass! He said *ass!*"

Em was tempted to disappear into the darkness on the beach. The woman with the twins was yelling at them to get out of the water. MyBob was headed off to find someone from maintenance while Lillian clutched Suzi and started to pray. Trish and Kiki encouraged Pat to duck under the falls and help the security guard. Big Estelle was bearing down on them along a path from the lobby.

"Uh oh. Time to split." Little Estelle put the Gad-About in gear and shot out the other end of the cave.

Roland walked over to Em.

"They're still holding Jackie for questioning, and they can't stall him much longer without charging him. I've got to go."

"Please. Take me with you."

He shook his head no but smiled a slow smile.

"What? And have you miss all this fun?"

30

A Port in the Storm

At twelve forty-five that night Sophie Chin was going through the ritual of cleaning up behind the bar at the Goddess. She'd been on her feet for hours, toting buckets of ice from the ice machine to the bin beneath the bar, tapping kegs, stocking bottles of beer and wine in the small refrigerator, and was physically drained. At the end of the shift her feet were killing her, and all of the perkiness she had mustered for the long day was gone.

Bartending in a popular watering hole was hard work, but she was happy to have the gig. One day had bled into another and incredibly, she'd been here for nearly a year, longer than she'd ever worked anywhere else.

About an hour ago, rain had started drizzling, and the bar slowly emptied, so when she heard slippers slapping across the front lanai, she turned, about to say they were closing when Em walked through the door.

"I thought you were staying at the hotel," Sophie said.

They'd booked a room together for the festival and dubbed it Command and Control Central and planned to use it for R and R to escape the Maidens. Em had volunteered to spend tonight, and Sophie would stay tomorrow after the awards were announced.

"Should I drive in now?" It was the last thing she wanted to do at one in the morning in bad weather.

Em shook her head. "It's too late. You can head back in the morning. I'll stay and prep the bar for lunch and the evening crowd before I go in. I just had to get out of there." She looked around the bar. "I never thought I'd say this, but I'm sure glad to see this place."

"That bad, huh? What happened?"

"What didn't? After you left Kawika collapsed."

"Are you kidding? Really?"

Em nodded. "He's in critical condition at Wilcox. There was a lot of chanting and praying, and the show had to go on so a dancer named Raymond Leahe stepped in for Kawika. Kiki ran into Marilyn and started accusing her of making Kawika sick. While the others were watching the festival, Flora got naked and climbed behind the waterfall to perform. Little

Estelle commandeered the boom box. It took an hour to get Flora down."

"Naked? Flora?"

"Naked Flora." That's what everyone at the hotel's calling her now. "Actually they're calling her Naked Auntie Flora."

"Of course. I thought Pat was watching them."

"Have you ever tried to keep an eye on all of them at once?"

Sophie shook her head and wondered why on earth she'd agreed to help them in the first place.

"That's impossible." She leaned back against the back of the bar lined with booze bottles. "I dread tomorrow night."

"This whole thing is my fault." Em sat down on a bar stool. Elbows on the bar, she rested her head in her hands. "I'm so sorry."

"I could have opted out," Sophie said. "If I hadn't felt so sorry for them I'd have never agreed."

Em looked around. "Where's Uncle Louie?"

"He cleared the register and took the money over to the house to put it in the safe. Do you want something to drink?"

"No, thanks. Listen, I need to tell you something while he's gone."

"There's more? I'm not sure I can take it."

"The reason I pushed Kiki to enter in the first place was because Roland wanted me to infiltrate the competition. He has a feeling someone in Mitchell's *halau* got rid of Shari Kaui and then Mitchell. I didn't want to believe him, but now Kawika has collapsed. After snooping around a little, I'm beginning to think Roland might be right."

"So that's it. You're working with your detective." Sophie crossed her arms and watched Em blush under scrutiny. "Your sudden interest in the hula competition finally makes sense."

She grabbed a bar towel and started wiping down the bar. "You're going to owe me big time for this, Em."

"How about a week's vacation?"

"Paid?"

"Maybe, depending on how the rest of this weekend goes. You've earned it."

"Sounds like you have too."

"All I've done is keep my eyes and ears open."

"Any real suspects? Or can you tell me?"

"If you can keep it to yourself."

Sophie nodded, glad to have earned Em's trust. "Of course."

"Jackie Loo Tong. Their rivalry is well known. And Marilyn was there creeping around."

"For reals? Marilyn is a suspect?"

"Roland doubts it. Kiki's certain."

"Does Kiki know you're working undercover?"

"No one does but you. Besides, I'm really just helping."

"Maybe you're just an undercover lover."

"Knock it off."

"You're blushing. So who else is a suspect?"

"Maybe Raymond, the guy who just stepped in for Kawika. He was way down the pecking order in Mitchell's *halau* until now."

"Maybe they were all sick, and it's all a coincidence or just bad luck." Sophie thought for a minute. "Or maybe someone cursed Mitchell's *halau*."

"You don't believe that, do you?" Em frowned.

Sophie shrugged. "Hawaiian curses go way back to ancient times." She saw Em start to smile. "My *tutu* used to know all about that stuff."

"Roland says his grandmother was psychic. I hate to say it," Em said, "but if there's such a thing as a cursed *halau*, it's the Maidens."

Just then Louie walked in the back door. Em gave Sophie a look and they fell silent.

"Hi, Uncle Louie." Em lifted her cheek for a kiss when her uncle hugged her. "How is it going?"

"I didn't expect you home tonight."

"Marilyn's not here, is she?"

He shook his head. "No. She's at the festival."

"I saw her earlier," Em said.

"How did she look? Who was she with? Has she found someone new?"

Em shook her head. "She was all by herself. She looked fine."

Louie sighed. "That's good. Hey," he perked up. "Want a Two to Mango?"

Sophie could tell Em wanted to refuse but agreed for Louie's sake. "Sure, I'll have one."

"I'll have one too." Sophie reached way under the bar for two real champagne glasses and set them on the bar.

"Make that three," Louie said. "I'll join you."

He filled the flutes with his new concoction. Sophie sipped at hers while she cleaned up. Em finished and asked for a refill.

"This is good, Uncle." Em raised her glass and watched the champagne bubbles. "No wonder it was a hit at the sculpture showing. Fruity but refreshing."

"I'm having trouble writing the legend, since the engagement is on hold," he admitted.

"Maybe you should wait a while." Sophie didn't want Louie engaged to a murder suspect any more than Em did. She'd been jailed on murder charges herself not long ago, but thanks to Em and the Maidens it wasn't long before the real killer was behind bars.

Louie finished his drink. "I'd better head back. I was watching television with David Letterman and left it running. Man, that parrot gets testy when there's no one around to change the channels."

Louie left, and Sophie cleared up their glasses.

"I'm ready to lock up if you're ready to go over to the house. If you want to talk I can stay," she offered Em.

"No thanks," Em said. "You'll need to be rested for tomorrow night."

"I'm going over to the hotel early in the afternoon. Wally will be there to help me gather up the Maidens and get them ready for their performance."

"Louie's going to have to manage alone again for a few hours. Either that or we'll have to close on a Saturday night."

"He can do it. He's used to all the time. He's not as bad off as you think, Em. I called the guy next door to walk over and check on Louie and call us if there's a problem. I hope you don't mind. I gave Nat your cell number. Mine too."

"Good thinking. Louie seems so sad that I feel bad about the Marilyn thing. I sure hope she's not involved in this mess."

"Me too. Scary to think there's a psycho on the loose."

"Scary no matter who's behind it. Hopefully there's another explanation."

"I hope so too." Sophie came around the bar. "See you tomorrow afternoon," she said.

"I'll find you in the dressing room area and wish the Maidens luck before they go on."

Sophie paused in the open front door. "The Maidens will need all the luck they can get."

31

Last Minute Pandemonium

Kiki shoved aside the black curtain to the Maidens' dressing area and stepped out into the small corridor framed with a network of metal poles and curtains provided by the festival committee. She closed her eyes, took a deep breath, and tried to calm her herself before she went back inside the dressing room.

With time ticking down to their performance, anxiety was running high. The Maidens were at each other's throats and driving Wally Williams to the breaking point. Kiki had to deal with her own nerves or her heart would explode—not altogether a bad thing if it got her out of the competition.

She closed her eyes and muttered, "Keep it together, Kiki."

After a few more deep breaths she went back into the dressing room.

The small space was filled with Maidens in every stage of undress along with coolers full of their floral hair adornments. Garment bags hung suspended from the curtain poles. Rubber slippers and sandals cluttered the floor along with purses and tote bags full of water bottles, snack bars, hair brushes, mirrors and undergarments. There were only four folding chairs in the crowded space.

Big Estelle, in nothing but a long white slip, was fanning herself with a program and had commandeered one of the chairs. Suzi and Trish helping each other zip up their *muumuus*. Lillian struggled to pull her gown up over her hips. Flora was draped over two huge coolers, her head on her arm, sound asleep. She was still wearing the crumpled *muumuu* she'd taken off the night before when she had channeled Esther Williams. Pat Boggs was sitting on the floor shuffling a deck of card between her legs. She started laying out a game of solitaire.

Kiki watched a bead of sweat slowly inch its way down Wally's temple. His elaborate Trump copycat hairstyle was pancaked flat. He had barely arrived but was already wilting from the heat in the close quarters. Wally stood helpless beside an empty chair and clapped his hands.

"Ladies, listen up please. Who wants to be first?" He held up a small basket of makeup and hair products. No one paid any attention.

Pat scooped up the cards, straightened the deck and shoved it into her shirt pocket. When she stood up, Kiki braced herself.

Pat clapped her hands and yelled. "Laydeeez! Did you *hear* the man? He's ready for y'all to get your hair and makeup on. Now who's goin' first?"

"I will." Gown on, Trish was ready.

Kiki studied the costume. The fluttering felt taro leaves she and Wally had hand sewn all over the gowns were all right, but the shimmering turquoise background didn't sit well with her. It was too bright. She decided a contrasting dark green or better yet, the color of rich reddish brown Kauai mud would have been better.

"I can't get this dress on," Lillian whined. "It won't go over my hips."

"Anyone bring a shoe horn?" Pat Boggs slapped her knee and yucked it up.

As Kiki hurried over to Lillian, Big Estelle said, "I can't get mine on either."

Wally set the basket of products down and went to her aid. Kiki tugged and pulled at Lillian's gown.

Kiki mumbled, "Did you gain weight?"

Lillian sniffed.

Wally looked up from where he knelt on the floor under Big Estelle. She'd started from the opposite direction, trying to pull her dress over her head. It was stuck around her waist but wouldn't go any farther. Wally reached up and gingerly pinched the hem with his thumbs and forefingers.

"You're going to have to commit, Wally. Grab it," Kiki advised.

Wally blanched. He held his breath, reached up and grabbed the material with both hands. "I think all these leaves have taken up the give of the fabric." He turned a wide, frantic gaze to Kiki. "What are we going to do?"

"We're going to shove them in these gowns one way or another. Mine fits. No problem."

"Well, that's because *you're* just *perfect* Kiki," Lillian sniped with a rare show of gumption.

Kiki thought about smacking Lillian who had obviously lost her mind and put an end to the hysteria. Pat Boggs suddenly stepped between them.

"Let me give you a hand there, Kiki. We'll get 'er in." Pat grabbed the open front of the dress and Kiki took the back. They wrestled and wiggled and finally heaved it up around Lillian's shoulders. It was like stuffing meat into a sausage casing.

"Suck it in," Pat commanded. Lillian sucked and Pat rammed the zipper home. "There ya go. Not so bad, was it? Go get in line Lil. Wally will fix your hair and makeup."

Lillian's face was hibiscus red. "I can barely breathe," she gasped.

"You don't need to breathe. You just need to dance," Kiki went on to help Wally with Flora.

Once Flora was awake and zipped in, they put her on a chair at the front of the line waiting for makeup. Wally picked up his little basket overflowing with pins and hairspray, cotton balls and mascara, took one look at the Maidens waiting for him, and panicked.

"What time is it? I'll never get them all done. There's too much to do." He started to hyperventilate. "I'm only one person."

"I don't wear makeup so don't worry about me. Just pin up my hair," Trish said.

"You have to wear makeup," Kiki yelled. "You have to." She glanced down at Lillian perched on the chair. "Take those glasses off."

"I have to wear my glasses. I won't be able to see the edge of the stage." Lillian looked around for support.

"You're in the back row. You don't have to see the edge. You just have to hula." Kiki planted her hands on her hips and refused to be swayed. "It's bad enough you have pink hair, Lillian. We'll probably get marked down for it."

"The *lei* on her head will cover most of it." Suzi patted Lillian on the shoulder.

Lillian moaned. "I don't want to do this. Where is MyBob? I need him."

"This is the dressing room. Men aren't allowed back here."

"Wally's here."

"Wally doesn't count. He could care less if we were all twenty years old again and stark naked. Now close your mouth and let him put your makeup on."

When Lillian finally closed her mouth, Wally tried to apply darker lipstick, but her lower lip was quivering like a windowpane in a hurricane.

Kiki realized none of the dancers in the dressing rooms around them were making such a scene. She heard dancers moving around, zippers zipping and occasional hushed whispers, but none of the other *halau* members ever carried on like the Maidens.

"We're such a bunch of *haoles*," Kiki grumbled under her breath.

"Where's Sophie?" Trish snapped a photo of Wally and Lillian.

"She went to make sure Danny and the band is ready. She said she'd be right here."

"Where's Little Estelle?" Pat looked to Big Estelle. "Who's watching your mother?"

"She's parked next to the front row in the ballroom. One of the ministers from Hanalei volunteered to keep an eye on her."

"You kidding me? She'll run all over him."

"It's the best I could do without hiring a security guard."

Kiki took Lillian's hair adornment out of one of the coolers. "Here you go Wally, pin this on Lillian's head."

She handed it over. She, Trish, and Suzi had been up until three a.m., finishing all the *haku*, the thick braided *lei* worn just above the dancers' foreheads. Big Estelle couldn't help them because she'd had to keep an eye on both her mother and Flora after the waterfall incident. Pat was exhausted and spent an hour in the laundry area last night waiting for her black jeans to dry before she went to bed. Lillian and MyBob tried to help, but Kiki ended up ripping out their efforts and ruining the leaves. The whole evening had been a nightmare.

"I'm out of hairpins!" Wally shook the basket. "How can I be out of hairpins already?"

There was a moment of panic until Pat Boggs handed him three full hairpin cards.

Kiki passed out all the other *leis*. Wally pinned, ratted, combed, and fussed. Trish finally gave up and let them put makeup on her. In no time the air in the small space was thick with hairspray.

"Don't anyone light a match in here or we'll go up in flames," Kiki warned.

Flora's *lei* slipped down to her nose and knocked off one of her false lashes. Wally threw up his hands and started to cry. Trish and Suzi helped him to an empty chair.

That was when the curtains parted and Em Johnson peeked in. "Howzit going?"

Kiki grabbed her arm and pulled her into the dressing room.

"Thank God you're here. Can you do hair?"

"Would I wear a ponytail all the time if I could do hair?" Em checked out all of the Maidens and smiled. "You guys look great."

"This is no time for your effervescent perkiness. It sets my nerves on edge." Kiki couldn't help herself. This whole idea was a fiasco, and it was all Em's fault. "They do not look great," she said. "Not yet anyway. We still need to finish hair and makeup and pin on the head *lei*. I need Sophie. Where is she?"

"Last minute band check, remember?" Pat reminded her.

"My face feels like it's on fire." Kiki started fanning herself with both hands. "I need a drink."

"No drinking before the performance," Pat reminded her.

"Who made that stupid rule?" Kiki glared at Boggs.

"You did, Kiki," Trish reminded her.

Em was already headed for the exit. "I'll find Sophie and send her back. Maybe she can help Wally with hair. I'll get you a kava smoothie, Kiki. That'll help calm your nerves."

"If Sophie knew anything about hair, her head wouldn't be covered with tinted spikes. And I'm *not* touching a kava smoothie," Kiki yelled as Em disappeared behind the curtain.

32

Killer Beans

Em made it into the ballroom just in time to watch the opening ceremony. She found Sophie standing near the exit door nearest the craft fair.

"Hi," Em whispered. "Kiki needs you."

"We can't leave now. I'll run right over as soon as they open the doors again. How's it going?"

Em thought a minute. "About as well as you might expect."

"That bad?"

"Let's just say they need you. I'm going to get Kiki a kava smoothie. She needs to calm down."

"If she won't drink it, I will."

"Is Danny here?" Em didn't see the trio anywhere in the room.

"The boys in the band are ready and waiting in the hallway back stage."

Em spotted Little Estelle parked at the end of the front row right where she was supposed to be. A nice looking older gentleman with steel gray hair and glasses was chatting with her. Em hoped the minister could hold his own.

The lights in the ballroom went down, and the crowd hushed as Raymond Leahe took the stage. He seemed a bit more composed than last night, but not much. He blinked into the spotlight before he found his notes on the podium.

"Welcome to the second night of the Annual Kaua'i Kuku'i Nut Festival Competition. We've got some great performances in store for all of you." His voice sounded as if it was computer generated and slowed down to a crawl as he went on.

"Tonight you will be treated to two remaining solo dancers and then the Kupuna division will begin. What a treat. You all know how those aunties and tutus can shake it, right?" The line might have been followed by a few laughs if he wasn't speaking in a monotone.

"Someone needs to put that poor guy out of his misery. They need a new emcee," Sophie said.

Em leaned close and whispered, "After what happened to Kawika and

Mitchell, who would rush in and take over?"

"Duh."

Raymond paused for a moment then looked up again.

"Before we start the performances, I'd like to ask *Kumu* Blake Honuhonu from Oahu to lead us in a prayer for Kawika. We've just received word from the hospital that he's still in critical condition and in a coma, but he is hanging in there."

The *kumu* from Oahu was seated near the front of the room. He took his time unfurling his six foot four inches as he stood. He smoothed his long curly black hair back with both hands then shook it out again before slowly making his way to the stage. He strolled along like royalty, acknowledging people in the audience with slight nods of his head. To most of those who knew him by reputation, he was considered one of the crown princes of hula. He took the mic from Raymond and made a grand, sweeping, bow.

"He should be the emcee," Em noted.

Sophie whispered, "I'm sure he'd like that, but this is a Kauai event. There's protocol, you know."

Em had already learned there was protocol for just about everything that went on in the islands. Certain toes were not to be stepped on. Ever.

The prayer lasted a good four minutes. Finally Raymond had the mic in hand again and announced that the doors should be open once more before the first dancer took the stage. Em and Sophie slipped out and parted ways.

When Em reached Tiko's booth, Tiko wasn't there, but her cousin Charlotte was calmly and efficiently handling the line. Em waited her turn, marveling at the people in line waiting patiently for smoothies. She silently congratulated Louie for trying Tiko's Tastee Tropicals at the Goddess. From what she'd seen this weekend they were sure to be a hit—but she'd have to police the rum.

Then she remembered the whole idea had been Marilyn's.

She reached the front of the line and waited as Charlotte wrote flavors and initials on the smoothie cups with a marking pen. A male teen dancer in costume was standing beside the booth. She handed them over to him with a smile.

"There you go," Charlotte said. "One Bananafanarama and one Monster Mocha."

"*Mahalo.*" The handsome young man winked at Charlotte and wandered off.

"Aloha, Em. What'll it be?" Charlotte smiled. Tonight she was wearing her long hair tied back and a Tiko's apron over a pair of shorts and a tank top.

Em's gaze wandered to the marking pen in Charlotte's hand. Something nagged her memory.

"Em?"

"Oh, sorry. I'd like a Kava Kooler."

"Which fruit juice?"

"What goes best with kava?"

"You can't go wrong with liliko'i."

"Perfect."

Charlotte wrote L for liliko'i on the cup and then "Em" and started to dump ingredients into the blender. She reached below the table for a small container and carefully measured out the kava with a teaspoon.

Em felt a presence at her shoulder and looked up to find Roland standing there in yet another aloha shirt and black slacks.

"Kava? Really?" he said.

"It's for Kiki. I hope it relaxes her. I've never tried it."

"Makes your lips kind of numb."

Em liked the way he was staring at her mouth. He was welcome to make her lips numb anytime—if and when she could work up the courage to give him the go ahead.

Charlotte had been listening. "It's not as bad in the smoothie as drinking it straight. You should try one, Detective Sharpe."

He turned his megawatt smile on Charlotte, and Em missed its glow.

Charlotte was smiling back with her even, pearly whites. Em wondered if every woman on the island knew his name.

When Charlotte handed Em the smoothie, Roland walked with her toward the exit.

"I heard Kawika is still critical." She asked, "What about Jackie Loo Tong?"

"We cut Tong loose. He has an alibi, and we can't hold him on threats overheard in a hallway." He lowered his voice and looked around. "Kawika's doctor called to alert us there are traces of ricin in his system. They have no idea how much he ingested or how, but a dose the size of a grain of salt is capable of killing a hundred sixty pound man. The victim starts vomiting, has diarrhea, shock and convulsions. Pretty soon the internal organs shut down."

"Somebody poisoned him? That's horrible." Though Roland suspected something was going on, Em still couldn't believe it.

"They're certain he ingested it. What we need to find out is where and how he got it."

"Where would anybody get something like that except in a lab?"

"Easy. It comes from castor beans."

"As in castor oil?"

"Yes, from castor bean plants. They're weeds that grow all over the islands."

Em pictured Kiki stringing the snail shells. *"You can use anything for leis,"* Kiki had said. *"Seeds, nuts, berries, flowers, leaves. Whatever."*

"Is there an antidote?"

"Nope."

"What are you going to do?"

"Figure out who Kawika was with and what he ate for the past few days. He's been here involved in the festival for days. It can be fairly fast-acting, so I think it's safe to say our suspect or suspects are right here at the competition."

"So you're right back where you started."

"But now I know my intuition was right."

"Thanks to your *tutu* you may be psychic."

He glanced at his watch. "I'll catch up to you later. Right now I want to check in with Kawika's doctor again before the program starts."

"Are you going on tonight?" She could almost smell the coconut oil.

"I'm closing the evening after the final entries are all *pau*. It'll give me the opportunity to hang out behind the scenes without tipping anyone off that we're on to them."

"*We* meaning more than just you and I, I hope."

He nodded. "We've got undercover patrols here as well as the two uniformed officers."

Condensation was running down the sides of the smoothie cup in her hand. "I've got to get this to Kiki."

He lifted his hand. For a second she thought he was going to touch her cheek. But his hand kept moving. He smoothed a lock of his hair off his forehead.

"Be careful, Em." He wasn't smiling. "We're not going on hunches anymore. This is serious business now."

"Don't eat any beans," she said as he walked away.

33

Sophie's Pep Talk

Sophie walked into the Maidens' dressing area and into complete chaos. Trish, always the professional photographer, was trying to line the Maidens up for a pre-performance shot but no one would stand still. Pat Boggs had lost control and was pacing back and forth a three foot space mumbling to herself and checking her watch.

"Thirty minutes and fifteen seconds, Laydeez," Pat barked.

Suzi refused to wear her hair up, and Kiki had her backed into a corner.

"*Kupuna* should always have their hair up for dancing. I don't care what you do with it at home," Kiki told her.

Suzi stuck out her chin. "Who says?"

"It's an unwritten rule," Kiki shot back.

"I'll put my hair up when they write it down."

Wally was suffering from the shakes.

Sophie worked her way to his side through the mess on the floor. "Are you all right?"

"No. No I am not. I am on the verge of a nervous breakdown. Not that any of these she devils gives a damn." He was trying to pin Flora's hair in a French twist, but it was thick and heavy and kept sliding out.

"Here, let me do that," Sophie offered. He handed her pins and a brush, staggered over to a cooler and sank down on it.

Lillian went to his aid. "Have some bottled water, you poor thing. I'd hold your hand, but I can't sit in this dress."

Sophie somehow managed to get Flora's hair to stay put. She seated the *lei* on Flora's head and stood back.

"Looking good, Flora."

"*Mahalo*." Flora smiled up at her. "You missed my solo last night."

"I heard about it from Em."

"I was great."

"You were naked," Kiki reminded her.

"How'd I look?" Flora struck a pose with her hand on her hip.

"Fat, and you almost drowned a security guard."

Pat Boggs yelled, "Listen up, Laydeez! It's time. Line up. We're goin' backstage."

Sophie's stomach dropped to her toes. She glanced over at Kiki. "Is it really time?"

"This is it, I'm afraid." Kiki started lining them up in the order they were to go on stage. Even though it would only take a few minutes to walk around to the backstage area, she and Sophie had decided the sooner they were in place the better.

Finally, blissfully, the Maidens fell silent. They were scared speechless, staring straight ahead as Kiki and Sophie tweaked their *haku leis* and snail shell necklaces.

"Do not touch your *haku*. If it falls in your eyes, or heaven forbid, breaks and falls off, just keep dancing. If anyone near you flubs up, keep dancing. If anyone falls off the stage or passes out, what do you do?"

"Keep dancing!" Pat was the only one who answered but she had enough gusto for all of them.

"Remember, *aka'aka*. Keep smiling."

"Do we have time to run through the dance one more time?" Lillian looked at Sophie. "Just once?"

Pat held up her hand. "Let me get this," she said.

"Be gentle," Sophie whispered.

Pat marched up to Lillian then eyed each dancer. "If you don't know the friggin' dance by now, you're all dumber than a herd of simpleminded Billy goats."

Sophie sidestepped Pat. She couldn't let the girls go out on such a low note.

"Ladies, you do know your dance. You've been working on it nonstop for almost three weeks. You all look lovely." She glanced over at the cooler in the corner. "Thanks to Wally."

Her compliment fell on deaf ears. His eyes had rolled up in his head, and his legs were spread-eagled.

"You are going to redeem yourselves from last time," Sophie said, "but most of all what you are going to do is go out there and have fun. Once the music starts, let yourself get carried away. Don't think about the judges or the audience or your nerves. Just listen to the music and let yourself go."

"Yeah. Do what she says. Now follow me." Pat's key chain rattled as she led them out of the dressing area.

Kiki would be the last one on stage. She brought up the rear and stopped beside Sophie.

"No matter what happens out there, thanks for all your help. I couldn't have done this without you."

"No worries." Sophie put her hand on Kiki's shoulder. "Now, break a leg."

Kiki sighed. "Hey, at my age that's exactly what I'm afraid of."

34

The Hunch

Smoothie in hand, Em hurried through the craft fair toward the dressing area thinking about watching Charlotte use the marking pen to write on the smoothie cup and then suddenly remembered Tiko making "special" smoothies for both Jackie and Kawika. She had Charlotte deliver them—and shortly afterward, Kawika had collapsed.

I wrote Kawika's name and drew stars on his. He hates chocolate, so I put coffee bean chips in his. Please don't get them mixed up.

Em stopped in her tracks. *Coffee bean or castor beans?*

She passed a trash can and tossed in the kava smoothie.

Would ground castor beans look like coffee beans?

She wished she knew more about ricin poisoning but it was crazy to think Tiko capable of something so sinister. Tiko had danced with Mitchell's *halau* members and knew them all personally. It was easier to imagine Marilyn chopping castor beans to poison Kawika than Tiko. Marilyn would be doing it for Jackie. But Tiko had been a loyal member of Mitchell's troupe. Besides, Tiko was into promoting health. Her grandmother was a healer.

"Em!"

She turned at the sound of her name and saw the Maidens filing out of the spa doors in a single file line led by Pat and Sophie. She waved and hurried over to join them. None of the Maidens, not even Kiki, acknowledged her. Their gazes were focused straight ahead.

The felt taro leaves on their fitted turquoise gowns fluttered. Each of them wore two strands of apple snail shell and kukui nut *leis*. They clanked against each other with every step.

They passed the hotel security guard, who let them into the backstage area. Their bare feet didn't make a sound as they walked along the cold linoleum floor in the narrow hallway. Bare florescent light bulbs shone down on them as they moved without talking down the corridor. The clank, clank, clank sounded like rattling chains.

Em leaned close to Sophie. "Why do I feel like we're reenacting a scene from *Dead Man Walking?*"

"They could be walking to their doom," Sophie whispered back. "The Japanese are performing right before us, and we have to wait in the wings. They're always so precise. I wish we didn't have to watch."

The Maidens trailed Em and Sophie up a short flight of stairs and waited in the wings stage left. Huge black draperies hid them from the audience, but from their vantage point they had a full view of the Japanese *halau* on stage. When the Japanese finished they were to exit on the opposite side, and the Maidens were to file on behind them. The group after the Maidens would line up and wait to go on.

The seniors from Tokyo were performing a traditional ancient *kahiko* hula, chanting and moving in unison to the beat of an *ipu heke*, a gourd drum fashioned in the shape of an hour glass. Each woman wore a skirt hand crafted of *ti* leaves. Each long green leaf had been picked, washed, deboned and then tied to a *ti* band. Sophie told Em that each dancer had to have picked one hundred leaves.

They had more than likely been up all night long, but not one of them showed any sign of fatigue. They were all in step, moving side to side, up and down, forward and back, as one.

"Oh boy," Sophie sighed.

"They're great." Em hated to admit it. She glanced over at Kiki, whose expression was one of resignation.

Another *halau* wearing tasteful indigo velvet *muumuus* moved into place behind the Maidens blocking the exit. There was no turning back. Participants were lined up like four o'clock traffic through Kapa'a. Em was sizing up the stage and saw Tiko slip behind the curtains into the wings directly across the stage to join Raymond Leahe. Raymond, who was suddenly front and center in Mitchell's *halau*, was talking to Tiko, the one who just might have put him there.

Em's first instinct was to call Roland and run it by him. She hadn't seen him in the backstage area anywhere. Come to think of it, she hadn't seen any KPD officers around, just the hotel security guard they passed entering the backstage area.

"Can I get around to the other side of the stage from here?" She whispered to Sophie.

Sophie nodded. "Behind the main curtain. Cut that way." She pointed behind them. "Where are you going? Is this about, you know, that thing Roland needed help with?"

"I just want to talk to Tiko a minute." Em smiled, hoping to reassure Sophie.

"You're a terrible liar. What's going on?"

"I'll be right back."

Em slipped past Pat Boggs, who was pacing the Maiden line up, and ducked behind a series of curtains, ropes and pulleys. She went behind the main curtain and felt the pulse of ten Japanese dancers all moving in time to the beat of the *ipu heke*.

She made it to the other side, intending to step out from behind the curtain to talk to Tiko.

She paused when she heard Tiko say, "You should be proud to be the leader of the *halau*, Raymond. You're finally getting the recognition you deserve."

Raymond mumbled something Em couldn't hear. Tiko's reaction was perfectly clear; "That's ridiculous. It's not your fault the others are dead," she said.

"Kawika isn't dead." Raymond's voice registered shock.

"He's dying. You'll be made *kumu* now."

Em found the spot where the edges of two curtains met. She separated them by a fraction of an inch, just enough to peek through.

"I don't want to be *kumu*. Not ever, and especially not this way."

"The number one *halau* on Kauai needs you." Tiko grabbed his arm, tried to make him turn and look at her.

"I never wanted to be a *kumu*," he repeated.

On stage, the drums grew louder and more frantic. Em had to strain to hear.

"This is your time, Raymond. Step up and take the lead."

Raymond shook her off, started to turn away, and then he stopped and stared at Tiko.

She grabbed his hand. "Listen to me, Raymond. Maybe I am crazy. I'm crazy in love with you . . . but you've never seen it. You've never seen *me*. That's the real reason I left the *halau*. I couldn't bear to be ignored by you, to see you date other dancers. I couldn't stand it anymore than I could bear to watch Mitchell elevate the others before you."

Em reached for her cell to text Roland. As much as she hated to admit it, she'd been wrong about Tiko. She should have called him when she first put two and two together.

"Listen," Raymond was saying, "Mitchell came to me. He did want to move me up, but I refused his offer. I told him just like I'm telling you now, I *like* being part of the whole. I don't want to be the leader. It's just not in me. Can't you see how nervous I am on the mic? I love to dance, Tiko. Just dance, that's all." He grabbed her by the shoulders.

Tiko didn't respond. For a long moment she could only stare up into his eyes, and then a dark shadow crossed her face. She looked torn and confused.

"Tiko?" Em stepped out from behind the curtain. "Did you put something in that smoothie you sent backstage to Kawika yesterday?"

Raymond's eyes widened. "I saw Charlotte hand it to him and heard her tell him it was especially for him."

Tiko was looking around frantically. Em stepped toward her, afraid she would bolt.

"Did you do it, Tiko? Did you poison Kawika and the others?"

Tiko shook her head and started backing away from Em. "No. Of course not. *No!*"

Her shout was drowned out by thunderous applause. The Japanese *halau* was finished. They would be coming on to this side of the wings.

Tiko tried to shove past Em.

Em tried to grab her, but Tiko struck her hands away and knocked Em's cell to the floor. It slid across the bare wooden floor. On stage the Japanese dancers were taking their bows, and their heads bobbed up and down like hens hunting centipedes.

Em saw Sophie across the stage beside Pat and the Maidens. Em raised her arm and tried to signal Sophie at the same time bobbing and weaving to keep Tiko from getting around her and slipping out the back. Tiko tried to make a run for it. Em lunged for her, grabbed with both hands and hung on.

"Let me go!" Tiko's voice was drowned out by the thunderous applause of the crowd.

The Japanese *halau* was still taking bows.

35

If All Else Fails: Go Down Swinging

"We're sunk. Torpedoed," Pat Boggs said. "Can we get out the back way before it's too late?"

Sophie shook her head. "Not funny."

She thought she'd seen Em waving at her on the other side of the stage. She couldn't really tell what Em had been doing. The Japanese on stage hadn't budged. As per instructions they were waiting for the emcee to take the stage and thank them before they walked off.

"What's the holdup?" Pat asked.

"Why aren't they getting off the stage?" Kiki leaned around Pat. "Show hogs."

Sophie saw Em launch herself in a tug of war with Tiko and clamp her arms around her. The women wrestled back and forth for a few seconds, then Sophie saw Raymond try to break them apart.

Em was holding on for dear life. The applause had finally ended, and the *halau* from Tokyo was still standing awkwardly on stage. Finally their leader barked an order, and they began to file off just as Em and Tiko came reeling out and crashed into three of the dancers. They went down like bowling pins.

The audience gasped.

Sophie told Pat, "Em needs help."

Pat turned to the Maidens. "Emergency! Charge!"

With Sophie in the lead, they all darted across the stage.

"What are we doing?" Kiki hollered.

By now the Maidens were center stage. The audience started cheering.

"Em's in trouble!" Sophie yelled.

"Outta my way!" Kiki hiked up her gown with one hand and forearmed one of the visiting dancers who stumbled back and yelled something in Japanese. Outnumbered two to one, the Maidens were quickly engulfed.

Sophie had almost reached Em who was entangled with Tiko. Kiki and the others started battling it out. Grunts, squeals and groans accompanied hair pulling and fabric ripping. *Ti* leaf skirts and *lei* were torn apart. Leaves and blossoms went flying. *Kukui* nut and snail shell *lei* broke and the nuts went rolling. Flora wrestled two of the smaller women to the stage floor and sat on them.

"What are we doing? What are we doing?" Trish grabbed Suzi and shoved her out of harm's way as a woman charged toward them with teeth bared.

"Em's in trouble!" Kiki called out.

Trish sidestepped, stuck out her foot and tripped the dancer from Tokyo.

Sophie reached the right side of the stage where Em was rolling on the ground clinging on to Tiko. One of the Japanese started yelling and pounding Em on the back.

Em clung to Tiko like a fisherman wrestling with a record-breaking tuna.

Sophie tried to pull the Japanese dancer away from Em. She looked around for Pat, but she couldn't find her in the melee. Lillian was in the middle of the crowd. Her face and scalp were crimson, which made her hair glow even pinker. She grabbed a short woman by the shoulders and flung her away then charged toward another.

"Help me!" Sophie called to Raymond Leahe. He was hiding behind the podium.

Suddenly out of nowhere, Roland vaulted up on to the stage followed by two uniformed policeman. The hotel security guards realized the brawl wasn't part of the show and waded in.

Sophie shoved the Japanese dancer away, and Roland extracted Em. He barked out orders, and one of the policemen grabbed Tiko by the arm.

"Are you okay?" Sophie looked Em over. Other than a swelling mouse on her cheek, she appeared to be all right. "What happened?"

"I think Tiko poisoned Kawika's smoothie," Em whispered.

Roland pulled Sophie aside along with Em. "Can you handle the Maidens? I need Em to come with me." He directed an officer to escort Tiko out back to a squad car.

"Raymond should come too," Em told Roland.

Sophie ran over to Raymond. "Detective Sharpe wants you," she said.

Raymond held up the mic. "But . . . I have to . . ."

Sophie took the mic out of his hand. "Bettah you go."

Raymond followed Em and Roland.

Sophie turned around. All over the stage, women were still scratching and screaming like cats in a bag. There wasn't a Japanese dancer left with a full skirt of leaves. The stage was littered with an explosion of foliage. Bedraggled felt leaves torn from the Maidens' gowns lay scattered among the real ones.

The lone uniformed policeman aided by the security guards and visiting *kumu* stood back and let the women duke it out. Pat Boggs swung a dancer around by her hair. Big Estelle, on hands and knees, her gown in shreds, crawled off into the wings. Kiki screamed at the top of her lungs and charged at two of the dancers. They took one look at her and fled behind the curtains.

Finally a *kumu* in the audience grabbed a gourd drum and climbed on stage. He stood next to Sophie at the podium.

Ta-ta Dum.

He beat the drum with the standard call to begin, a call for the dancers' attention. Sophie turned on the microphone.

Ta-ta Dum. Louder this time. *Ta-ta Dum.*

One by one, the Japanese dancers and the Maidens stopped thrashing each other. Slowly they backed off and looked around, blinking as if awakening from a nightmare.

Ta-ta Dum.

This time, all of the dancers, including the Maidens yelled, "*A'i,*" and stood perfectly still. The *kumu* started chanting. Sophie watched Kiki limp over. While the *kumu* chanted, no one else moved, not the police officers, the dancers, nor anyone in the audience.

Kiki's nose was swelling, and one of her acrylic nails was hanging half off. Most of the fabric leaves had been ripped off her turquoise gown. Her head *lei* dangled over one eye, her *kuikui* nut and snail shell *lei* was missing. She shoved her head *lei* into place and gestured toward the audience.

Sophie followed her gaze and saw Marilyn Lockhart. She was staring at the stage in shock and awe with the rest of the audience, but she was still wearing her huge hat and sunglasses.

"She did this," Kiki mumbled. "Somehow she's responsible, and I'm going to get her if it's the last thing I do." She looked around. "Where's Em? Is she all right? What in the hell happened?"

"Roland took Em to the police station. They think Tiko poisoned Kawika."

Kiki looked around. "What are you talking about? Tiko? No way."

The *kumu*'s chant finally ended. The troupe from Tokyo fell into line and limped off the stage. Some were crying, others cradled their arms or wiped bloody noses. Sophie signaled Pat to round up the Maidens.

"Let's get out of here quick," she told Kiki. "We'll take the girls to Command and Control, and I'll fill you in."

36

All You Need Is Proof

Em found a bench outside police headquarters and sat down beneath a quarter moon and a sky spattered with stars. One of the assistants in the office had made her an ice pack. She pressed it to her cheek and tried not to worry about the catastrophe she'd started back at the competition. More than anything she wished she was headed back to the North Shore. She was craving a long hot shower, a good night's sleep and her morning ocean swim. She needed to forget about the Maidens and Tiko, and more than anything, she wished she'd never agreed to help Roland.

He found her a while later. She hadn't budged. The ice in the Ziploc had melted.

He sat down on the bench beside her. They stared at nothing for a minute.

Finally Em asked, "Did she confess?"

"She swears she didn't poison anyone. I had officers shut down the booth the minute I took her into custody. We've obtained a warrant to haul everything in and go through it. If there are any poisonous substances among her supplies, then we've got her. Without proof or a confession I can only hold her for twenty-four hours without charging her."

"So she denies it. Then why did she run when I asked if she poisoned Kawika?" Em inspected her cheek with her fingertips.

"The swelling's gone down." Roland tucked a strand of hair behind her ear. She'd lost her elastic ponytail band in the riot.

"I've single handedly ruined the Kukui Nut Festival and a friendship. She must hate me."

"If she murdered three people, do you really care what she thinks?"

Em swallowed. "If she did murder three people, and you can't find anything to charge her with, then that's just a little worrisome." Em studied his profile in the dark. "If she is innocent, then I've ruined her life and her business."

He shrugged. "This is Kauai. A crowd of supporters gathered at her booth when we shut it down, and the officers thought they were going to have another riot on their hands. Tiko has quite a following. Not only do people love those smoothies, but she grew up here. She's got friends all over the island. Look what happened to business at the Tiki Goddess when that body ended up in your luau pit." He shrugged.

He was right. Business had been booming ever since the notoriety.

"Go figure." She sighed. "If she's innocent, I hope you're right."

"She did admit she is in love with Leahe and wanted to see him move up the ranks. We questioned him, and he verified what you overheard."

"How did you come to the conclusion she poisoned Kawika?"

"I saw her make two smoothies yesterday. One for Jackie, and one for Kawika. She said Kawika's was special. She made them and wrote the names on the cups herself and had Charlotte deliver them. She wanted to be certain Kawika got the right one."

"Charlotte is her cousin," he said.

"Right. She just moved back here from the mainland."

Roland leaned forward, rested his elbows on his knees. "Leahe claims he didn't want any part of *kumu* status."

"You don't think he could have done it, do you?"

He shook his head no. "I saw him on stage. He doesn't have it in him."

"But you think Tiko does? Could she have been doing it all for him?"

Roland sat back and shrugged. "Depends on how obsessed she is with this guy."

"Enough to kill for him?"

"Yeah."

Despite the warm tropical night, Em shivered. "I convinced Kiki to enter the Maidens in competition to redeem themselves. Now their reputation will be worse than ever."

"Disaster follows them around. It's not entirely your fault."

"They wouldn't have been there if not for me."

"You can blame it on me. I'm the one who asked for your help."

"I could have said no." She noticed he was still dressed in his aloha shirt and black pants. "You missed your gig again. Did they cancel the rest of the performances?"

"I heard they cleaned up the mess on stage and carried on. The Maidens' number was scratched, though."

"Great. That makes me feel even worse."

She turned to him when he touched her arm. "They'll get over it. If you're ready, I'll drive you home."

"I'm more than ready." As much as she wanted to go home she had to face the music. "But you'd better take me back to the hotel."

37

Assessing the Damage

"Little Estelle, would you please go refill the ice bucket?"

Sophie carried a padded faux leather ice bucket across the hotel suite she and Em named Command and Control. The double king suite with its attached sitting room was littered with dresses and makeup bags, wine glasses and wine bottles. Trish and Suzi had already limped off to their room. Wally hadn't been seen since he escaped the fight, but there was a Do Not Disturb sign hanging from his room's doorknob.

Sophie stepped over Pat, who was sitting on the floor in cut-off denim shorts, legs spread wide, lining up cards for a game of solitaire. MyBob was beside his wife on the sofa lending Lillian his support.

"Why do I have to go get ice? I might miss something." Little Estelle eyed the bucket Sophie was holding out to her but didn't reach for it.

"Because it's at the far end of the hall. You can drive down there. Besides, look around." She waved her hand. Flora and Big Estelle were sprawled on the beds. Flora was opening another emergency bag of Cheetos. Big Estelle had brought along a supersize bag of Peanut M&M's.

"Do you really think you'll miss something?" Sophie asked Little Estelle.

"If I could have driven up on stage, I could have rammed the Gad-About into those crazy *wahines* from Japan. I'm going to write the Mayor and then the Governor and complain on behalf of elderly and handicapped folks everywhere. I'm going to write the Office of Hawaiian Affairs, the Bureau of Land Management and the Department of Defense." She wagged her finger in the air. "And don't think the hotel manager is going to come out smelling like a rose. I'll start with him."

"There's stationery in the desk. How about you start right after you get more ice? The girls need it."

Little Estelle mumbled a couple of four letter words then reached for the ice bucket, propped it on the steering wheel and headed out the door.

Kiki was splayed across an armchair holding a washrag pressed against a cut on her forearm. Her nose had stopped bleeding. "I sure hope I don't get staph."

"Or flesh eating disease." Pat stacked a card.

"That's not funny." Kiki lifted the rag and stared at the cut a second. "When do you think Em will get back?" she asked Sophie.

Sophie wondered how much, if anything, she should tell them. Before she could answer, Big Estelle spoke up.

"I saw Em walk out with Roland." Big Estelle was surveying the front of her gown. The right strap was ripped and the material sagged, exposing her bra.

"Roland took her to the police station. Did you hear from her, Sophie?" Kiki asked.

"I keep leaving voicemail messages, but she's not picking up."

Lillian's mascara had smeared into two huge blobs encircling her eyes. Her upper lip was swollen, her bouffant hairdo plastered to her head. MyBob was holding a hand towel full of ice against her lip. She looked like a huge frightened panda.

She said something muffled by the towel. MyBob translated. "Em got arrested?"

"No. Em got *Tiko* arrested," Kiki explained.

"Tiko?" Flora had lost the entire ruffle off the bottom of her gown. She rolled over, and the king bed undulated beneath her. "Tiko arrested? Ah, shoots. I loved those smoothies. I musta had four a day."

"Em thinks Tiko gave a poisoned smoothie to Kawika yesterday," Sophie said.

"Then good thing you aren't dead too, Flora." No stranger to a juicy brawl, Pat was in far better condition than the rest of them.

"What actually happened?" Big Estelle wanted to know.

Sophie said. "I was in the wings waiting with all of you, and I looked across the stage and saw Em grab Tiko, and they went down. I didn't wait to see what was going on. I went to help."

"That makes no sense," Big Estelle popped another handful of M&M's into her mouth.

"That *haole* is *pupule*." Flora twirled a Cheeto-stained finger next to her temple.

Pat lined up another card. "Nothing wrong with Em 'cept she probably came out of the same nut roaster y'all did. Not to mention that Tiko chick. I never met a health food junkie I liked. Som'pin wrong with people who don't eat fat or sugar, if you ask me, which you didn't so I'll just shut up."

Little Estelle scooted in tooting her horn. "What'd I miss?" She handed Sophie the ice bucket.

Everyone was still talking at once about Tiko and Em and how such a thing could have happened.

"Quiet!" Sophie clapped her hands, and the room fell silent.

She told them about Roland's suspicions about Mitchell and Shari's deaths and how he had asked Em to hang around the competition and see if she heard anything that might help him.

"That's about all I know," she finished.

"So that's why she pushed us into the competition." Kiki was working up a full head of steam. "She wanted us here because Roland needed *her* here. It wasn't about us bettering our scores or redeeming ourselves."

"Now we'll never know if we're any better." Big Estelle sighed.

Flora tugged the remains of her gown up. "My brother-in-law's kid says we won the fight. He saw the gals from Japan in the lobby crying and making big *huhu*."

"Oh, great." Sophie so wished Em would come back. She'd been alone with the Maidens too long.

Lillian shoved aside the towel and held up her hand. "Can they sue us? I didn't hit anyone, I swear." She looked around the room. "I think I need some wine."

"You mean whine?" Pat sniffed.

"You sound like Louie, Lillian. Paranoid about lawsuits," Kiki said.

"Well, can they?" MyBob asked.

Kiki shrugged. "What for? We were defending ourselves. And Em."

Flora washed down a mouthful of Cheetos. "Why would Em think Tiko poisoned Kawika?"

"I'll let her tell you when she gets here." Sophie collected Kiki's damp rag, carried it to the bar sink, rinsed it out and handed it back. Kiki sniffed and pressed it to her arm.

"We're almost out of M&M's." Big Estelle rattled the bag when it came back around to her. She looked into it and frowned.

"I'm not going after more." Little Estelle had parked next to the TV and was channel surfing.

"Mother, turn that off. I have a headache," Big Estelle said.

"I wanna see if maybe we made the news." Little Estelle kept surfing.

"Oh my stars. I hope no one in Iowa sees me," Lillian sniffed.

"They don't even broadcast our hurricanes or tsunamis on the mainland," Big Estelle grumbled. "You actually think they'd put our little hula throw down on national news?"

"We could go viral on Your Tubes," Pat said.

Just then Em came walking through the door. "Oh, no. We're on YouTube?" Sophie walked over and whispered, "I didn't know how much to tell them."

"I'll handle it," Em said.

"So what's up?" Kiki looked irked. Her arm was scraped with three long scratches but no longer bleeding. "Talk."

While Em filled them in, Sophie finally filled a glass with ice and white wine for herself. Big Estelle offered Cheetos, but Sophie waved the bag away and sat on the foot of the bed.

"Tiko swears she's innocent," Em told them.

"I can't believe she did it, but then again, didn't Marilyn introduce you two? Maybe they're in cahoots," Kiki said.

"Kahoots? Is that by Koloa?" Flora burped.

"It's on the mainland." Little Estelle laughed uproariously.

Pat slammed a card down. "C-a-h-o-o-t-s. It means they were in on it together."

"But *why*? I can see Marilyn doing it, but why Tiko?" Kiki wondered.

"That's what we don't know for sure," Em said.

"Something must have made you suspect her," Trish said.

"The investigation is ongoing, so I can't really say any more right now." Em looked exhausted as she lowered herself to the floor and leaned against the wall. Flora tossed her a bed pillow. She wedged it behind her.

"I so wish I'd never gotten myself into this," she said.

"I'm having the time of my life." Little Estelle shut off the TV. "If we're lucky we'll nab another murderer."

Lillian whimpered.

Certain this night would never end, Sophie grabbed a handful of Kleenex and carried it over to Lillian. "How about some M&M's, Lillian?"

Just then Raymond Leahe knocked on the open hotel door and stuck his head in. Away from the mic, he seemed perfectly at ease.

"*E komo mai*," Sophie welcomed him. He was carrying a handful of forms and smiled at all the ladies.

"Are those warrants?" Little Estelle eyed the papers. "I'm innocent. I wasn't fighting. I'm a helpless ninety-two-year-old. I can't walk, and I can barely see."

Raymond smiled down at her. "No worries Auntie. I just came to tell you ladies that you'll get to perform your dance tomorrow."

"What?" Kiki walked over to Raymond and glanced at the forms. "We're performing our competition number? Tomorrow?"

He nodded. "The Festival committee didn't think it was fair for you not to have a turn to perform. Only thing is, we can't use the ballroom. There's a big Rhino convention checking in tomorrow. They'll be here all week."

"What's a Rhino?" Flora licked orange off her fingers.

"You never heard of the Rhinos Club?" MyBob asked.

The Maidens shook their heads.

"It's a men's service organization like the Lions, the Elks and the

Shriners. We had a big crush in our town in Iowa."

"You had a crush on a Rhino?" Pat sat up.

"A crush *of* Rhinos. A.k.a. a herd." MyBob smiled.

Raymond handed Kiki the papers. "Whatever they are, this place is going to be choke with the Rhinos and their families tomorrow. So you folks will perform your competition number out by the pool at one. We'll set up chairs for the audience, and the judges will be front row."

"What about the Tokyo group? Will they be there?" Kiki ignored the forms.

"Their scores were recorded before the . . . well, before the incident. You were the only *kupuna* group who didn't get to perform. So we're holding up your division's awards until your scores are added. They'll be tallied right on the spot, and we'll announce the winner of your division poolside."

Kiki handed the papers back. "That's very considerate of the committee, but I'm afraid our gowns are ruined. We won't be able to perform."

Sophie put a hand on Kiki's shoulder. "Wait a minute, Kiki." She turned to Raymond. "Given the circumstances, can they wear something else?"

Kiki leaned close to Sophie. "We didn't bring anything else."

"I'm sure we can come up with something," Sophie said.

Lillian clapped her hands. "Oh! We could use the drapes like Scarlett O'Hara."

When Kiki actually checked out the drapes Sophie whispered, "Don't even think about it."

"They look too heavy anyway," Kiki whispered back.

"We'll think of something," Sophie promised. "If nothing else, I'll make a run up to the North Shore at dawn and pick up clothes for all of you at your places."

"How about the gift shop downstairs?" Suzi suggested. "You think they might have seven of something that matches?"

"I don't know," Kiki said. "I have a bad feeling about this. Besides, the gift shop is closed for the night."

Em was on her feet. The bump on her cheek had gone from red to light blue. "I'll go down and look in the window. And there might be some crafters who haven't packed everything up yet."

Sophie could see Kiki's mind turning.

"You don't have to go, Em," Sophie said. "Stay here. I'll go with Kiki. We'll check it out."

Em pulled her hair back off her face. "This is my fault. I should go."

"You look ready to drop." Sophie gazed around the room. "In fact, you all need a good night's sleep if you're going to pull it together tomorrow. Clear out, and go back to your rooms. Kiki and I will go down to the lobby and see what we can find." Sophie turned to Raymond. "Can we make a decision and let you know in the morning?"

"Find me by ten. We need to hold the judges here and get the chairs set up."

"That would be great. I'll walk you out."

Sophie left the Maidens in the process of helping each other off the beds and cleaning up the wine glasses and empty bottles.

Stiff and sore in places she hadn't known she'd been hit, Em got off the floor and walked out into the hall. She wanted to talk to Raymond before he was gone.

"Can I ride down to the lobby with you?" she asked him.

His smile faded once he was outside Command and Control.

"Sure," he nodded. They walked to the elevator in silence. He pushed the down arrow, and the car opened immediately and they stepped in.

As soon as the doors closed, Raymond said, "How is Tiko? What happened at the station?"

"She swears she's innocent."

"I feel terrible." His voice was so low she barely made out the words.

"I feel worse than terrible, but I saw her mark those cups and make a big deal out of which was for Kawika, and now we know he was poisoned."

"She sent them to all the *kumu* every night. Same thing each time—Kawika's cup had his name and big stars written on it."

"*Both* nights? Did you tell Roland?"

He nodded. "I did."

"Nothing we can do but wait to see if they find anything in her smoothie supplies."

"She's smarter than that."

"I know." Em sighed.

"This is all my fault. I had no idea she was in love with me."

The elevator stopped, and the doors opened. The bright lobby lights made Em squint. Across from the elevator, a maintenance man was on a ladder holding one end of a huge purple and white banner that read WELCOME RHINOS! Another man was giving directions from the floor.

"It's not your fault," Em put her hand on Raymond's sleeve. "The trouble is she's probably still in love with you, so be careful, okay?"

"*Mahalo,*" he said, then he added, "you too."

38

A Crush of Rhinos

Kiki met Sophie in the hall at nine the next morning to look for costumes in the gift shop. Sophie handed her a mug of steaming hot coffee, and they stepped into the open elevator.

"I hope we don't find anything," Kiki confessed.

"Oh, come on. You've all worked too hard not to dance today."

"We have no *leis*, no hair pieces. Everything was ruined last night. I think we should give up."

"The girls are counting on you," Sophie reminded her.

The elevator door opened, and they stepped out into chaos. The place was full of men, women and children in matching T-shirts printed with the logos of various Rhino crushes all over the world. The men wore hats fashioned like Rhino horns. Some had on gaudy aloha shirts, and most of them had on Bermuda shorts with dress shoes and black socks.

Three Rhinos approaching the elevator stopped and stared at Sophie's neon spikes, tattoos and pierced eyebrow.

One leaned close and said, "Hey, Honeybunch! We don't see anything like you in downtown Duncan, Illinois!"

"Oh yeah?" Kiki grabbed Sophie by the elbow and started ushering her away. "We hunt Rhinos for sport on Kauai," she called over her shoulder.

Overnight the hotel staff had set up a portable Tiki Bar in the lobby. It was situated between Kiki and Sophie and the gift shop. Rhinos three deep were swarming their new watering hole.

"Louie would love this," Kiki said.

"Let's tell the bartender and concierge to spread the word. If the Rhinos take day trips to the North Shore this week, they should stop by the Goddess."

"Good idea."

They made it a few more feet before music came blaring over a loudspeaker. "Put your right hoof forward, put your right hoof back, do the Rhino hop. Hop, hop, hop."

"Look out!" Sophie pulled Kiki out of the way just in time. They ducked into the gift shop and watched the Rhino conga line cavort past the window.

"Crazy buggahs, yeah?" The clerk, a local gal, watched with them for a few minutes. "Pretty soon they'll be running around naked. We've all got bets on how long it takes." She shook her head and walked back to the register. "How can I help you ladies?"

"We need six matching dresses," Sophie said.

"But I'm sure you don't carry various sizes of any one dress, do you?" Kiki crossed her fingers.

"Oh!" The woman studied Kiki. "You folks from the *halau* that was fighting on stage last night?"

"That's us." Kiki shrugged.

"I heard you folks won. Congratulations."

"Oh, no. They haven't performed their competition dance yet," Sophie said. "That's what we need the dresses for."

"I heard you ladies won the fight, not the competition." The woman smiled.

"*Mahalo.* I guess," Kiki sighed.

"So, I'll show you the dresses I've got. What sizes you need?"

"Two XXLs, two XLs, one medium and one small." Kiki turned to Sophie. "I'm not getting one for Little Estelle."

"No need," Sophie agreed. "Just be prepared for repercussions."

Before the clerk could show them the dresses, two Rhinos came rolling in. Sophie told the men to go first.

"We need some scissors, disposable razors and shaving cream," the taller of the two said.

"It's a pain you can't bring that stuff on the plane, eh?" Kiki watched one of them adjust the tusk on his head.

"Naw, it's not that. One of the guys from our crush just passed out, and we're gonna shave him before he wakes up." He laughed like a school boy.

"Wow. I'd like to be there when he wakes up bald." The clerk handed them some scissors and walked over to a display of disposable razors.

"Oh, we're not shaving his head." The shorter man snorted. "Rhinos' heads are sacred. That's where we wear our horns."

The tall one said, "We're shaving his—"

"Stop!" Kiki yelled.

"We get the picture," Sophie said. "And I hope it fades fast."

39

The Big Performance

Self-conscious of her role in igniting last night's debacle, Em bought a black baseball cap. Like Marilyn in the disguise, she wore it with sunglasses to watch the Maidens' competition number by the pool. Em picked up *leis* at a table in the lobby for all the Maidens and Sophie and Pat and looped them over her arm.

Rows of banquet chairs were lined up out in the open garden area by the pool. Though the mid-day sun was beating down on them, many of the seats were already filled with tourists, a few of the Rhino contingent and other *halau* from the Kupuna division anxiously awaiting the final results to be announced.

All twelve of the Japanese *kupuna* were seated together. There were twice as many of them as there were Maidens, but they were definitely the worst for wear. One had her arm in a sling, and most of them were sporting black eyes. One even had a bandage over the bridge of her nose.

Em spotted MyBob in the second row. There were still empty seats beside him, so she hunched down and scooted toward him.

"Are these saved?" she asked.

"Just one for the Sarge." He patted the seat beside him. "You can sit here."

She sat down, and MyBob pointed out Danny Cook's band near the stage. Sophie and the Maidens were lined up nearby. The women were outfitted in items that could be found in most gift and tourist shops on the island, matching *pareau* in various shades of green and two strands of brown *kukui* nut *leis*. Thick *haku lei* made of various green leaves surrounded their heads. Lillian shaded her eyes with her hand. Flora and Big Estelle were fanning themselves with *ti* leaves.

"Where's Little Estelle?" Em had a sinking feeling in her stomach. The Gad-About was nowhere to be seen.

MyBob shrugged. "I don't know. With any luck they locked her in the van."

Em couldn't count on it. Her luck hadn't been running on high lately.

Over in the nearest pool one of the Rhinos was tossing his head and making rhinoceros sounds in the water. A woman seated in the audience close to the pool yelled, "Enough already!" A hotel security guard walked over and ordered him to quiet down or get out.

Back at the platform stage set up for the performance, Raymond Leahe welcomed the crowd. Em watched the Maidens come to attention as Raymond asked everyone present to join him in a prayer for Kawika who was still in critical condition but hanging on. Once the prayer finally ended, he explained that the Hula Maidens from the North Shore had not had a chance to perform and so they would do so now. Thankfully he didn't go into why they'd missed their turn, but most of the crowd knew about the fight, just as they knew the contents of Tiko's smoothie booth had been confiscated and she'd been hauled in for questioning.

"And now," Raymond said, "the Hula Maidens from the North Shore, under the direction of Kiki Godwin and accompanied by Danny Cook and his band, will dance to '*Kalo O'Hanalei.*' The taro of Hanalei."

The audience was silent as the women filed up the steps and took their positions. Sophie and Pat stayed right next to the stage. The musicians started, and someone in the audience yelled out, "Go aunties!"

Everyone started on time except for Lillian. Beside Em, MyBob groaned. The song was simple, fun and the choreography basic. Lillian found the beat half way through, and the Maidens executed the moves perfectly to the end.

Em found herself holding her breath until the finale. She turned to the judges who were stone-faced and serious as they marked their judging forms.

The Maidens exited carefully. Pat was there to help them down the three steps to the cement walkway. They remained in line and walked back toward the lobby doors.

"Now the judges will tally the scores, and in ten minutes we'll announce the winners of the Kupuna division of the Kukui Nut Festival Hula Competition," Raymond announced. "Sit back and enjoy the sounds of Danny Cook and the Tiki Tones."

Em stayed put. The sun was hot, but it felt great to be outside in the trades. On stage, Raymond looked more at ease than the nights before, but he wasn't comfortable ad-libbing or bantering with the audience between songs. Em found herself wondering if he was really shy or if he had been harboring secret aspirations that had turned deadly?

Finally the head judge stood and waved a sheet of paper. Danny and the band stopped playing.

Raymond said, "It looks like the judges are ready." He waited while the judge with the tally sheet walked to the stage, accompanied by three women carrying koa trophy bowls.

The crowd shuffled in their seats. The Japanese dancers sat up straighter.

Afraid the Maidens would miss the announcement, Em saw them standing with Sophie and Pat at the back of the audience behind the last row of chairs.

"We'd like to say a big *mahalo* to all of the entries in the Kupuna division. Keep dancing, ladies. How about a big round of applause, folks?" Raymond waited for the crowd to clap, quiet down and then began again.

"And now, in fourth place, the *halau* from Tokyo, *Hula Halau o' Ka La.*"

Em saw Kiki break into a smile. The Maidens weren't going to be fourth out of four. The Japanese sat in stunned silence while the crowed clapped politely. Finally the *kumu* from Tokyo rose and limped up to accept a Certificate of Merit.

"In third place, from Kauai, The Hula Maidens!"

MyBob gave off a shrill whistle and jumped up. Em yelled, "Whoohoo!"

Kiki went to the stage to graciously accept the trophy bowl. She carried it in front of her like an offering to the Gods as she walked back to join the others.

The *halau* from Oahu took second, and Mitchell's *kupuna* took first place.

After Raymond invited all of the division's competing *halau* back next year, he called on one of the judges to lead the crowd in singing Hawaii Aloha. Then Em and MyBob made their way to where the Maidens were still waiting at the back of the audience.

"Congratulations!" Em hugged each Maiden and hung a *lei* around her neck.

"Good work, Kiki!" she said.

"We did it," Flora shouted. "We didn't come in last."

Em walked next to Sophie as they all strolled through the garden to the lobby. They had checked out earlier, and their bags were already packed in their cars. Finally it was time to head back home.

"Are we all here?" Sophie looked around to make sure they hadn't left anyone behind.

"Where's Little Estelle?" Em asked.

Big Estelle was looking around as if she'd forgotten all about her mother. "I thought she was at the pool with you."

"I haven't seen her," Em said.

"Me either," MyBob added.

They all searched the lobby. The Tiki Bar was deserted. Most of the

Rhinos had broken up into various conference rooms for lectures. A few Rhinos were sitting around with their families looking over maps and rack cards of Kauai activities. Others were checking out trinkets for sale at a whole new craft fair with vendors who catered more to visitors than hula dancers.

Em looked through the open doors of the hotel entrance. An EMT ambulance was parked out front.

"I've got a bad feeling," she told Sophie.

"Why?"

Em nodded toward the ambulance.

"Uh oh," Sophie whispered. "You think someone else has been poisoned?"

"As far as I know, Tiko is still in custody."

"Which would mean someone else *is* responsible. Have you seen Marilyn around?"

"No. Not since last night." They both looked around the lobby.

Just then there was a commotion at the front desk where a man's voice was raised in anger. He was a middle-aged Rhino in a yellow T-shirt, safari pants and a Rhino horn.

"Don't tell me to hang loose," he yelled. "I haven't seen my father in over two hours. He's eighty-five and blind as a bat. He could have fallen, drowned, wandered down the beach . . ."

Big Estelle ran over to Em and Sophie. Pat and Kiki joined them, and they huddled together.

"We have to find my mother," Big Estelle whispered. "Quick."

"She's probably snockered in the bar," Pat said. "I'll go look."

Trish and Suzi came strolling up.

"Wait, Pat," Trish said. "We just left the bar. She's not there."

Just then a service elevator opened and the EMTs were inside transporting a gurney with an elderly man strapped down and moaning. The Maidens watched as the EMTs cleared the elevator. Wedged in behind them was Little Estelle on the Gad-About with a Rhino horn on her head.

The man at the reception desk saw the EMTs. "That's him! That's my father." He ran over to the gurney. "Dad? Dad what happened?"

The Maidens edged toward the front door. Em heard the EMT say, "Sorry, brah. He had a heart attack. We're taking him to Wilcox Hospital, and they'll fly him over to Honolulu."

"Where was he?" The son was still frantic.

"He was having sex in an empty conference room. No idea who called it in, but when we got there he was all by himself."

They rushed out the door to the waiting ambulance.

Big Estelle pressed a hand over her heart. All of the Maidens watched

Little Estelle put the Gad-About in neutral. She folded her hands on the steering wheel and smiled.

"Mother . . ." Big Estelle stared in shock at her mother. "Please tell me you didn't."

"Oopsie." Little Estelle patted her hair into place and adjusted the strap on the horn.

"How could you? The poor man is blind," Big Estelle cried.

Little Estelle shrugged. "I know, so I told him I was thirty. If he dies, at least he'll go with a smile on his face."

Cute Clit

40

Em Heads Home

By the time all the Maidens took off for the North Shore, Em was exhausted.

She walked out to the parking lot and got into her Honda Element. She found the bright blue pre-owned car listed in the *Garden Island* and bought it with money from the Porsche she got in her divorce from her ex, which was about all she got out of her nine year marriage. The Honda wasn't the Mercedes she'd had in Newport Beach, but then again, Kauai wasn't Newport, and the Element was great for tooling around the island.

She unlocked the car, slipped behind the wheel and was almost out of the parking lot when she spotted Tiko's van a few rows over. Tiko was beside it with a porter from the hotel who was loading her folding tables. Em turned in the opposite direction and drove to the entrance of the hotel lot. Shaken, she pulled over beneath the spreading branches of a *kamani* tree.

She hadn't seen any boxes in Tiko's van. Everything but the tables had been confiscated by the police.

Em reached for the straw purse on the seat beside her and started fishing around inside for her phone. Obviously Roland hadn't had enough evidence to charge Tiko with Kawika's poisoning. If she'd been wrong, Em would never forgive herself.

Her phone wasn't in her purse, which explained why she hadn't gotten any calls from Roland. She gripped the wheel and closed her eyes and remembered it fell to the floor backstage. She made a U-turn and headed back to the hotel entrance, told the valet she'd be back in a second and ran in to ask at lost and found.

No one had turned her phone in. When she asked permission to go backstage to look for it, the reception clerk called the manager over. The woman stared at the bruise on Em's cheek and said, "Sorry. The Rhino Conference is using the ballroom."

"If I could just go backstage . . ."

"You're with those Hula Maidens, right?"

"Well, yes, but . . ."

"I'll have maintenance look for the phone. If they find it, we'll call you. What's your number?"

Em thanked her and gave the number to the Goddess then headed back to her car.

Tiko's van was no longer in the lot, but when Em turned onto the highway headed north she spotted it ahead of her in traffic. When Tiko turned up the hill toward home, Em pulled into the left turn lane. With three cars between them, Em hung back. She had no idea what possessed her to follow Tiko home other than a massive attack of guilt. They passed Opaeka'a Falls and the Wailua River lookouts. The parking lot was full of rental cars and buses, and the car in front of Em turned off. By the time they reached the Wailua Country Store, there was only one car left between her and Tiko. She pulled into the store parking lot and stalled to give Tiko time to get home. She'd be sure to notice Em right behind her.

Five minutes later, Em pulled onto the road again. She drove by Tiko's without slowing down. The house sat in the middle of the wide open acreage, and she saw Tiko's van was the only vehicle in the driveway. Still hoping Tiko wasn't guilty, Em found herself wishing Tiko hadn't had to return to an empty place.

The Goddess was usually quiet on Sunday evenings, at least it was quiet compared to the usual chaos. Em and Louie had an early dinner together after the bulk of diners left. It was a comfortable relief to talk about something other than the competition or to think about her part in Tiko's arrest. They sat near the stage where Auntie Irene's life-sized painting smiled down on them.

"I came up with another drink to celebrate the Maidens placing in the competition," Louie announced. "The Kookookie Kooler. Have you noticed how Pat slaughters Hawaiian? She says koo-kookie instead of *kukui*."

"She slaughters English, too. That's a cute idea, Uncle. What's in it?"

"Rum, macadamia nut liquor and a couple other special touches. I'm keeping real *kukui* nuts out of it, given what happened with Marilyn and the *inamona*."

Em noticed he'd been toying with his teriyaki chicken and not really eating.

"Are you feeling all right?"

His expression drooped. "I really miss Marilyn. I know she messed up with Kiki and the others, but if you could just talk to them, convince them she didn't mean it. I know Marilyn is sorry."

Em sighed, her own appetite suddenly vanished.

"This is your place, you know. If you want Marilyn here, then Kiki will have to live with it, but there's something you should know. Something that happened this weekend."

She didn't know how much to tell him, and she was sort of surprised he hadn't heard about Tiko and the smoothie incident yet.

"Tiko was taken in for questioning on suspicion of poisoning one of her old *halau* members."

"What?" His brow wrinkled.

"She may have put something in one of the smoothies."

Louie leaned back in his chair and stared at Em. "You're kidding."

"I wish."

"Did she do it? Is she in jail?"

"She's been released. I saw her leaving the hotel earlier."

She still hadn't connected with Roland, but she filled Louie in on what she knew. "Roland must not have found enough evidence to hold her. They're probably still going through her smoothie stand ingredients." Em ran her finger down the condensation on her ice tea glass and didn't tell him about her involvement. He'd hear about it soon enough.

"I think we should take the smoothies off the menu for a while. Until this all dies down," she suggested.

"You're probably right," Louie was actually smiling again. "In a way this turned out great."

"Great?" Em felt far from great about it.

"Kiki could be blaming Marilyn."

Em couldn't bear to tell him that she wasn't so sure about Marilyn's innocence either.

"Marilyn introduced us to Tiko," she reminded him.

His expression drooped. "You're against her too."

"I don't know what to think about any of this, Uncle Louie. I just want you to be happy and safe. Give it a few more days. Let Kiki and the girls enjoy their success before you invite Marilyn here again. Things will settle down."

Em almost laughed. Things hadn't settled down since she moved to Kauai. All she could hope was that before too long the KPD would make some kind of a discovery and arrest.

"Hey, there's Nat." Louie waved their neighbor over to the table.

"If you're closed I'll come back." Nat walked in anyway. "I just stopped in to say hi and find out how the Maidens did in the competition."

"They came in third." Em indicated the seat across from her. "Have a seat. Are you hungry?"

He shook his head. "Thanks anyway. I already ate. So they came in third."

"Out of four," Louie added.

"That's great," Nat laughed. "I'm sure they're happy."

"More than happy. Kiki called Kimo and said she's already working on next year's number," Em said.

Louie stood up. "Would you like a beer or something?"

"Sure, a beer would be great. Corona if you have one."

While Louie stepped behind the bar and opened a beer, Nat focused on Em. Louie came back, set the beer down on a cardboard Goddess coaster and immediately started to clear their dishes.

"I'll get those, Uncle Louie," Em said. "No hurry."

"No problem. I've got it. You've had a hard weekend. I'm going to head back and turn on television for Dave. He loves *Celebrity Apprentice*. You kids go ahead and chat."

She watched him walk away. Hard weekend? He didn't know half of what she'd been through, thanks to Roland.

"Kids?" Nat laughed.

"To him we are." She relaxed back in her chair. "We're planning a celebration party for the Maidens. Louie will be introducing a new drink. Be sure to walk over," Em told him.

"For sure. Just let me know when."

He smiled at Em. He was a handsome man, not drop dead ruggedly handsome like Roland, but good looking. Nat seemed solid, capable, steady and intelligent. More importantly, in the months he'd lived next to the Goddess, there hadn't been a steady stream of women in and out. After her divorce, the last thing she was interested in was a player.

Screen writing was as exciting a profession as being a detective, but it certainly wasn't dangerous. At least not as far as she knew.

"I've got something to run by you." He leaned his forearms on the table and started playing with a coaster.

"Shoot." She took a sip of water.

"I'm seriously thinking about pitching a reality show about the Goddess. Would you and your uncle be up for it?"

Em was no stranger to *People Magazine*. She knew what happened to the lives of people who entered the unreal world of "reality" shows.

"I can't speak for Louie, but I'm not excited about the idea. Besides, do you really think there's enough going on around here?" She indicated the shadows of the empty bar.

"You kidding me? Since I've been back you've had an artist showing body parts made of bread that were so realistic a woman fainted. The Maidens are a whole show in themselves."

"Unfortunately they'd be thrilled about the idea."

"And I don't know if you've heard yet, but Buzzy is dating a dolphin."

She kept a perfectly straight face. "And you find that odd?"

He shrugged. "I guess it's no weirder than finding a body in your luau pit."

"Oh that?" She waved as if brushing off the thought. "That was months ago."

"Really, Em. Do you realize the money you'd make if a show was centered on this place?"

"What about our local customers? They might not want to be filmed."

"Oh, right. You'd have a line out the door and down the highway the minute people heard about it. Everyone wants fifteen minutes of fame. That's why YouTube and Facebook are so popular. Everyone can become a celebrity overnight."

"I don't know."

"Just think about it, okay?"

She shrugged.

"And run it by your uncle."

Intuition warned her Louie would love the idea.

"But don't think too long," he added. "I have to pitch it when I go back in two weeks."

"You're leaving so soon?"

"Now that *CDP: Hawaii* has been cancelled, I need to get back. LA is where it all happens." He looked out the window into the dark tropical night. "I love it here, though."

"Do you love it enough to want a film crew next door twenty-four-seven?"

He thought about it for a minute. "It would sure be a great commute."

She watched him for a minute and thought about his work.

"Writing for *Crime Doesn't Pay*, did you have to do a lot of research?"

"A fair amount. A lot of the crimes were 'ripped from the headlines' as they say. We had a team of experts in forensics and crime investigation." He gazed around the bar. "The only research we'd have to do for a show set here would be on Hawaiian lore, music and tropical cocktails. And tourism, of course," he added.

"You might be surprised." She leaned forward. "Do you know anything about ricin poisoning?"

"Ricin? We did a show on ricin poisoning. Espionage stuff. Supposedly a small grain of it can kill."

"What about the castor plant? What about eating castor beans?"

"Nothing good would happen." He thought about it a minute and then glanced toward the kitchen door. "Should I be worried about the pulled pork I had for lunch?"

"Not that I know of." It took her a few minutes to fill him in on what had really happened at the competition. When she finished, he leaned back.

"Wow."

"I know. Wow." Em sighed. "I guess I just added fuel to the reality show fire."

"You bet, but this is no laughing matter. Whoever poisoned that *kumu* means business. Was ricin only found in one case?"

"Yes. The woman who died first had advanced immune deficiency, and the leader of the group had a very serious heart condition that was deteriorating."

"So." He tapped the table with his thumb. "No one suspected anything at the time of their deaths."

"No. Both had been under doctors' care. Only Detective Sharpe had a feeling something was going on. But if there been ricin poisoning in those first two incidents, wouldn't the victims—if they were victims—have shown the same symptoms as Kawika and arouse suspicion?"

"Apparently they didn't."

"Roland says castor plants grow all over Hawaii. But as far as the first two deaths, there's no way of knowing what really happened now."

Nat finished off his beer. "I'll find some information on the web and print it out for you."

"That's really nice of you, but I can look it up myself. You're here to relax."

"Look it up in your non-existent spare time, you mean? I'm on break, and I love to research. Especially when my own work *isn't* involved," he said.

"If you really want to I'd appreciate it."

"I do. No problem. I'll have some information for you in the morning."

He studied her so long she blushed.

"Would you go to dinner with me sometime?" Nat asked.

"You mean actually have dinner somewhere other than here? What a concept."

He laughed. "Do you ever get a night off?"

"Not routinely. I did just take most of the weekend off."

"Being with the Hula Maidens isn't exactly relaxing or time off."

"A night away from all this chaos sounds great."

"So how about it? Is tomorrow too soon?" he asked.

"How about Wednesday?" She needed a couple of days to check their inventory and cut Sophie and Kimo's paychecks. The Tiki Tones needed to be paid. There was a stack of inquires about catering estimates and schedules to go over.

"That sounds great. You can let me know which night is best tomorrow. In the meantime, I'll look up some information for you and bring it by." He pushed back and got up.

Em rose and walked him to the door.

"Any particular place you'd like to have dinner, Em?"

"Somewhere without a hula dancer or a paper umbrella in sight."

"How about Kintaros? No Hawaiian music, plenty of *saki*."

The Japanese restaurant was a good forty minute drive away in Waipoli, but the food was great and the service A-1.

"That sounds perfect. I'll look forward to it."

The words were barely out of her mouth when Roland came walking through the door. He glanced around the deserted room and paused just inside.

"I was just driving by and saw the door open. If you're closed . . ."

"No," she said quickly. "I'm . . . we're not."

She introduced the two men. Nat offered his hand and they shook.

"I'll see you tomorrow," Nat told Em before he headed out the door and across the parking lot.

Roland watched him leave.

"So what are you looking forward to?" He leaned against the bar.

"What do you mean?"

"I heard you say you were looking forward to something."

"Playing detective?"

"Always."

She walked back to their table, picked up the empty beer bottle and carried it over to the bar.

"He's going to do some online research on ricin and poisons for me."

"You told him what's going on?"

She moved closer to him.

"That's all right, isn't it?"

"By now it's no secret," he said.

"So I told Nat about the ricin poisoning and asked what he knows about it. He was a writer for *CDP: Hawaii* for years."

"Solving fictional crimes on television."

"Is that sarcasm I hear, Detective?"

"I'm just saying."

"They can't just make things up, you know. He's worked with forensic doctors and all kinds of experts."

He pushed off the bar. "I get paid to know when people are evading the truth."

"What do you mean?"

"I heard you say 'That sounds perfect. I'll look forward to it.' Are you really that thrilled about getting research material?"

"Thrilled? I sounded *thrilled?*"

"Okay, maybe not thrilled."

She thought for a minute he was kidding and then realized he was dead serious.

"I can't believe we're having this conversation. If anyone overheard they might think you were jealous. Seeing as how you've never actually asked me out on an official date, I find that pretty amazing."

He took a step closer. "Is that what you'd like? To go on an official date?"

She tipped her head back to look up at him. "You're psychic. You tell me. Besides, I am going out on an official date. Nat asked me out to dinner."

"I meant do you want to go out on an official date with me?"

"Well . . ."

Without warning she found herself pressed against him, his hand cupping the back of her head, and he was kissing her. He kissed her until she felt it down to her toes, and she was pretty sure her flip flops were starting to melt right before he abruptly let her go.

"I'll call you, and we'll set up something for Friday night." He acted as if he hadn't just kissed her senseless.

"What was that all about?" Em tried to focus. She was actually dizzy.

"That was something to think about while you're on that official date with your fictional crime solving neighbor."

41

How Does Your Garden Grow?

The week started with the kind of brilliant blue sky that made Kauai locals forget that it could rain buckets on the North Shore. Light trades kept the occasional cloud passing by with no more than a misty sprinkle. Em woke up Monday morning and padded through the house barefoot looking for Louie. He was gone and so was his truck, so she figured he'd taken off for the post office and to pick up groceries.

She slipped into her Speedo swimsuit, grabbed her towel, mask and snorkel and hit the beach. The coral in front of the house had conveniently formed an underwater ring that created a huge natural pool. It was Em's favorite place to do her workout. Wearing a mask allowed her to see a rainbow of tropical fish.

But today the fish went unnoticed. With every stroke she thought Roland, Roland, Roland and had to stop herself. She checked her watch, and once she'd put in the obligatory thirty minutes, she swam to the shore and got out of the water. It was only eight in the morning. There was a mound of work piled up on the desk in the office, but she didn't have to get to it until nine. Work could wait.

Em pulled off the mask and snorkel, and after shaking out her hair, spread her towel and sat in the sun, content to take a few minutes to watch the waves lap against the shoreline. The sun was warm. The trade winds rustled the palms that lined the property. Em closed her eyes, cleared her mind and thought of the images of the surf as the earth's heartbeat. The constant, even rhythm lulled her into a relaxed stupor, and she actually stopped thinking about Detective Sharpe and the way he'd kissed her last night—until she felt someone in the sand beside her.

Em opened her eyes, expecting to see Roland.

But it was Nat sitting cross legged in the sand in khaki shorts and a white T-shirt with a *Crime Doesn't Pay* logo of a microscope and a pair of handcuffs printed on the front.

She sat up. The trades and the salt water had played havoc with her loose hair. She brushed it back off her face.

"You're up early." She glanced at her watch again. Twenty minutes had flown by.

"I try to stay on mainland time while I'm here. Easier to adjust when I go back."

She glanced at the pages in his hand.

"These are for you." He handed them over, and Em glanced at them. "Already?"

Nat shrugged. "I told you I like to research. I've been up since five."

On the top page was a photograph labeled Castor Bean Plant. Nat pointed to it.

"Those grow like weeds all over the world. You'll even find them in parks and gardens. They're originally from Eastern Africa."

"And they're all over Kauai."

"Right. Drive down the road, and you'll start to recognize them."

She turned a couple of pages and stopped. "Tiko has a tree like this . . . or maybe it's a bush . . . in her garden. It was so beautiful I asked about it." She tapped the picture. "This is poisonous?"

"Yes. It's called angel's trumpet."

"So she told me." She read the description next to the photo of the lovely white trumpet or bell-shaped bloom and then went down the list of poisoning symptoms.

"What's mydriasis?"

"Pupil dilation," he said.

Em read the rest aloud. "In large amounts it causes flushed skin, tachycardia, delirium, hallucinations, urinary retention, nausea, vomiting, and diarrhea. This reads like a laundry list of symptoms you don't want to have."

"With care and knowledge, the plant is also to treat asthma," Nat said.

"Tiko told me her grandmother was into herbal cures."

"It's also known to cause euphoria and hallucinations. There was a lot of interest in it in the seventies when LSD was first popular."

"I wonder if Buzzy's tried it."

"You think he'd remember?"

She shook her head and looked at the list again. "Tachycardia. Rapid heartbeat isn't something you'd want if you had a severe heart condition like Mitchell Chambers. He'd have had to have ingested a large amount of the toxin."

"Stems, roots, and blossoms can be boiled into tea."

She flipped through the pages and studied pictures of Kauai's poisonous plants.

"Poinsettia, plumeria, oleander, be-still." Em shook her head. "These plants are everywhere, not just in Tiko's garden. We have plumeria and poinsettia right over there." She pointed to the plants around Louie's house.

"Oleander and be-still seeds are highly poisonous. Even inhaling the dust can cause damage to airways."

"*Pua kala.*" She tapped another photo of a lovely white bloom.

"Hawaiian poppy. Did you see any of those?"

Em shook her head. "I don't think so. Could be."

"It says here they're mostly in botanical gardens."

"I'm not kidding you, Nat. This woman's yard is a botanical horror show."

He reached over her and turned the pages until he found the photo he was looking for. "Did you see any pokeberries? The roots are really deadly. So are the leaves and stems. It says tea brewed from pokeberry plants is highly toxic."

Em read aloud. "People use the plant as greens despite the danger." She shook her head. "Are they nuts?"

"No they're berries."

She nudged her shoulder into his. "Ha ha. Not funny, considering."

"Anyone already under a doctor's care for something like congestive heart failure or any major heart problem could ingest one of these poisons brewed from the angel's trumpet. Mitchell Chamber's heart might have sped up fast enough for tachycardia to kill him," he said.

"And there wouldn't be any toxicology tests?"

"Not if he was under a doctor's care and suffering from extensive heart disease." His expression was thoughtful. "What disease did you say the woman had? The first one to die?"

"An autoimmune disease. Roland said hemolytic anemia."

"I thought that's what you'd say. It's associated with heart problems, including heart failure. Under the right circumstances, any poisoning that caused heart failure in that case could go unnoticed."

"As with Mitchell."

She lined up the edges of the stack of pages in her hand and looked at the man beside her. Nat had leaned back on his hands, legs stretched out and crossed at the ankles and was staring out at the ocean. The trades ruffled his curly light hair. She guessed he was in his early forties, but his hair showed no sign of thinning. He had a great career and was obviously interested in her.

So why did she want to call Roland right now? Was it to tell him about Tiko's bouquet of poisonous plants, or because she couldn't stop thinking about his kiss? She dug her toes into the warm sand.

"Have you had time to tell Louie about the reality show idea?" Nat asked.

"Not yet. He was up and out early, but I'll talk to him soon, I promise."

"You don't like the idea."

"I'm not sure I'd like the invasion. Our neighbors in Newport rented out their home to a film company once. The street was closed and crowded with huge trucks, the film and catering crews, not to mention all the trailers for the stars' dressing rooms. All that would wipe out our parking lot, and then where would our customers park?"

"It wouldn't be as much as all that. The 'stars' are all of you. No need for dressing rooms. The crew can park in my yard."

He had a solution for every reservation she had.

Em glanced at her watch. "Kimo gets in around nine-thirty, so I'd better get going."

"Are the Maidens coming in to practice?"

"Not today. I think the weekend did them in." Em stood up. She waited for Nat to rise before she picked up her towel and shook the sand out of it. "Thanks again for all this great info."

"Easy. Let me know if you need anything else."

She was still focused on calling Roland when Nat asked, "Are we still on for Wednesday night?"

"Sure, why not?"

Nat smiled. "Just checking."

As he headed down the sand toward his yard next door, Em thought about the wide open windows in the Goddess and wondered if he'd seen Roland kiss her last night.

Em showered, dressed, and was in the office by nine-thirty. The phone on the old wooden desk Louie had had for over forty years was ringing when she walked in, and there were six messages on the answer machine.

"Tiki Goddess Bar and Restaurant." She grabbed a pencil and notepad.

It was the concierge at the Island Holidays Hotel giving her a heads up that there were two minivans full of Rhinos headed their way for lunch tomorrow. She thanked him and made a note to tell Kimo and Sophie the minute they walked in. She listened to the messages and made a couple of call backs.

She was able to put off calling Roland until she'd handled the messages, but before she got into calling food and liquor distributors, she turned to the stack of poisonous plant materials and hit his programed number on her cell.

"Sharpe," he answered.

Yes you are, she thought.

"My neighbor brought over the ricin information this morning."

"And . . ."

"Are you too busy to talk right now? If so, I can call you back."

"Nope. I got a call and was out late. You woke me up."

"I'll call back."

"I'm up now."

"And grumpy."

"I need coffee."

She heard him shuffling around, the sound of water running and imagined him barefoot in the kitchen making a pot of coffee.

"*Wala'au.* Talk story," he said.

"He printed up a lot of information on other toxic tropical plants. I could take a stroll through our yard, mix up some tea and possibly take out a whole lot of people."

"Hopefully you won't."

"Tiko's garden is a death trap. I saw plants that match the photos on the information sheets."

"Can you meet me for breakfast someplace? Unofficially?"

"By unofficially do you mean an unofficial date or that I'm working on this unofficially?" She caught herself smiling into the phone.

"Both. You'll know when we're on a real date."

"I can't today. I'm slammed with paperwork, and we have two van loads of Rhinos coming in tomorrow."

"You're cell is cutting out. I thought you said rhinos."

"I did. Rhinos. They're like Elks and Lions."

"Pretty exotic menu."

"I'll explain later. I still don't want to believe Tiko did this, but I wanted you to know that she has the means to have poisoned Mitchell and Shari without using castor beans."

"Thanks, Em. I appreciate this."

She found herself stalling, not ready to end the call. "How's Kawika?"

"Hanging on. It's almost been forty-eight hours. He may make it."

"Is he conscious?"

"Not yet. We don't know any more than we did, just that there wasn't anything suspicious in Tiko's smoothie supplies or packages."

"What about her cousin Charlotte? She worked in the booth. Maybe she saw something."

"We interviewed her. She was only helping Tiko out because of the size of the festival crowd. She's working for Garden Island Vacation Rentals, has great references and said she hasn't been back on island very long."

"She may have unknowingly delivered the poisoned smoothie."

"She's got no motive," he reminded her.

Kimo stuck his head into the office. Em waved him in.

"Listen, Roland. I've got to go."

"Can you fax me a list of those plants? Save me some time?"

"Sure."

"Great."

She thought he was going to say goodbye but he said, "Remember you're saving Friday night for me. Officially."

"Got it," she said.

"Unless I get a call and have to work."

"Right."

Hopefully nobody else would be poisoned or run off with a chicken suit on Friday.

42

Kiki's New Attitude

The weather held. Tuesday morning was as bright and sunny as the day before, except for the occasional misting trade shower. Kiki pulled into the lot at the Goddess promptly at eight twenty. She wanted to get there before the other gals, who were due to arrive at nine. Louie was on the lanai waiting to greet her.

"*Aloha kakahiaka*, Kiki."

"Good morning to you, Louie. You're looking dapper as ever."

She wasn't just blowing smoke. With his head full of white hair, perpetual tan, quiver of aloha shirts and white linen pants, he was every bit a dashing man-about-the-island. If she was older and single she might have gone after him herself.

"Congrats on winning third place at the competition."

"*Mahalo.* Our scores weren't half bad. Nowhere as bad as before, anyway. I'm actually thinking next year's number already." She felt as light as a champagne bubble for a change.

"Can't start too soon."

"What are you up to?" She followed him inside the bar and set the boom box and CDs down on the edge of the low stage.

"I'm working on a new drink. We've got a bunch of those Rhinos coming in for lunch today, and I thought I'd make up something special. In fact, I was just going to take a sample over to Letterman and let him try it."

"Can I watch?" The parrot tasted and approved of all of Louie's creations, but she had never seen David Letterman at work.

"Sure. Come with me."

He led her back through the office, out the door and across the parking lot to the house. The place was comfortably worn in, not posh like the newly remodeled or recently built homes on the beach. The screen door banged shut behind them. They walked across the lanai and into the wide, airy living room. Louie stepped behind the tiki bar in the corner of the room beside the tall iron cage where the macaw spent his indoor hours.

"I'm calling it Coconut Rum Rhino. How's that sound?"

Kiki pictured Little Estelle with the horn strapped to her head.

"How about Horny Rum Rhino?"

Louie shot his fist in the air. "Perfect!"

"What's in it?" She leaned on the bar and watched him read ingredients off a scrap of paper before he measured them out.

"Three kinds of Jamaican rum, light and dark, along with some cream of coconut and some pineapple juice."

The minute he dumped ice into the cocktail shaker David Letterman started pacing back and forth on his perch bobbing his head.

The bird screeched, "Lime in da coconut! Lime in da coconut! Shake it tall up!"

"Hang on there, Dave." Louie finished up with the splash of pineapple juice and started shaking. "Line up two glasses and one of those tall shot glasses for me," he said.

Kiki walked behind the bar and got out two old fashioned glasses and set them on top.

Kiki didn't like the way the blood red parrot was staring at her.

"Like I'm going to steal your share," she mumbled at Dave as she set down his shot glass.

"How old is he?"

"He's around sixty. Macaws can live to be a hundred, so I'm leaving him to Em."

"I'll bet she's thrilled."

Louie filled the glasses with ice and strained the samples into them. He filled the tall jigger, then opened the door to Dave's cage.

"Down the hatch! Down the hatch!" The parrot bounced up and down in a frenzy as Louie poured the drink into an empty drinking cup hooked to the side of the cage.

Letterman grabbed the bars with his claws and hung upside down, guzzling the cocktail until it was gone. He got back on his perch, reared his head back then leaned forward and made a spitting sound.

"Yuck! Yuck! Patooie!"

"He hates it." Louie tasted his own sample. "I don't get it. I think it's pretty good."

Kiki watched the parrot act as if he'd been poisoned by spitting and yucking it up. She lifted her glass and took a sip.

"I think it's good. Considering it's not nine in the morning yet, it goes down pretty smooth. It's a pretty creamy color. What's not to like?"

"It needs a bit of adjustment." There was still some in the cocktail shaker. Louie made a note on the scrap of paper, poured a little more dark rum into the shaker and shook it. The parrot matched the motions and bobbed up and down.

Louie refilled Dave's empty water dish and waited.

Letterman took one sip and then another. Soon the extra water container hooked to the side of the cage was empty. The parrot was a little slower in responding but he still wasn't satisfied with the mix.

"Patooooie." He followed up with choking sounds that reminded Kiki of one of her cats before it hurled a furball.

"Shoot." Louie tasted the second batch. "I think it's pretty good."

Kiki leaned close to the cage, and the bird started shrieking like a stuck pig.

"Did you ever think maybe he's playing you?"

Louie paused with a bottle of light rum in his hand. "What do you mean?"

"I mean, do you think he might just be *pretending* not to like the first two or three batches so that you'll keep giving him more?"

Louie stared at the parrot for a minute. "You wouldn't do that, would you Dave?"

"Lime in da coconut!" Letterman shouted. "Drink it tall up!"

Kiki heard a car pull into the Goddess parking lot and downed her sample. "I've gotta get back over there. The girls will be waiting." She started for the door. "Thanks for the sample. I think the Rhinos will love it."

"Great. By the way . . ." He put down the shaker and walked over to where she waited by the open door onto the lanai. "I hope you can put what happened with Marilyn behind us and give her another chance. Don't be upset if she starts coming around again."

"Upset? Someone poisoned a *kumu* at the competition and who knows how many before that? As far as the police know, it could be anybody, even Marilyn."

"Or you."

"*What?*"

"I'm just saying that it's not Marilyn. Blaming her is as crazy as blaming you. Em told me they questioned Tiko but they released her. Until the police find some hard evidence, don't go around blaming someone who's innocent."

Kiki was mad enough to yell patooie.

"The Goddess is your bar. You can welcome anyone you want. Just don't blame me if you wind up poisoned by that black widow someday."

She stomped out and let the screen door slam behind her. Inside the house, Letterman started squawking up a storm. By the time Kiki got back to the bar she had gotten a grip on herself. She wasn't about to let Louie or Marilyn ruin her good mood.

Trish and Flora were already inside waiting for the others. Trish had spread photos out over one of the tables.

"Are those from the competition?" Kiki leaned over to get a better look.

"I had a friend in the audience taking still shots with my camera."

Kiki couldn't believe what she was seeing. "Our arms are all up at the same time."

"I know." Trish was beaming. "We look great in every shot."

"Did you take out the bad ones?" Kiki scanned the photos. Something had to be up.

"Two. That's all."

As soon as the others arrived and had time to ooh and ahh over the photos, Kiki signaled Pat to call them to order. She beat on her Crisco can and yelled, "Laaadeeze!"

The Maidens stood at the ready.

"Some of the Rhinos are coming in for lunch today," Kiki smiled, thrilled to be able to announce the surprise. "I say we practice a few of our numbers and dance for them. I've got all the CDs, and we're good to go."

"But we're not dressed for a show," Lillian whined.

"It's what we call *impromptu*, Lillian. It's going to be fine." Kiki picked out a CD and loaded it on the boom box. She was lining them up on stage when Big Estelle walked in with Little Estelle rolling along behind her.

"Sorry we're late," Big Estelle apologized. "Mother was chasing the meter reader down the street."

Little Estelle shrugged. "He was cute."

"Whatever she's taking, I need some," Pat mumbled.

"Get on the stage, Big Estelle. We're doing a lunch show for the Rhinos. It's a dance-as-you-are show. No time to change."

"The Rhinos?" Despite the crowded space, Little Estelle executed a perfect donut on the Gad-About. "Whoohoo."

Kiki held up her hand. "Stop riding in circles. How about scooting outside and cutting some song of India for to wear in our hair? I brought extra pins." Kiki dug around in her basket purse and pulled out some pruning shears and handed them to Little Estelle.

Trish started digging in her bag. "I think I have some pins in here some place too."

Little Estelle drove back outside without a word of argument.

"What if she doesn't come back?" Lillian asked.

Big Estelle sighed. "Oh, she'll be back. She tried to get me to take her back to the hotel this morning to score another horn for her collection."

They practiced for almost two hours. When Em came in, Kiki waved her over.

"We heard about the Rhinos coming, and we've got a show all worked up for them."

Em didn't respond with the enthusiasm as Kiki had hoped for, but nothing was going to burst her bubble today.

"We'll need a lot of tables for them." Em looked around at the Maidens. They had broken into twos and threes. Their things were spread out all over the room. Little Estelle was back with a bag full of green and white variegated leaves. Her assignment accomplished, she was sipping on a tall Huli Huli Boolie, a drink that was strong enough to even make Kiki's head spin. Kiki signaled Big Estelle over.

"I'm not so sure that's a good idea," Kiki nodded toward Little Estelle.

"You try to stop her." Big Estelle went back to where she'd been talking to Lillian.

"Hit it." Kiki told Pat. Pat pounded on the drum and the women fell silent.

"Pick up all of your things and haul them out to your cars *wikiwiki*. Then meet back here, and we'll pin leaves in your hair. Em needs help with the tables. She'll tell you how to arrange them." Kiki turned to Em. "There. Easy, see? Exactly how many Rhinos are coming?"

"Twenty to twenty-five. Depending on how many they can squeeze into a van."

"You can tell how big a Rhino is by the size of his horn," Little Estelle yelled.

"Kiki, this is not a good idea." Em looked decidedly worried.

Kiki waved away her concern. "I'll take care of her. Trust me."

Sophie walked in from the kitchen. "Kimo wants to know what to serve for the lunch special."

"What do we have the most of?"

"Yesterday's teriyaki chicken and mac salad."

"That's the special."

Sophie hesitated. "Should we offer the smoothies and cut the price? We might be able to use them up on the Rhinos. The locals won't be so anxious to order them once the story gets out. Besides, none of the Rhinos is in line to be a *kumu*."

"Good idea," Kiki agreed. "Louie has a new cocktail ready for them, too."

"I don't know." Em glanced toward the kitchen. "You better tell Kimo about the special."

Sophie hurried toward the kitchen.

Kiki put her hand on Em's shoulder. "Don't look so worried."

"I just don't know about serving those smoothies."

"You think Tiko might have put something in them?"

Em shook her head. "No, but I hate to find out I'm wrong."

"Then go for it." Kiki smiled.

"You sure are happy today," Em noted.

"I'm still riding the high from our performance."

Em's gaze shifted to Little Estelle. "What should do about her?" she whispered.

"Have Sophie fix her a double Huli Huli Boolie. With any luck she'll pass out and we can take her away before the Rhinos pull into the lot."

The double Huli Boolie worked better than a tranquilizer gun on Little Estelle. Once she passed out, Kiki convinced Big Estelle to leave her mother on the Gad-About and roll her into Em's office to sleep it off.

The Rhinos arrived and commenced doing what Rhinos did best—partying. After an hour Kiki took refuge in the hall between the bar and the bathrooms. Across the room Em yelled to Sophie, "Eight more Rum Rhinos!"

When Louie walked up beside her, Kiki said, "You'd think they would have all passed out by now."

Together they watched Sophie, an island of calm in a hurricane of chaos, as she lined eight tall glasses up on the bar and started pouring.

Near the banquette, a half dozen Rhinos were yelling, "Chug, chug, chug," over one of their brothers who was lying on his back across a table. Three others found a broom in the restroom and used the handle to take turns doing the limbo.

In the far corner, two Rhinos squared off. Heads down, horns pointed and strapped on tight, they pawed the ground. Then they charged each other, completely missed and fell over.

"Too many Rum Rhinos to do any damage," Louie commented.

"Good thing they came in vans with drivers or you'd have to cut them off," Kiki said.

Louie laughed. "They've definitely broken a record. We've never sold this many specialty drinks at once other than on luau night. I had to send Buzzy to town for rum, and he cleaned out the shelves at Hanalei Liquor and the Big Save."

"I guess I should get the girls up and dancing before the audience passes out."

Kiki tried to announce the Maidens over the din. They lined up on stage and danced their hearts out, but the boom box was barely audible even on the highest volume. None of the Rhinos paid any attention.

"I hate these guys," Flora told Kiki. She stopped dancing and walked off the stage.

Lillian and Suzi followed. Kiki and Big Estelle looked at each other, shrugged and stopped too. Kiki unplugged the boom box and was wrapping up the cord when a middle-aged Rhino wearing a horn with the word BULL printed on it came staggering over.

"Aloooooha!" he shouted at her.

"Aloha to you too."

He crooked his finger and had her bend down so that she could hear him.

"Can I use your microphone?"

"I think you're loud enough," she said.

He wagged his head from side to side. "I gotta make a speech. It's impotent."

"I can imagine."

"No really."

"How *impotent* is it?"

He signaled one of his brother Rhinos over, pulled off the man's horn and waved it around. "Gotta make a special presentation. To the guy who owns the place."

"Oh, in that case," Kiki handed him the mic. "Be my guest."

"Whas'sis name?"

"Louie Marshall."

"Where are we again?"

"You're in Hawaii. At the Tiki Goddess Bar."

"Oh, yeah. Right."

He climbed onto the stage, held the mic to his lips and made a loud, long moan. He kept moaning like a rhino in heat until every Rhino in the room stopped yelling and faced him in reverent silence.

"Brother Rhinos! Here ye, here ye." He held up the horn and waved it around. "Can we have Mr. Louie Marshall come forward?"

He waited until someone ran into the kitchen and found Louie and sent him into the bar. Two Rhinos marched Louie to the stage and placed him beside their leader.

The man drew himself up, stopped weaving for a second and turned to Louie.

"As Bull Rhino of the Cincinnati Crush, it's my privilege to present you, Louie Marshall, creator of the Horny Rum Rhino, with an honorary Rhino horn."

He handed the horn to Louie. "Go ahead. Strap it on."

Ever the genial host, Louie took off his Panama hat, smoothed back his hair and strapped the horn on his head.

"Here's to Brother Louie!" the bull from Cincinnati hollered.

There wasn't a dry-eyed Rhino in the room as they raised their glasses and moaned.

It was another hour before the Rhinos stampeded out to their vans, leaving the place in such a mess the Maidens volunteered to help clean up.

"Gather 'round, ladies," Louie said when they were all finished. "I can't tell you how grateful I am for your help. You've gone above and beyond the call."

"We're happy to do it," Kiki said. "After all, this place is our second home."

Big Estelle said, "I'd better wake up mother and get going."

"Just a minute." Louie pulled off his honorary horn.

Kiki and the other Maidens followed them into the office where Louie carefully strapped the horn to Little Estelle's head. She snorted but didn't wake up. They rolled her back into the bar and parked her near the stage.

Big Estelle gently shook her shoulder. "Mother, it's time to go home."

Little Estelle blinked and looked around in confusion. She touched the strap under her chin, then reached up and discovered the Rhino horn.

"That was some party," she mumbled. "I don't even remember putting another notch in my belt."

She had a smile a mile wide on her face when Big Estelle finally rolled her and the Gad-About onto the van lift.

43

Just Another Quick Trip to Town

"Thanks for loaning me your truck, Uncle Louie." Em was almost out the door, keys in hand the next morning.

It was a gray day, overcast but not raining. After the fan belt broke on Sophie's rust bucket last night, Em had loaned Sophie her car. She hated to have to borrow the truck and leave Louie on his own, but she was determined not to be gone long.

"Sophie said she'd be in early," Em reminded him.

She only planned to go as far as the Island Holidays Hotel and pick up her phone. The manager had called last night after the maintenance crew found it backstage. When she thanked him, he asked if *"those women"* had been in any more fights.

Happily, she told him no. But then again, it had been less than forty-eight hours.

"Would you mind picking up a battery for my watch?" Louie crossed the room and handed her a slip of paper with the number of the battery he needed. "And Kimo needs a bulk pack of Sterno for the catering job we're doing on Sunday," he added.

Em sighed. "I guess I can go all the way into Lihue."

"As long as you're running around," he was on a roll, "you might as well stop at Napa Auto Parts and pick up a fan belt for Sophie's car. Otherwise you'll have to drive her back and forth until she can get one. Either that or let her keep your car."

Em pulled a pen out of her purse and wrote Sterno and fan belt on the slip of paper he'd handed her.

"I'll walk you out and take the old belt off her engine. Just hand it to the guy at Napa and he'll get you the right one."

Louie followed her to the parking lot, removed Sophie's fan belt, and Em carried it over to his compact Toyota truck. An older model, it was a faded blue, but it ran like a top. Em turned the key, and it started right up. She lowered the window on the driver's side and Louie hovered.

"Thanks again. I'll be back as soon as I can." She was anxious to leave before anyone else rolled in and added another stop to her list. "Don't forget to call the people we're catering for on Sunday to see if they decided on chicken and teri beef skewers or chicken and shrimp."

"I will. Right after I take my beach walk. Don't worry. And watch the road."

It was seven thirty when she finally left the parking lot. With the stop to pick up her phone, it would take an hour to get to Lihue. She popped a CD into the player and settled back to enjoy the road and the view. Folks here complained about traffic, especially the old timers, but she never minded the slow drive, what with the lush green mountains on one side of her, the ocean on the other and an occasional rainbow in between.

Her cell phone was at the front desk at the resort right where it was supposed to be. Em thanked the manager and turned it on. The battery was dead, but she'd grabbed her car charger before Sophie took off last night so now she hooked up charger to the phone.

Headed for town again, she was singing along with Celine Dion on an old CD of Louie's until she passed a white panel van and felt a rush of adrenaline. She side-eyed the driver, afraid it was Tiko, but it wasn't. It took her heart a minute or two to slow down.

If the police couldn't tie Tiko to Kawika's poisoning, it was a given on an island the size of Kauai that Em was bound to run into her again.

She'd never forgive herself if she'd jumped to conclusions and Tiko was completely innocent. Though Tiko denied any wrongdoing, the image of her garden with its bouquet of poisoned plants kept popping into Em's mind.

As she neared town, Em found herself wondering what was happening with the members of Mitchell's *halau*. How many had defected, as Kiki put it, to other *kumu*?

At her first stop in town Em checked her phone. There were old messages from Sophie from the night of the fiasco performance and a couple from Roland but none since Sunday. She stopped everywhere on the list and was headed back home in record time when a red convertible Mustang pulled out in front of her with little room to spare.

She didn't get a good look at the driver, but she thought it looked like Tiko's cousin, Charlotte. The car was the same make and color she'd seen Charlotte driving at Tiko's.

Em adjusted her visor, hoping to hide her face. Her sunglasses surely helped. She doubted Charlotte would recognize her anyway, and she certainly wasn't paying much attention to her rear view mirror. Charlotte was too busy tailgating the car ahead of her, weaving to the left side of the lane, trying to see if there was room to pass. On the strip of highway known as Blood Alley was a forty mile an hour zone. Passing here was a pretty stupid idea.

Em backed off the accelerator and watched Charlotte pull one impatient move after another, until they crossed the Wailua River bridge. When Charlotte slid into the left turn lane that headed up Kuamo'o Road toward Tiko's house, Em jogged in behind her. The light turned green almost instantly, and soon they were able to turn *mauka,* inland.

Charlotte punched it, and the Mustang raced ahead, up the hill past the falls and round the curving road that followed the cliff above the Wailua River valley. The woman was in a hurry. Her obvious destination was Tiko's. Em had nothing to lose but time, so she hung back but kept Charlotte in sight.

When the red Mustang turned right at the Wailua Country Store, Em was sure Charlotte was headed to her cousin's. A car pulled out of the store lot and fell in between them.

Em drove right on by when Charlotte whipped into Tiko's empty driveway and went as far as two lots up, then she made a U-turn and headed back. She pulled over on the side of the road and parked in the shade of a huge mango tree. From there she could see Tiko's vanilla colored house bordered by the gardens around the open lawn. Tiko's van was nowhere in sight.

If Tiko was in the house and looked out the window, she wouldn't recognize Louie's old truck, nor would Charlotte. Em watched Charlotte get out of her car and open the trunk, then she ran up the driveway toward the back of the house and disappeared.

Em picked up her cell and hit Roland's number. All she got was his voicemail. She left him a message, told him to call her ASAP and shoved the phone into her pocket.

She drummed her fingers on the steering wheel, wishing she had the information Nat printed out for her. Her gaze drifted up the hill to the empty land crowded with wild growth behind Tiko's property, where countless castor bean plants were probably growing there like the weeds they were. Closer to the yard, the angel's trumpet was still in bloom. Tiko's garden was a potpourri of potential poisons.

A fine mist of rain hit the windshield. She turned on the wipers for a second and the moisture was gone. The passing cloud had already drifted by. Suddenly Charlotte appeared in the driveway. Still in a hurry, she was rolling a carry on suitcase. It bumped along the gravel drive until she reached her car and tossed it in the trunk and then ran back toward the rear of the house.

"Call me Roland," Em mumbled to herself. "If you're so psychic then pick up on this."

Em was tempted to move her truck further up the road so she could see down the driveway. Was the carry on Charlotte's, or was she picking it up for Tiko? If Tiko was trying to leave the island, then Charlotte was an accomplice.

Em pulled her cell out of her pocket, dialed Roland again and left another voicemail.

"Call me ASAP."

Charlotte appeared again, this time carrying two recyclable grocery store totes that appeared to be heavy. She put them in the trunk with the carry on and closed the lid. Then she looked over her shoulder, scanning the road. Em slumped down, but Charlotte didn't look at the truck. She got back in the Mustang, started it up and backed out of the driveway so fast that she left a spray of gravel behind.

She braked at the end of the drive, forced to wait for a passing UPS truck, then surprised Em by heading north and not back toward the airport. Em reached over and opened Louie's glove compartment, ignoring the flurry of old receipts and Snickers bar wrappers that fell out. She looked down as Charlotte flew by focused on the road.

Em started the truck, drove a few yards down the road and turned far enough into Tiko's driveway to get turned around. Now that Charlotte was headed in the opposite direction from the airport, it was hard to tell where she was headed. Maybe Tiko was hiding out at a friend's place.

If Tiko was innocent and terrified, she should know better than to run. Neither Tiko nor Charlotte was stupid. Tiko was a savvy entrepreneur. And Charlotte . . . Em realized she didn't know much about Charlotte other than that she'd just moved back from the mainland and worked for Garden Island Vacation Rentals.

Em slowed down for a truck piled high with green waste, frustrated when the driver continued at a snail's pace. She drifted toward the center line to see around him and watched Charlotte round a bend in the road. Em was tempted to go around the truck. She took a deep breath and put on her turn signal, but luckily the truck slowed down and turned into a driveway.

She let out a sigh of relief, clutched the steering wheel and went as fast as she dared around a curve and asked herself what in the heck she thought she was doing.

"Go home, Em," she said aloud.

She still had a lovely bruise on her cheek from Saturday night's brawl and didn't need to tempt fate, not while things were calm at the Goddess, and Kiki and the Maidens were still riding high from their triumphant third place award at the competition.

Up ahead, Charlotte had reached a crossroad. Em expected her to turn right and head to Kapa'a, but she made a left and headed inland toward

Kawaihau. After hesitating for half a second, Em followed, hanging back.

They just entered a neighborhood when Charlotte made a right turn into a dead end street. Em slowed down. Wood frame homes with carports stuffed with boxes and coolers, toys, surfboards, bikes, and here and there fishing boats on trailers lined the street. Em crept along at a crawl while up ahead, Charlotte pulled over. She parked and hurried into a house in the middle of the block.

Em drove past the house thinking, *now what?* It was a short block. Em parked on the opposite side of the street behind a boat on a trailer. As she slid down in the seat, she glanced at her watch. Before long Louie would start to worry if she didn't check in. She pulled out her cell, left Roland yet another message and then dialed the Goddess.

"I'm almost to Kapa'a. I made a couple of detours," she told Louie.

"We're doing great. Sophie is here, and Kimo's got the place smelling like barbeque sauce. Ribs are tonight's special." He paused a minute and then said, "By the way, I called the people who booked us for Sunday night. They wanted to know about hiring some hula dancers. They want a fire knife dancer too."

"Nothing like planning ahead." She rubbed her forehead and tried to iron out her frown lines with her fingertips. "I'll see if Roland is free. I'm sure the Maidens will do it if we can't find a couple of young local dancers."

She couldn't book the Maidens without warning the hostess that they wouldn't be getting what visitors thought of as typical hula dancers. It wasn't worth risking customers going into cardiac arrest when a bunch of middle-aged *haoles* showed up in *muumuus* with stolen shrubbery pinned on their heads.

"Uncle Louie, I'll take care of it when I get back. I'll see you soon."

"Great. Be careful."

She smiled until she shoved her phone back in her pocket and looked around. Thankfully school was in session, and there weren't any kids playing on the street and no one was working in any of the yards right now, either. On a dead end street like this one, a *haole* lady sitting alone in a truck spying on the neighbors was sure to be noticed.

She started up the truck, turned around and headed down the block toward Charlotte's car. As she cruised slowly by she nearly hit the brakes when she noticed what was parked in the driveway in front of the Mustang.

Jackie Loo Tong's metallic silver truck.

Kumu Jackie Loo Tong. Mitchell's rival.

"What the . . . ?" Em pulled over again.

Why was Charlotte here? If she stopped to pick up Tiko, why would Tiko be here? Unless Tiko had been sabotaging her old *halau* for Jackie's benefit?

Tiko's van wasn't in sight, but it could be hidden in Jackie's garage.

Common sense told Em she should head home, wait for Roland to call, tell him what she'd seen and let the professionals take over. But by then Tiko might make a run for it. How easy was it for a murder suspect to get off the island?

Jackie had threatened Kawika and now Tiko could be tied to Jackie, but that still didn't prove Tiko had poisoned anyone.

Em had to get out of the truck, but she needed a destination and to look like she belonged.

She was two houses away from Jackie's. The house in between had a For Sale sign out front. The yard needed a good weeding. The hedge was out of shape and the faded blooms on the ginger plants needed cutting.

She looked into the small narrow cab behind the driver's seat. Louie had left a rain jacket with a hood in the car. It was overcast and not too hot, so she might not look too suspicious in a windbreaker. She spotted an old U of Hawaii baseball cap, put it on and threaded her ponytail through the opening in back.

If anyone saw her snooping around the house next to Jackie's, they'd think she was just a lookie-loo, and if questioned she could say a realtor sent her. With luck she'd be able to sneak into the yard unseen and get closer to Jackie's place by walking around to the back.

Before she got out, she picked up the receipts that had fallen out of the glove compartment. She was about to shove them back in when she noticed one was from Roberts Jewelers. It was a layaway receipt for an engagement ring.

A very pricy engagement ring.

It was dated just last week. Louie had put money down on a ring for Marilyn after he'd supposedly put the engagement on hold.

"Oh, Uncle Louie," Em whispered. "You can't afford this." She stared at the receipt again then shoved it into them all into the glove compartment.

Her hand was on the door handle when she remembered to set her phone to vibrate. Once she was on the street she kept her eyes focused on the house that was for sale and acted as if she were checking out the yard and then walked up to the front lanai. After peering in the windows—the place was completely empty and forlorn—she walked around the side of the house that was opposite Jackie's and continued around to the back yard.

Once she was on Jackie Loo Tong's side of the property, she was only eight feet from his open windows and could hear the conversation inside. It definitely wasn't a happy chat.

"I never made you any promises," Jackie said.

"No?" The female voice wasn't Tiko's. It was Charlotte's. "What about Las Vegas? You made it pretty clear you were serious about us."

"If you call that clear then you'd better get your eyes checked." Jackie laughed. "That was an affair, Charlotte. A-f-f-a-i-r-e. No big t'ing. I have 'um all the time."

"Yeah, I heard." Her voice went up a notch. "Tiko told me they hauled you in for questioning on Friday night, *after* they found you at the Leilani Motel with some dancer from Oahu. I was busting my butt at the festival and you were playing around behind my back."

Em heard their footsteps on the bare floor as they moved from the front of the house to another room.

Charlotte's voice sounded desperate and angry. "I quit my job for you, Jackie. I moved back to Kauai for you."

"I never asked you to."

"Please, just tell me I'm not wasting my time," Charlotte said.

"That depends on what you expect from me. You've found a good job here and you're back home. If you want to have some fun, no strings attached, I'm up for that."

"I had a good job, and I loved Las Vegas. It's boring as hell here."

"Then go back."

"But I love you, Jackie."

"You hardly know me." There was a pause. "Look, honey, I'm sorry, but I'm just not a one woman man. Ask anyone."

There was the sound of an ice dispenser dropping cubes in a glass.

"At least look at me," Charlotte said.

"Want some water?" Jackie sounded as cold as the ice in his glass.

"No, thanks. Here, finish this if you like."

"What is it?"

"Starbucks latte."

Em heard the sound of some liquid being poured and then the tinkle of ice cubes.

"Maybe you can get your old Vegas job back," he suggested.

"I don't want my job back. I've gone way too far to turn back now."

"All you have to do is pack up and go back."

Charlotte laughed again. The sound gave Em the chills.

"I could have done that a couple of months ago, but not now," Charlotte said.

Em heard Jackie say, "Where's Tiko? How about I call her for you?"

"Tiko? What do I need her for?

There was a hesitation then Jackie said, "Maybe you need to talk things out with someone. Some girl talk. Advice."

Charlotte laughed but there was no joy in the sound. "It's too late for talking. Way too late."

44

You Can't Always Get What You Want

There was a plastic chair a few feet away on the lawn of the deserted house. Em tiptoed over, picked it up and set it down without a sound beneath Jackie's kitchen window. She climbed up on the chair and had just put her fingertips on the edge of the windowsill when she heard a vehicle coming down the street.

She froze and saw a white van go past the space between houses. The engine stopped. Inside, Charlotte and Jackie fell silent. The van door slammed, and then Em heard flip flops slapping against the walk.

Tiko's voice called out, and there was a knock on the door.

"Jackie, it's me. Are you in there, Charlotte?"

Em peered over the windowsill. If they were expecting Tiko, they both looked surprised. Jackie, with a glass in hand, was eyeing Charlotte who was next to the kitchen sink.

"What's she doing here?" Charlotte asked him.

"Heck if I know," he shrugged.

"Charlotte? I know you're in there. I can see your car in the driveway." The screen door banged. Tiko must have walked in.

Charlotte headed for the front room while Jackie trailed along carrying a tall glass full of ice and a short bottle of Starbucks latte. Em stepped off the chair, picked it up and carried to the front window. She climbed up, peered over the windowsill.

Tiko looked frantic. "What are you doing here, Charlotte?"

"How did you find me?"

"I've been looking for you since Sunday and put the word out. My neighbor's second cousin lives a block over. She saw you drive by." Tiko's gaze cut to Jackie. "What are you drinking?"

"Latte," he held up the bottle.

"Did she give it to you?"

"Yeah." Jackie stared at the glass.

"Put it down," Tiko said.

Jackie set the glass and bottle on a side table. "Why?"

Tiko's gaze cut back to Charlotte.

"What's the matter with you?" Charlotte walked further into the living room.

"I think you know." Tiko never took her eyes off her cousin. "I've been looking for you since I was released. You haven't been at work, and you haven't been to your condo. You aren't answering my calls. We need to talk. Outside."

Charlotte glanced at Jackie then turned back to Tiko. "What for?"

"I think you know." Tiko was three inches shorter and twenty pounds lighter, but she wasn't budging. She walked over to the table where Jackie had set his drink and picked up the bottle.

"What's going on?" Jackie's gaze flashed from one woman to the other.

"I came to talk to my cousin. To help her," Tiko said.

Charlotte lowered her voice, stepped closer to Jackie and put her hand on his arm. "She's dangerous."

"Funny stuffs have been going on, you know," Jackie said to Tiko. "Maybe you ought to take off. If she wants to see you, she knows where you live."

"I know funny 'stuffs' have been going on," Tiko said. "That's why I'm here. I need to talk to Charlotte. Alone."

Em's cell phone vibrated, and she almost fell off the chair. Catching her balance, her hand shook as she tried to pull the phone out of her pocket. Finally. It was Roland.

"What's up? I got your messages," he said.

She whispered into the phone. "I'm at Jackie Loo Tong's. You need to get over here right now."

"Address?"

"I have no idea. I followed Charlotte here. It's way up above Kapa'a somewhere."

"What's going on?"

She heard his car door slam and the engine start up over the phone. He was on the move.

"Tiko is here too. And Jackie."

"Where are you exactly?"

"Crouched down on a plastic chair between two houses. Something's going on. I thought Tiko was going to leave the island. It's a long story . . ."

She heard him sigh. "Sit tight. I'll track down the address. We're on the way."

"Thanks," she whispered.

"Em?"

"What?"

"Don't do anything crazy." He hung up.

Em hopped back up in time to see Jackie walk over to a cane bottomed chair near the front door. He sat down, wiped his upper lip and then his brow and doubled over.

"Jackie?" Tiko ran to his side. "What's wrong?"

Jackie held out his hand. "I'm shaking. My legs won't hold me."

Tiko leaned over him, touched his wrist. "Your pulse is racing." She looked over at her cousin. "What did you give him? What have you done?"

Charlotte grabbed her purse off the table. Em's mind was racing. *What did you give him? What have you done?*

Charlotte had been working the smoothie booth all weekend with Tiko, but that wouldn't account for Shari and Mitchell's deaths, unless Charlotte had already moved back from the mainland before Shari and Mitchell died.

Charlotte had access to Tiko's garden. Charlotte had learned herbal lore from their grandmother too. She'd been working in the smoothie booth the night Kawika was poisoned and was the one who delivered the tainted smoothie to the *kumu*. Charlotte could have easily put ground castor beans in *after* Tiko handed it over for delivery.

It was clear why Charlotte was furious at Jackie, but was she mad enough to poison him? And what motive would Charlotte have for killing off members of Tiko's old *halau*?

While Em clung to the window ledge, now aware she'd suspected the wrong cousin of murder, Charlotte bolted out the front door.

Tiko stayed with Jackie.

"I'm gonna be sick," he covered his mouth.

"Can you make it to the bathroom? Try to vomit."

He got up and staggering across the room. Tiko ran out after Charlotte. Em dialed 911.

"It's an emergency. I don't know where I am." She thought her phone had GPS. She jumped off the chair and ran around to the front of the house. Tiko was yelling at Charlotte who was already behind the wheel of the Mustang. Em read the numbers on the house into the phone. "I'm up above Kapa'a somewhere. Somebody's been poisoned."

A woman across the street stepped out onto her porch to see what was going on.

"What's the name of this street?" Em yelled to her.

The woman said something that sounded like Popopokia or Polopokia. Em said both into the phone as she watched Tiko try to open the driver's side door on the Mustang. Charlotte started the car, and as she pulled out of the driveway, Tiko was forced to let go and jump back.

When Tiko turned around and saw Em standing there, she hesitated

Jill Marie Landis

for a split second.

"We've got to stop her," Tiko started running for her van.

"Roland is on the way."

Tiko started crying. "Call him. Call Detective Sharpe again and tell him to hurry."

Em dialed Roland again.

"Are you all right?" They were the first words out of his mouth. Em nodded as if he could see.

"Em?"

"I'm good. Charlotte. It's Charlotte who poisoned Kawika. She just gave Jackie Loo Tong something toxic. Tiko tried to stop her but she drove off."

"Charlotte or Tiko?"

"Charlotte. Charlotte is in a red Mustang convertible. She's up here somewhere around Kawaihau."

"She won't get off the island."

"Are you sure?"

"Don't worry. I'll get more cruisers up here. Did you call 911?"

"Yes."

"Sit tight with Jackie. We'll take it from here."

"Red Mustang. Convertible," she reminded him.

"Got it. Stay put."

She hung up and ran to tell Tiko. "He's on the way and he's got patrol cars coming. He said to stay with Jackie."

Tiko was already at her van. "I'll try to follow her. I want to be there when they catch her."

"What about Jackie? You know better than I do what he needs right now."

"I need to find out what she gave him. It's crucial. You stay with him. Keep giving him water even if he can't keep it down." She ran down the sidewalk toward her van. Em jogged along beside her.

"Tiko, I'm sorry. Really. I'm so sorry I suspected you. I didn't want to believe it . . ."

Tiko stopped with her hand on her car door. "You were almost right."

Em ran back to Jackie's, expecting to find him heaving into the kitchen sink. He wasn't there.

"Jackie? Where are you? It's Em Johnson." She walked down a narrow hallway calling his name until she heard a moan and then loud gagging.

"Bathroom."

She followed the sound to a closed door and tried the door handle. It

206

was locked.

"Don't come in!"

"I can't get in."

From the variety of sounds he was making, rushing in to help wasn't high on her list of choices anyway.

"Tiko said you should be drinking water." She had to yell over the sound of the flushing toilet.

"*Awe*," he moaned. "I'm dying."

"You aren't going to die." Then she mumbled, "At least I hope not." The blissful sound of sirens shrilled in the distance. "Hang on, okay? The EMTs are almost here."

She ran through the house and out the front door to flag them down. A fire truck, an EMT ambulance and a police cruiser pulled up. Six hunks in navy blue uniforms swarmed after her into the house asking questions.

She told them Jackie had swallowed something toxic but she had no idea what it was. They had the bathroom door open in less time than it took Louie to shake a cocktail.

Em got a glimpse of Jackie Loo Tong as they rushed in to help him. The gambling, playboy *kumu* was on the floor hugging the toilet, with his pants down to his knees. With the crowd of men in the bathroom, she figured Jackie was in good hands. When she returned to the living room, a KPD officer in uniform was waiting for her.

"Are you Ms. Johnson?"

"Em. Em Johnson." Now that the EMTs were here, Em realized she was shaking.

"Detective Sharpe says to stay put until he calls you."

"Did he catch Charlotte Anara?"

"I don't know, ma'am."

A fireman came down the hall. "Do you know what he ingested?"

"Is he all right?" She wished she knew more.

"He's suffering from violent vomiting and diarrhea, but he hasn't lost consciousness. Do you know what he had or how much?"

She showed him the Starbucks bottle and the glass on the table.

"I don't know if it was a full bottle when he got it. He poured it over ice."

There was still a quarter of a bottle of latte left. Condensation had puddled beneath the glass and the latte that was left had been watered down with melted ice.

"Hopefully he didn't drink that much," she stared at the bottle. Charlotte must have twisted off the cap, tampered with the latte and put the cap back on.

A premeditated crime of passion.

Two more firemen came out of the bathroom and down the hall. Em waited with the silent police officer. The firemen came back with two ambulance drivers and a gurney. They loaded Jackie up and wheeled him out, eyes closed but moaning.

His neighbors and some of his dancers had gathered out front. Cars were being turned away from the crowded dead end street by another patrol officer on the corner.

"*Kumu, kumu!*" Two young girls ran alongside the gurney as the attendants rolled it to the back of the ambulance. A half dozen more young men and women, most of them with waist length black hair, crowded around Jackie, crying.

The ambulance attendants stood by impatiently as the dancers cried over their *kumu*. When one of the women started to chant, they all joined in. The attendants quickly loaded Jackie into the ambulance and closed the doors then drove off. The dancers were chanting in the street as the ambulance disappeared around the corner.

45

Bad News Travels Fast

Kiki hurried up the lanai stairs at the Goddess and was breathless by the time she walked into the bar.

She leaned on a table for support and asked Sophie, "Where's Louie?"

"I'm right here." He came walking in from the office.

"What's wrong?" Sophie filled a glass with water and set it next to Kiki's elbow.

Kiki stared at it. "I don't drink water," she said.

"Take a sip. You look like you're going to have a stroke. Pretty soon you won't be able to talk again."

Kiki downed half the glass.

"Have you heard?" She looked at Sophie and then Louie.

"Heard what?" Louie sat on the barstool next to Kiki.

"Jackie Loo Tong has been poisoned."

"No kidding?" Sophie clicked her tongue stud.

"Where did you hear that?" Louie looked skeptical.

"Vickie Tamaguchi has a police scanner, and she was parked at the fruit stand when her husband called and said he heard it broadcast. She was standing out there telling everyone in the Big Save parking lot when two seconds later the news hit Facebook. Some of Jackie's *halau* was outside his house crying and chanting and taking videos and photos and posting them."

"Was it Tiko? Did she do it?" Sophie waved at a couple having lunch in the corner. "I'll be right there," she told them.

"I guess. The big news is Em was there at Jackie's house up by Kawaihau. I saw her in the crowd in one of the Facebook posts."

"Was she all right?" Louie was patting himself down, searching for his phone in his baggy linen pants pockets.

"She looked okay."

"What was she doing up there?" Sophie wondered. "She said she was only going into town to run a few errands." Sophie paused a minute.

Louie looked befuddled. "You don't think *she* did it, do you?"

"Of course not!" Kiki scoffed. "The story is all mixed up, and folks are a bit confused. Some say Tiko poisoned him. Others say it was her cousin or both of them together. There was a police chase through the back roads and they probably wouldn't have caught them except that feral pig ran out in front of the car. Wrecked it up pretty bad too and killed the pig."

"Anybody pick up the pig?" Kimo had wandered in from the kitchen to listen. "I could use for the luau."

The customers at the back table got up and walked out.

"What's with them?" Kimo shook his head.

"Impatient *haoles*." Sophie waved it off. "Either that or it was the luau road kill idea. Whatevah."

"Hey, dis ain't the mainland," Kimo grumbled as he walked back into the kitchen.

"I'm calling Em," Louie said.

Kiki glanced at herself in the mirror behind the line of liquor bottles. Her cheeks were flushed. Sophie might be right about the stroke. She finished the glass of water. It wouldn't do to start speaking in tongues with so much gossip flying.

"Em? Are you all right?" Louie yelled into the cell. Kiki hung on every word. "Good. Good. Where are you?" He looked at Kiki and Sophie and said, "She's at the police station in Lihue."

He was speaking to Em again. "Don't worry about my truck. We can pick it up. You will? Okay, if it's no trouble. Take your time and call when you're on the way home, okay? What? Oh, Nat? Okay, I'll tell him." Louie hung up.

"What's going on? Why is she at the police station?"

"They're going to take her statement. She's a witness."

"To what? What was she doing at Jackie Loo Tong's in the first place?" Kiki couldn't stand not knowing all the details.

"She said she'd tell us everything when she gets back."

"Well, I can't wait that long." Kiki was starting to itch all over.

"It could be hours," Sophie said.

Louie nodded. "She said I should go over to Nat's and let him know she can't go out to dinner with him tonight."

"She was going out with him? Tonight?" Kiki hated being this far out of the loop.

"Yeah. She left my truck at Jackie's. Roland will drive her by to get it once she's through at the KPD." Louie absently fingered his phone. "I should have known something was up. She should have been home a couple of hours ago."

Kiki's cell rang. "Hi, Suzi. Thanks for calling back. I need you to start an emergency phone chain. Let the girls know Jackie Loo Tong has been poisoned." Kiki held the phone away from her ear until Suzi stopped screaming. "No, I don't know if he's dead or alive yet. I haven't checked Facebook for a few minutes." She signaled for Sophie to make her a martini and held up two fingers.

"Does that mean you want a double or two olives?" Sophie reached for the vodka.

"A double and three olives." She went back to the conversation with Suzi. "Whoever can go should meet at the Princeville Library parking lot in twenty minutes. We'll carpool to town and be there when Em walks out of the station so we can get the story first hand. Right. Yes. Like we did when Sophie was arrested and we were there in the parking lot to show Hula Maiden solidarity when she was released. We'll have to hurry, though."

Kiki listened as Suzi tried to reorganize the plan. "Okay, okay. Tell everyone twenty-five minutes then, but no later. I'll grab the boom box."

Sophie set a martini with three olives threaded on a green plastic sword sticking out of it in front of Kiki.

"I'm not so sure this is a good idea, Kiki," Sophie said.

"The martini?"

"That and going to meet Em at police headquarters."

"You loved it when we were there for you, didn't you?"

Sophie didn't respond for a second but then she said, "Em hasn't been arrested. She's just a witness."

"But she'll have the whole scoop. I'll bet she was working undercover for Roland."

Louie stopped staring at his phone. "Em's been working undercover? If it comes out that she's a secret agent for the KPD think of the press we'll get."

Sophie held up her hand to stop him. "She's no secret agent. She was just helping Roland out at the Kukui Nut Festival."

"No one tells me anything," Louie put his phone in his pocket.

Kiki was upset to think she was getting minimal information herself. She tossed back half of her martini and slid an olive off the little sword.

"That's because you're so close to the Defector." She popped the olive in her mouth. "We can't tell you anything secret and have you tell *her.*"

Sophie turned to Louie. "Kiki and I didn't know anything about the undercover thing until the festival was almost over."

Kiki speculated, "I thought they'd lock Tiko up, and if not her, then Marilyn. Now Jackie's been poisoned. Pretty soon there won't be a live *kumu* left on Kauai."

She polished off her drink. "I'd better get going. You want to go with us to the station, Louie?"

"No, I'll leave the festivities to you girls. Tell Em I love her and I'll see her later."

Sophie picked up Kiki's empty martini glass. "I think you should reconsider, Kiki. Why not be here to welcome Em home when she drives in?"

Kiki chewed up the remaining olives and smacked her lips.

"I've already started the Hula Maiden emergency phone chain. Once that *pig* is in the *imu* there's no pulling it back out."

46

Confession is Good for the Soul

Em was ushered into a small room at KPD headquarters where she gave her witness statement to an investigative services officer. She'd yet to see Roland, and she'd been there an hour and a half already.

Her statement was clear and concise; she'd seen Charlotte Anara racing along the highway and followed her to Tiko's where she watched her load a carry on and some tote bags that appeared to be full into the trunk of her Mustang convertible. She thought Charlotte might be helping Tiko leave the island. She called Detective Sharpe and left him a voicemail. From Tiko's she followed Charlotte inland to somewhere near Kawaihau where she turned into a small street and recognized Jackie Loo Tong's truck in the driveway.

She was embarrassed to admit she'd donned her uncle's baseball cap and snuck around the property of an empty house to listen in on Charlotte and Jackie's conversation. She heard the two argue about Jackie not wanting to make any romantic commitments. Charlotte was furious. During the conversation Charlotte offered him a Starbucks latte, which he accepted. Then Tiko showed up and wanted to talk to Charlotte alone. Charlotte refused. Then Jackie got ill and sat down. Charlotte ran out of the house. Em said she called 911 and Roland again.

When she was finished Em thought it all sounded perfectly logical, and it was definitely factual. She signed her statement and was told to wait. Detective Sharpe would be in soon.

Fifteen minutes later, Roland opened the door and walked straight to where she was sitting. He put his hand under her chin and tipped her head up. He searched her face with his eyes.

"Are you all right?" he asked.

Em was shocked to find she was suddenly all teary eyed.

"I will be when you stop looking at me that way."

"What way?"

"All worried. It's not like you at all," she said.

He sort of smiled.

"What's happening?" she asked.

"We're booking Charlotte for the murders of Shari Kaui and Mitchell Chambers and the attempted murders of Kawika Palikekua and Jackie Loo Tong, though she swears she only wanted to make Jackie suffer a bit, not kill him."

"How is he?"

"He'll be fine. He's at Wilcox right now, but he's listed in good condition."

"She confessed? To all of it? Shari and Mitchell, too?"

Roland pulled out a chair and sat down.

"She moved back right before Shari died. It took a while but with Tiko's help, we finally convinced her things would go easier for her if she made a full confession, especially since Kawika came out of his coma this morning. I was at the hospital interviewing him when you kept calling me. He said that on Friday night at the festival he didn't have time for dinner. He drank the smoothie Tiko sent an hour or so before he collapsed."

"But why target Mitchell's *halau*?"

"For Jackie. They met in Las Vegas and had an affair that lasted over a year and a half. He hooked up with her every time he flew over to gamble. She decided to move back here to be with him and was determined to make Jackie the top *kumu* on Kauai. Unfortunately, Mitchell and his *halau* were in the way."

"So Charlotte decided to get rid of his competition," Em said. "Did Tiko know?"

"Not until the night you confronted her backstage and questioned her about the smoothies she'd given all the *kumu* that night. When you asked if she had poisoned Kawika, she was terrified that it might have been Charlotte who did it and was desperate to find out before she accused her cousin.

"As soon as we took Tiko in, Charlotte disappeared. Tiko finally tracked her down at Jackie's. You know the rest, thanks to your talent for getting yourself caught up in the middle of things you should leave to the experts."

"You got me into this," she reminded him.

"I asked you to keep your eyes and ears open at the competition, not start a brawl trying to apprehend a suspect, or go snooping around on private property."

"If you'd called me back sooner you could have talked me down off the plastic lawn chair."

"I was at the hospital interviewing Kawika."

"So how did Charlotte do it? Castor bean concoctions for all of them?"

"No. She was more cunning than that. She stopped by to watch Mitchell's hula practices and kept telling him she was interested in joining because Tiko had been one of his dancers and spoke so highly of him. Everyone knew Tiko, so naturally, Mitchell was thrilled. Charlotte took them all sample smoothies, not poisonous, of course. Then one day she used the angel's trumpet plant to kill Mitchell. It sent his already weak heart into tachycardia and caused heart failure."

"And Shari?" Em pictured the lovely, frail young woman she'd seen in the photos at Kawika's home.

"Charlotte gave her a smoothie she had doctored with a brew made from leaves and stems of the oleander. The symptoms from oleander poisoning matched those she would have suffered had her hemolytic anemia worsened: fatigue, dizziness, shortness of breath and eventually, heart failure."

"I guess Jackie should consider himself lucky that she was in love with him."

"For sure. She only used enough poinsettia sap to make him wish he was dead. He was interviewed at the hospital and said when she handed him the Starbucks bottle, a third of it was already gone so he assumed she'd been drinking out of it—which was exactly what she wanted him to think."

"The next time I'm in the middle of an argument and somebody offers me a drink, remind me to turn them down."

He leaned back and stretched, then got to his feet. "Ready to go?"

Em looked at the clock on the wall behind him. It was already late afternoon.

"It's been a long day." She stood up. Roland pushed her chair back under the table.

"I'll drive you back to Jackie's to get your truck." He held the door open for her. "Think you'll make it home in time for your official date with the writer?"

"I've already cancelled."

He stopped. "Really."

"Careful. Your smug is showing."

He guided her toward the lobby. "Sorry we have to go out the front entrance."

"I'm not going to run into Charlotte, am I?"

"Worse. Word's going around that the Hula Maidens have assembled in the parking lot."

"Let me guess. They're lined up to dance for me."

"You got it."

Em sighed. "You know something? After everything I've been through today, I'll be happy to see them."

47

Happy Daze Are Here Again

The Goddess rarely closed for private parties, but Louie insisted that with everything they all had to be thankful for, that he was going to rent a tent and throw a beach bash.

Once word got out, it turned out to be as private as a party can be on the North Shore. It rained the day before, but the night of the party the weather was perfect. Clear with enough of a breeze to keep things cool. Tiki torches flickered around the outside of the tent as partiers gathered just before sunset.

"This is a great idea, Uncle Louie." Em surveyed the crowd seated at picnic tables beneath the party tent. "The Maidens are excited to have a chance to perform their competition number and show off their third place *koa* wood trophy bowl."

"I'll call Kiki up to the stage before they start dancing later."

"Where is she?" Em looked around.

"Over by the bar." They'd rolled the tiki bar out of the house and set it up at one end of the tent. Sophie had volunteered to bartend. She told Em she'd rather mix drinks than just sit.

"Has Kiki seen Marilyn yet?"

"I think so. I saw Kiki's face turn four shades of furious when Marilyn walked in."

"I'll do my best to make sure Kiki doesn't cause trouble," Em promised.

"I'll do my best to keep Marilyn occupied."

"I'll bet you will." Em had noticed the diamond on Marilyn's hand the minute she walked in. It was hard *not* to notice since Marilyn entered the tent with her left hand out in front of her. The diamond was inside before she was—a diamond that Louie couldn't really afford.

The Maidens brought along their significant others. Wally was there with a young male hula dancer he'd met at the Kukui Nut Festival as he was running off the stage. The neighbors had all been invited to keep them from complaining about the noise.

"Nat's over by the bar," Em told her uncle.

"Great. I'd love to talk to him some more about the reality show pilot. It all sounds really exciting," Louie said.

"Do you really want to go ahead with it? Are you sure? Won't publishing the tropical drink recipe book be enough?"

"Sure, I want to go ahead with the show. Why not?"

"For one thing, we could come off looking like a bunch of idiots."

"Oh, pooh. Us? Don't let your ego stand in the way of success. People will be lined up all the way down the highway to get into the Goddess once we hit prime time."

"That's exactly what I'm afraid of—hitting prime time," she said.

"Nat said the idea might not get picked up. If it does they could start shooting in four to five months."

"It would sure be great to have some cash that was flowing in and not just out for a change," Em said.

"I know. Marilyn has some great ideas for expanding the restaurant."

"I'll bet she does." Em noticed Buzzy was running out of the far end of the tent. "Where's Buzzy going? You think he's all right? I've never seen him move that fast."

Louie laughed. "He's supposed to be down at Tunnels standing on the beach every night at sunset to tell his fiancée good night or she gets jealous."

"The dolphin."

"Who else. And they said it wouldn't last."

After Louie wandered away, Em pressed her fingertips against her frown lines. She was still pressing when Roland walked up beside her.

"My mom used to wear little sticky triangles above the bridge of her nose to smooth those things out. Maybe you can find some somewhere."

"*Mahalo* for that." She dropped her hand.

He surveyed the tent. "Looks like a good crowd."

"It's a crowd. I'm not sure how good they are."

"When does the entertainment start?" He glanced at his watch. "I'm on the late shift and can't stay much longer."

"As soon as we get everyone served and seated. I hope you at least have time to eat."

"Sure do."

She turned toward the long tables filled with chafing dishes at the far end of the tent where Kimo was waving a dish towel in circles above his head.

"Looks like the chef is ready," she said. "I'll go tell Louie to get on the mic and have people refill their drinks and start lining up. Will you save me a seat?"

"For sure."

Em told Louie to announce the buffet line was open, and when he stepped up to the mic next to the portable dance floor, Marilyn was right beside him with her arm linked through his. Searching the crowd, Em found Kiki next to the bar whispering to Sophie. As long as Sophie had an eye on her, thing would be all right. She hoped.

"*E' komo mai* everybody. Welcome to our celebration!" Louie was shouting into the mic but no one seemed to care that it was so loud. "As most of you know, we're here to toast the Hula Maidens' success at the Kukui Nut Festival. They did us proud all right." He picked up the *koa* bowl that was on display next to the mic stand. Let's hear it for their big third place title in their division. After we eat I'll have Kiki tell you a bit about the event, and then the Maidens are going to perform their award winning number for us. Won't that be great?"

Everyone cheered and raised their glasses in a toast.

"How do you like the Kookookie Koolers? I'd say they're definitely not for the timid. Plenty of rum in those babies."

David Letterman was nearby on his outdoor perch by the front door. In his best pirate imitation he started squawking, "Rum! Rum! Yo ho, ho!"

Louie had to pause until the laughter died down.

"Now that I've got your attention, I'd like to turn the mic over to Detective Roland Sharpe of the Kauai Police Department. Most of you know Roland as our fire dancing detective, but tonight, though he's not going to be able to perform for us, he would like to say a few words on behalf of the KPD."

Em wondered what was up and watched Roland walk over to Louie who handed off the mic.

"As you know, we recently apprehended a murderer here on Kauai. As sad as it is to know that bad things can and do happen in our community, it's also a great thing to know we have citizens who are willing to go above and beyond to help the police out when we need it."

Roland gazed around at the crowd until he found Em.

"One person in particular was instrumental in helping us apprehend the perpetrator in our hunt for the *Kumu* Killer as folks are calling the accused. The person who helped us is someone most of you know well. If you don't, be sure to introduce yourself and tell her *mahalo*."

Em thought about sliding under the picnic table but the Maidens and the people who had heard she'd been helping the police had already turned her way.

Roland reached toward Danny Cook who bent down and picked up something in a frame behind the drum. He handed it to Roland.

"Em Johnson, if you'd come up please?"

Em looked around and realized there was no way she was getting out of this one. She slid off the bench and headed for the stage. When she was beside Roland, he turned the frame around so that she and the crowd could see the certificate of appreciation matted inside.

"I'd like to present this Certificate of Appreciation and Gratitude from the Kauai Police Department to Em Johnson for answering the call to help. It's signed by the police chief and the mayor."

The crowd broke into thunderous applause when Roland handed over the framed award and said, "*Mahalo*, Ms. Johnson, for a job well done."

Em glanced over and saw Louie nearby with tears in his eyes. All the Maidens, led by Kiki, were headed for the stage carrying *leis*. Sophie was giving her a thumbs up from behind the bar, and Pat Boggs had her fingers in her mouth and was letting off ear splitting whistles.

"Thanks for the warning," Em whispered to Roland.

"It wouldn't have been a surprise if I'd warned you."

The Maidens reached the stage, and one by one they crowded in close, hugged Em and hung *leis* around her neck until they were piled up to Em's chin.

The crowd was still on its feet. Louie took the award from her and put a Kook-Kookie Kooler in her hand.

Danny and the Tiki Tones tried to play "For She's a Jolly Good Fellow" but they didn't know the tune so it ended up sounding like "Happy Birthday."

"This is great. Does this mean I can turn in my badge?"

"The sooner the better," Roland said. "I don't like having you in harm's way."

"Oh no. I was just going to ask if you'd mind coming back when your shift is over and teach me how to twirl flaming fire knives on the beach."

"No fire allowed, but have a few more of those coolers, and when I get back I'm sure we can find something for you to twirl around."

More Tropical Libations from Uncle Louie's Booze Bible

Two to Mango

A fruity, fizzy cocktail dedicated to Louie's fiancée, Marilyn Lockhart, aka "The Defector" as she has been unlovingly referred to by the Hula Maidens ever since she left them to join another hula halau (hula school). Louie popped a bottle of champagne for this one, but will their love last? Or is this "black widow" just after the Tiki Goddess Bar?

Per cocktail you will need:
1 Lime wedge
Sugar
2 oz. Mango nectar
Champagne

Glass: Champagne flute

Fill a saucer with a bit of sugar. Moisten the rim of the champagne flute with the lime wedge and dip into the sugar. Pour 2 oz. mango nectar into the bottom of the glass and fill with champagne. If you like mango, drop a chunk of fresh mango into the glass before you add the liquid ingredients.

Horny Rum Rhinos

When the Rhinos Club convention hit Kauai and three van loads full of Rhinos arrived at the Tiki Goddess during their tour of the North Shore, Uncle Louie had this cocktail all ready to honor the hard working, hard partying "crush" from the mainland. (Rhinos don't travel in herds, they travel in "crushes"... look it up!) They were so delighted (not to mention inebriated) they gave Louie his own horn and made him and honorary Rhino!

Per cocktail you will need:
3 oz. Mango nectar
3 oz. Dark rum
1-1/2 oz. Sweet and Sour
1/4 oz. Curacao

Glass: Rocks glass (aka lowball).

Shake all in a cocktail shaker and pour into a rocks glass over crushed ice.

Kookookie Kooler

Louie concocted this drink to immortalize the Maidens' Third Place triumph at the Kukui Nut Festival and Hula Competition. The Kookookie Kooler has a hint of a nutty flavor but don't worry, there's not even a smidgen of a real kukui nut required to make this version.

Per cocktail you will need:
1 oz. Trader Vic's Macadamia Nut Liqueur
2 oz. Pineapple juice
2 oz. Orange juice
1 oz. Dark rum (Louie prefers Myer's).

Glass: Cocktail (aka margarita glass).

Pour the juices and the liqueur into a cocktail shaker with ice. Strain into a chilled margarita glass and float the dark rum on top. If you can't find the macadamia nut liqueur, you could use Amaretto but Uncle Louie would advise you keep searching for the real island delight.

Uncle Louie's Lazy Man's Mai Tai

In 1944 Victor Bergeron aka "Trader Vic" mixed his first Mai Tai which included lime juice, two kinds of rum, bitters, a sprig of mint, a maraschino cherry and a pineapple wedge. Uncle Louie is a busy man and the Tiki Goddess Bar makes up their luau night 2 for 1 mai tai mix by the pitcher full so tourists aren't caught waiting in a line at the bar for a refill.

Per cocktail you will need:
2 oz. Light rum
1/2 oz. triple sec
1 oz. orange juice
Splash of Orgeat syrup
Splash of sweet and sour mix
1 oz. Myer's rum to float on top (optional)

Glass: Uncle Louie uses a hurricane glass, but any tall glass will do.

Shake ingredients in a cocktail shaker, strain and serve over ice in a tall glass. Optional: Add a float of dark rum. Garnish with a pineapple wedge, maraschino cherry and if you're in a party mood, a paper umbrella, an orchid blossom, or both.

Where The Story Began...

MAI TAI ONE ON

Book 1: The Tiki Goddess Mysteries

Excerpt

They would have found the body sooner, if it hadn't been two-for-one mai tai night . . .

Six months ago, if anyone would have told Em Johnson she'd end up divorced, broke, and running the dilapidated Tiki Goddess Bar on the magical North Shore of Kauai, she would have told them to shove a swizzle stick up their *okole*.

As if all that isn't bad enough, when an obnoxious neighbor with a grudge is found dead in the Goddess luau pit, suspicion falls on Em and the rest of the Goddess staff. With the help of a quirky dance troupe of over-the-hill Hula Maidens, Em and the cast of characters must band together to find the killer and solve the mystery before the next *pupu* party.

Praise for Mai Tai One On

"I want to be a Hula Maiden, too! Reading this fresh, funny mystery made me yearn to hang out at the Tiki Goddess, sip one of Uncle Louie's drinks and watch a certain super sexy fire dancing detective entertain the crowd. This is a story for anyone who's ever been to Hawaii, dreamed of going to Hawaii, or wondered what it would be like to live in our 50th State. I loved this book!"
—*Susan Elizabeth Phillips*

"MAI TAI ONE ON is that rarest of novels—one that is both emotionally satisfying and laugh out loud funny. As a part-time Hawaiian resident, I absolutely fell in love with Jill Marie Landis's spot on glimpse into a Hawaii that most tourists never see. Smart and sassy, fun and endearing, MAI TAI ONE ON will sweep you away. Once you meet the quirky, real-as-your-best-friend Hula Maidens, you'll wish the book would never end."
—*Kristin Hannah*

"Jasmine-scented jungle, jewel seas, white beaches; an irresistible glimpse at real life on the North Shore of Kauai. MAI TAI ONE ON is a fun and fabulous book."
—*Stella Cameron*

Mai Tai One On

Excerpt

They would have found the body sooner if it hadn't been two-for-one Mai Tai Night.

Before all hell broke loose at the Tiki Goddess Bar, Emily Johnson was hustling back and forth trying to wait tables and bartend, wondering if her uncle, Louie Marshall, had slipped out for a little hanky-panky. She couldn't care less that the seventy-two year old was romantically involved, but why did he have to disappear when the bar was the busiest?

Drenched in the perpetual twilight that exists in bars and confessionals, she sloshed an endless stream of sticky, pre-made mai tai mixer into hurricane glasses. Then, just the way Louie taught her, she added double jiggers of white rum and topped off the concoctions with a generous float of dark Myer's.

Six months ago, if anyone would have told her she'd be living on the North Shore of Kauai divorced, broke, and managing a shabby—albeit legendary—tiki bar, she would have told them to start spinning on a swizzle stick.

Em checked her watch. It was 7:45. Not only was her uncle MIA, but her bartender, Sophie Chin, was an hour and a half late. With no time to worry, Em convinced herself that sooner or later, Sophie would show. The twenty-two year old desperately needed the job. In the three months that Sophie had been working at the Goddess, she'd never been late, so Em didn't mind cutting her a little slack.

When Em's cell phone vibrated, she pulled it out of the back pocket of her cargo shorts and flipped it open expecting to hear Sophie's voice.

It wasn't Sophie. It was her ex.

"Em, we need to talk." His voice was muffled by the noise in the crowded bar.

"We've done all the talking we're going to do, Phillip." Em tucked the phone between her shoulder and ear hoping it wouldn't slip and fall into the ice bin beneath the bar.

She thought she heard him say, "I want the Porsche." Em laughed.

If he hadn't screwed half the women in Orange County they would still be married and he would still have his precious Porsche. Now they were divorced and she had sold the only asset she'd been awarded in the split.

She glanced over at the small stage in the back corner of the room where the musicians were about to start the evening's entertainment.

"I'm busy, Phillip. Don't call again." She snapped her phone shut, shoved it back into her pocket, and wished it was that easy to forget how he'd humiliated her.

A tourist walked up to the bar asking how long it would take to get his order. There was no time to dwell on Phillip. She had to focus on making drinks until Uncle Louie or Sophie appeared.

On stage, Danny Cook, singer and guitar player, began to warm up the crowd with his rendition of Tiny Bubbles. He reassured the audience he was not in any way related to the infamous voyager, Captain Cook, who discovered the islands and started the first real estate boom. Behind him, his cousin, Brendon, tried to keep time on a drum set that had seen better days.

Back in the ladies room, the Hula Maidens were fluffing and primping, adding final touches to their "adornments" before they took the stage. An enthusiastic group of mostly seniors, the Maidens relied on dramatic costuming to distract from their not-so-great dancing.

Em topped off the tray of tall shapely hurricane glasses with pineapple slices, cherries and lime wedges carefully skewered onto miniature plastic swords. For a final touch she added brightly colored paper umbrellas—warning flags that the drinks were packing a memorable headache.

She was about to heft the tray to her shoulder and step out from behind the bar when a ruddy cheeked, overweight female tourist with a sunburn and a bad perm burst through the front door screaming for help.

Em rushed around the bar. "What's wrong?"

The woman kept screaming. Patrons set down their drinks and stared.

Em grabbed a glass of water off a nearby table and tossed the contents in the woman's face.

The screaming abruptly stopped. The tourist gasped. "There's . . . there's . . . there's a man roasting . . . in the barbeque pit . . . outside!"

"That's Kimo, our luau chef," Em said. "In fact, we have plenty of tickets left so if you'd like to—"

"No!" The woman yelled. "He's not cooking. He's . . . burning up! You have to do something! It's horrible. It's . . ." The woman's eyes rolled up and she collapsed.

All over the packed room, chair legs scraped against the scarred wooden floor. Dozens of rubber soled thongs slapped skin as locals and tourists grabbed cameras and ran for the door.

There *was* a strange odor in the air. Em glanced around the nearly empty room. Danny Cook was still singing. Only Buzzy, the aging hippie who lived down the road, continued to gnaw on some barbequed ribs. Nothing had fazed Buzzy since he had some bad mushrooms back in the 70s.

Em propped the unconscious tourist against the carved tiki base of a bar stool and followed the crowd around the corner of the building to the back parking lot. Two and three deep, folks ringed the *imu*. Em hoped to God, Kimo, the cook, hadn't tripped and fallen into the luau pit where he roasted pig.

Em gagged and covered her mouth as she got closer. The air smelled like a mix of singed hair and burning rubber.

"Call 911!" Someone hollered.

"Did already!" At least five people yelled back.

Though the last thing she wanted was to see Kimo roasting, Em forced her way through the throng to get to the edge of the pit. Her pulse was hammering even before she saw a man's body lying face down atop the coals. Fully clothed in a pair of baggy navy blue shorts and a stained white T shirt, he was short and stocky with thick calves that showed above the tops of his black rubber work boots.

The melting boots gave him away.

"*Ohmygosh*, that's Harold," Em whispered. Afraid she'd pass out, she took a deep breath and immediately wished she hadn't. She gagged again and tried to concentrate on the crowd.

Kimo suddenly materialized at her side.

"Poor buggah," he mumbled. "Uh oh. Here comes Uncle Louie."

Em spotted her six-foot-three-inch uncle's thatch of white hair above the crowd. She shoved her way back out of the circle and ran to his side.

Louie was still spry, attractive, and the picture of health. He had been an impressionable eight-year-old when Victor Bergeron's Trader Vic's Restaurants were all the rage in his home town of San Francisco. At twenty, dreaming of exotic jungle haunts, tiki drums, and cocktails named after WWII bombers and airmen, he set off to explore Polynesia. Against his family's advice, he married an island native, settled down and established the Tiki Goddess Bar on the North Shore of the northernmost inhabited Hawaiian island. Then Louie Marshall sat back and waited for the world to come to him.

Every day he donned one of over fifty loud aloha shirts, a kukui nut necklace, baggy white linen shorts and flip flops. Most days he worked from sunup to well into the next morning. He was tan as a coconut and physically in great shape. He still surfed. Only his mind was failing, or so Em had been told.

"What's going on?" He tried to see over the crowd. When Louie looked down at Em, his expression went blank for a second, as if he had no idea who she was or what she was doing there.

Em glanced over his shoulder, half expecting to see Marilyn Lockhart trailing behind Louie. The Hula Maidens were convinced the woman they nicknamed "The Defector" was after him. Marilyn wasn't a young gold digger. She was sixty-five if she was a day. She had danced with the Maidens until she became fed up with their antics—she wasn't the first—and went on to join another troupe.

"Someone fell into the luau pit, Uncle Louie," Em could barely get the words out.

Louie's face may have paled. He was too tan for Em to be sure.

"Who?" he asked.

"Harold Otanami."

"Is he all right?"

"He's dead." Em figured there was no way Harold wasn't dead by now. "At least I hope so," she mumbled.

Roasting alive was too horrific to imagine.

"Dead! After all these years." Louie shook his head. "I can't imagine that old bastard gone."

The sound of sirens echoed along the coastline. The Kauai Police Department's substation and the Hanalei fire station were side by side, a good twenty minutes away.

Em's gaze drifted to the luau hut, a lean-to shelter built not far from the pit. Beneath the thatched roof, the remains of tonight's traditional smoked kalua pig lay spread out on a huge wooden table that served as a carving board. Seeing the roasted pig carcass complete with its head so soon after viewing poor smoldering Harold nearly did her in.

She noticed some folks were actually taking photos of Harold's remains. Others, pale and shaken, huddled together in small groups. Neighbors were starting to gather, swelling the crowd.

"We've got to get these people back inside," she whispered.

"Are the Hula Maidens ready?" Louie glanced over at the dark green, wooden building that housed the Tiki Goddess Bar and restaurant.

Em noticed most of the aging dancers had left their makeshift dressing area in the bathroom to join the crowd around the pit. The huge sprays of variegated leaves pinned atop their heads stuck out like spear tips. They looked like a squadron of tropical Statues of Liberty.

"When *aren't* they ready to dance?"

Without warning, Louie cupped his hands around his mouth and shouted, "Drinks on the house!"

Coming in 2013

Book 3 of The Tiki Goddess Mysteries

"Three To Get Lei'd"

About the Author

JILL MARIE LANDIS has written over twenty-five novels which have earned distinguished awards and slots on such national bestseller lists as the USA TODAY Top 50 and the New York Times Best Sellers Plus. She is a seven-time finalist for Romance Writers of America's RITA Award in both Single Title and Contemporary Romance as well as a Golden Heart and RITA Award winner. She's written historical and contemporary romance, inspirational historical romance and she is now penning The Tiki Goddess Series which begins with MAI TAI ONE ON and TWO TO MANGO. Visit her at thetikigoddess.com.

CPSIA information can be obtained at www.ICGtesting.com
Printed in the USA
BVOW08s0433090813

328062BV00002B/413/P